The
Morpheus
Project

Steve Kroska

Dedication

Dedicated to my wife Nami and my sons
Alex and Michael.

Special Thanks

A special thanks and appreciation to my parents Jerry and Jackie Kroska. I would also like to thank Kimberly Holborn and Marty Sanders for their help in editing this book.

Prologue

In the past three hours he had killed a man, stole classified files, and sabotaged the executive jet.

It was just past midnight when the Special Projects Director, Dr. Paul Valerius slipped out the side door of the top-secret research facility. The thin, sixty-four-year-old man with a comb-over crouched in the darkness and stared at the electrified fence.

The fence stood some twenty feet high and was topped with razor wire. He knew little of the island's security beyond the fence, but he counted on the fact that the facility was focused on preventing break-ins, not break-outs.

He scanned the area. With no sentries in sight, he hurried to the base of the fence, took a knee and placed four clips in a rectangular pattern on the chain links. With the electrical current rerouted, he cut a section with wire cutters, pried it back and stepped out. Now all he had to do was navigate down the steep jungle terrain to a speedboat waiting to pick him up on the water's edge.

He took no more than two more steps outside the fence when bright lights flooded the surrounding jungle and a deafening siren sounded—*Wah-Wah-Wah-Wah!*

"Damn!" he cried.

He hurried down the sloping landscape. Soon he felt his legs giving out. Being a scientist, he focused on intellectual pursuits, not physical activity, and for the first time in his life, he regretted it.

He ignored the ache and fatigue in his legs and ran faster, but he tripped over an exposed root and rolled down the hill, smashing through vegetation, striking rocks, and hitting fallen limbs.

After coming to a sprawling stop, he cursed the world and closed his eyes. His entire body hurt. He wasn't sure he could go on. Then he heard the dogs and his eyes snapped open.

He had forgotten about the dogs. Packs of wild dogs were left to roam the island as an added layer of security. Struggling to his feet, he pushed forward. When it seemed he couldn't go any farther, he stumbled out the jungle and onto the sandy beach.

He sucked in huge amounts of air and peered left and then right. In the water, patrol boats with flashing red lights were moving straight toward his position. He crooked his head and heard approaching dogs barking under the wailing siren. It was all coming down around him too fast.

Then, in the soft glow of moonlight, he spotted the speedboat anchored a short distance offshore. With what little strength that remained, he lurched into the surf. He pushed through the waves until the water was over his head and then swam.

When he reached the boat, a shadowy figure with a full beard and black knit cap helped him inside. Dr. Valerius plopped in a chair.

The speedboat engines roared to life. As the craft gained speed, the single hairs of his comb-over lifted and danced in the wind. The patrol boats gave brief chase, but the hired boat with its powerful motors soon put them far out of reach

Dr. Valerius was more exhausted than he had ever been in his life. As he leaned back in his seat and closed his eyes he let his fingers linger on the computer flash drives in his pocket. The files were going to make him a very wealthy man. But stealing the files was only step-one of his plan. Getting his hands on the cargo in the executive jet was the other.

Over the sound of the boat noise, there was a thundering in the sky. He looked back at the executive jet with a yellow tail taking off from the island.

As he watched the flashing lights of aircraft disappear into the dark sky, a slight smile creased his lips, for he knew...the plane, the VIP passengers and the precious cargo would never reach its final destination.

1

Belize Jungle

Alex McCade gazed out the window of the chartered helicopter as it soared above the jungle. It was a magnificent sight, a sea of endless trees that stretched all the way to the horizon. He yawned and stretched his arms. A little peace and quiet at the jungle resort was just what he needed.

Alex glanced over at his friend, Mike Garrison, asleep in the seat beside him. The two men had been friends since childhood. They both were thirty-two years old, yet vastly different.

Alex was cerebral and a ruggedly handsome man with an athletic build, short dark hair, and piercing dark eyes. Whereas, Mike was carefree and looked like a model from a surfboard ad.

He had bright blue eyes, chiseled cheekbones, wavy blond hair, and a smile that made women swoon. This annoyed most people, including Alex. What was more annoying was the man couldn't pass a shiny surface without admiring his own reflection.

Despite their differences, they were as close as brothers.

Alex turned and looked into the sky. A glint of light

caught his attention. Curious, he raised a pair of binoculars and looked through the lens. The reflection came off the surface of a small, executive jet with a yellow tail, nose down, on a collision course with the jungle.

His pulse raced as he jabbed a finger at the aircraft. "Hernando, get them on the radio."

The helicopter pilot, a man in his sixties with weathered brown skin, pulled down on the brim of his cowboy hat and reached for the radio. He attempted to contact the other aircraft but found only a high-pitch screeching in his earphones. "I don't understand it; the radio was working fine earlier."

Mike snorted. He sat up and wiped the sleep from his eyes. "What's going on?"

Alex pointed at the aircraft, but there was nothing they could do except watch the scene play out. In a matter of moments, the aircraft crashed into the trees and was gone, like it had never existed at all.

"Those poor bastards," Hernando muttered.

"Not so fast," Alex said. "There could be survivors."

The pilot shook his head. "*Senor*, I assure you, no one could survive that."

"We won't know for sure unless we look."

"But…"

"Look, we may be the only ones who saw the crash. Your radio isn't working, so you can't call in its location. By the time we report it to the authorities, it'll be too late. It's up to us. We have to go."

Hernando huffed. "*Senor*, even if there are survivors there is nothing we can do for them. I can't land this thing, you know."

"You have a winch, don't you? Does it work?"

"*Si*, but..."

"Then lower us down."

"Down there?" Hernando asked incredulously. "You want to go down there? *Senor*, it is too dangerous."

Mike leaned forward and grinned. "Let us worry about that."

"No, you don't understand, the area below us is cursed." The pilot made the sign of the cross over his heart as if to protect him to what he was about to say. "Centuries ago Spanish conquistadors named this stretch of land *Tierra de Demonios*--Land of Demons.

"They say evil spirits roam the shadows in search of victims. Even in modern times people disappear. A few weeks ago, an archeological expedition went missing and they haven't been heard from since."

Hernando saw the determination in Alex's eyes. He shook his head in frustration and banked the helicopter.

In the vicinity of the crash, Alex spotted narrow slips of smoke rising up through the dense jungle canopy. "There it is."

Hernando positioned the helicopter to within twenty feet of the jagged hole and hovered. "This is as far down as I go."

"Good enough," Alex replied. He unbuckled his seatbelt and tossed off the headset. He tapped the pilot on the shoulder and lifted the headphones off an ear. "Do you have a harness for the cable?"

"*Si*, back at the hangar. I was repairing it," Hernando replied. He grabbed Alex's arm in an attempt to stop him. "*Senor*, are you sure you want to do this? What about your vacation? What do I tell them at the resort?"

"Tell them we'll be there as soon as we can."

Alex moved to the back of the chopper. He located a couple of clamps in a cardboard box. Mike helped him form circular footholds in the cable while he used the clamps to secure them. When they finished the footholds, Mike opened the side door and hot winds swirled inside.

Alex tossed the end of the cable out the door and then signaled Hernando for more slack.

Wearing a t-shirt, cargo shorts, and athletic shoes, Alex sat on the edge of the open doorway with his legs dangling over the side. He reached for the cable and with a turn of his body, he lowered himself out the door and slowly down the cable. Hand over hand, he went until his foot slipped into the lower loop.

Looking up, he waved to Mike.

Mike descended the cable in the same fashion. Meanwhile, Hernando monitored their progress via a bottom mounted camera. When they were in position Hernando started the winch and the men began their descent to the inhospitable jungle below.

Alex slowly entered the gap in the leafy canopy. He could immediately see the angle the plane went in by the cracked branches and deeply gouged trees.

As he was lowered, he pushed off limbs and slipped around thick vines. He had been outside less than a minute, and already his shirt was soaked from perspiration. The heat and humidity were intense. Unfortunately, the lower he went, the more humid and darker the jungle became.

After descending more than 150 feet, he spotted the jungle floor. As he neared, he jumped and landed on a soft carpet of decomposing leaves. He waved away mosquitoes swarming around his face and scanned his surroundings. Filling his vision was a world of lush green vegetation, large trees, hanging vines, and deep, dark shadows. Mike landed beside him with a 'thud'.

Alex took the lead and moved quickly through the rugged terrain. Time was critical; seconds could mean the difference between life and death. Thirty yards ahead, he swept aside a wide palm and found the small executive jet lying at the base of a fat tree.

The fuselage, once glossy white was dirty, gouged, and dented. Both wings had been torn off, hung up somewhere in the trees. The nose of the aircraft was crushed in due to the impact with a fat tree. The passenger cabin, however, was intact.

Alex darted around the small, smoldering fires and arrived at the open boarding door. He swept aside vines, lowered his head and stepped inside the aircraft.

A quick glance into the cockpit told him the pilots were dead. Wheeling right, he stepped into the spacious four-seat passenger cabin and looked on in shock. The once elegantly styled interior was awash in blood. Blood was splattered on the seats, on the floor and even dripping from the ceiling.

Three passengers still buckled in their seats had horrific gunshot wounds to their heads. The wounds looked fresh, and the air was stagnant with the smell of burnt gunpowder.

Alex had seen his share of death in the military. Personally, he had no problem killing those who deserved it, but he was revolted by sick bastards who actually enjoy it. One shot would have been sufficient to kill these men, but for the madman who did this, one shot clearly wasn't enough.

Mike skid to a stop behind him. "Whoa, what the hell happened here?"

Alex said nothing. To his left, he eyed the man

seated in the front row. The dead man wore black slacks, a white blood-soaked shirt with a loosened tie around his neck. Alex reached down and plucked the ID badge off the man's pocket. He thumbed the blood off and looked at the photo.

The man appeared to be in his sixties, with thinning gray hair and glasses. He looked nothing like that now. The name on the ID read: Dr. James Llewellyn, United States Advanced Weapons Research and Development.

"Who is it?" Mike asked.

"A scientist."

Alex handed him the ID and turned his attention to the two men on his right, one seated in front of the other. They were United States military police wearing BDU's, or military battle dress uniforms. He noted their empty side holsters. "Most likely a security team for the scientist."

Alex looked down at the spent .45 shell casings. The floor was littered with them.

Mike dropped the ID on the dead scientist's lap and pointed to the empty seat behind the scientist. "The killer must have sat there. He killed everyone and ran off."

Despite the horrendous scene Alex couldn't help but smile. "Your deductive reasoning is truly astounding since that's the only empty seat on the plane."

"Thank you," Mike replied. "Some say it's a gift."

Alex stepped down the narrow aisle and looked at the empty seat. "Mike, you may want to return that 'so-called' gift of yours."

"What do you mean?"

"The killer didn't sit here."

"He had to." Mike walked to the seat and there on the wall, scrawled in dripping blood, were the words–

HELP ME!

Whoever sat here was now missing. Alex noticed an ID on the floor directly below the seat. He picked it up. The photo showed a woman in her late sixties, with olive colored skin, black hair, and dark eyes. The previous occupant of the seat. The name on this ID read: "Dr. Isra Farah, United States Advanced Weapons Research and Development."

"Another scientist?" Mike asked.

Alex nodded and paused. "So, if she didn't kill them, who did?"

"Maybe a stowaway?"

"Maybe." But Alex had his doubts. He dropped the ID on the seat. "Let's have a look outside."

As he stepped from the aircraft, he immediately spotted bloody boot prints on the ground. He couldn't believe he didn't notice them when he arrived. Although, at the time, it was a rescue mission, not a crime scene.

Mike put his foot beside the biggest boot print. "Look at the size of this. It's got to be at least a size twenty-one boot. This guy is huge."

"And he's a heavy one, too," Alex replied. "Look how deep the impression is."

Alex spent the next few minutes walking around and studying other boot prints. "I make out at least four separate prints, with different sizes and treads."

"For a total of four killers," Mike replied.

Alex absent-mindedly twisted the wedding ring on his finger, an act he unconsciously did when thinking. To sum up what he knew so far: the plane had four seats, and those four seats had been occupied by two scientists and two military guards. So who killed them? Stowaways? No, the plane was far too small to carry an additional four people.

The only logical explanation was that the killers had been waiting for it on the ground. But how did they know when and where it would crash? Were the pilots in on it? If so, that would be a suicide mission. But he could not rule out that possibility. The daily newspaper was filled with stories of men, women and even children in war-torn areas who carried out suicide missions.

Alex stared off into the trees. So, if the four killers weren't on the plane, where did they come from? And now that they have the scientist, where would they take her? There was nothing but jungle for hundreds of miles in any direction. When it came down to it, it didn't matter where the killers came from or how they got here. The woman scientist needed their help and standing idle wasn't doing her any good.

2

The two men followed the bloody trail deeper into the jungle. Unfortunately, the blood from the killer's boots soon wore off which forced them to search for more subtle clues. It wasn't easy. The jungle was vast and monotonous and finding clues of any kind took men with expert tracking skills; fortunately for the scientist, these were such men.

As experienced trackers, they shared the principle that all good trackers have, the belief that no one can go through an area without leaving some trace of their passing. It was important to know what signs to look for and be able to read those signs correctly. One wrong interpretation could mean going off in the wrong direction and getting hopelessly lost. In the jungle--that usually meant death.

As they moved forward, they examined bent and broken branches, trampled vegetation, and disturbed patterns of leaves on the ground. To the trained eye, even a broken spider web was helpful in determining the direction the killers went.

After an hour of steadfast pursuit, Alex smelled cigarette smoke wafting through the air. He stopped and pointed to his nose. Mike caught his meaning and nodded. They silently inched forward. A few yards ahead, Alex peered through the vegetation and saw three rugged men dressed in jungle fatigues, holding Russian made AK-47's. The AK-47 was an extremely dangerous weapon, capable of firing 600 rounds per minute.

Alex saw the scientist sitting on the ground with her back against a tree. Bathed in sweat and trembling, she looked frightened and exhausted from her ordeal. She survived a plane crash only to witness her fellow passengers murdered in front of her. And if that wasn't enough, now she was being dragged through the jungle by a group of murderous thugs.

Alex's attention was drawn to a man inhaling deeply on a cigarette. He was pacing back and forth while glaring at Dr. Farah. The man abruptly stopped and said, "We need to kill her. That bitch is slowing us down. Those damn natives are probably watching us, waiting to pick us off one by one like they did to the others. If we don't pick up the pace—we'll be next!"

"Keep it down or Veck will hear you," spat one of the men.

"I don't care! We need to kill her and get the hell out of here. I didn't sign up for this. None of us did."

"We can't kill her. Veck says she's a gift for Sebastian."

The cigarette man shook his head. "No, Sebastian only mentioned the case and we got that. Are we together on this, or not?"

The other men looked at each other and nodded their heads enthusiastically.

"Good, then when Veck comes back, we tell him."

Satisfied with his plan, the cigarette man walked about ten feet away. He scanned the jungle, then leaned his rifle against a tree and began to urinate. When he finished, he yanked up his zipper and darted back to the others. "Did you see anything?"

The men shook their heads.

The cigarette man laughed uncomfortably. "Jeez, I was so nervous, I nearly peed myself."

Suddenly, all three men stiffened as a large, hulking man lurched into view. Alex unconsciously backed away when he saw the man's massive size. The monster was at least 6 feet, 6 inches tall and weighed close to 400 pounds.

He had a bald fleshy head, small crinkled eyes, and a large, bulbous nose. His skin was as pale as a cadaver. He had an ugly slash of a scar under his right eye with rough edges that he probably stitched himself long ago. His gigantic body reminded him of an old-time professional wrestler; big, barrel-chested, and clearly strong.

He was dressed in jungle fatigues like the others and had a camouflage-patterned backpack strapped over his powerful shoulders. Around his enormous gut, he wore a holstered .45mm pistol; the same caliber weapon used to murder the men on the plane.

In the big man's left hand he carried a silver case. The case was oblong and resembled a portable synthesizer or electronic keyboard case, but Alex doubted these men were music lovers. What was inside? He wondered. Alex recalled the cigarette man saying, only a few moments ago, "…Sebastian only mentioned the case and we got that."

The giant strode to the men. "You three shut your gobs!" he bellowed in a raspy British accent, "we're leaving."

The cigarette man jabbed a boney finger at the scientist. "No, we need to kill her right now. She's slowing us down."

The big man grinned. "What? You afraid the natives

might get you, Rafferty?"

"Aren't you? They already took half of our number!"

"They were expendable—she's not."

"Then you stay with her. We're leaving without you."

Veck set the silver case on the ground. He placed his massive hands on his hips, and said, "All of you want to leave?"

"We do," replied the cigarette man firmly.

The giant shot nasty looks at the other two men whose only response was to lower their heads meekly. The big man laughed and turned to the cigarette man. "Looks like you're on your own, mate."

The cigarette man's eyes pleaded with his co-conspirators, but he was sold out. He pivoted. His rifle was still leaning against the tree where he urinated. He seemed to calculate the odds of reaching it before the big man could move, but time had already run out.

The monster pulled the .45mm pistol from his holster, jammed it between the cigarette man's widening eyes, and pulled the trigger.

The explosive sound echoed in the jungle. Birds screeched and flew from the trees as the bullet ripped through the man's brain and exited the other side. The body dropped to the ground and his lit cigarette landed beside his bloody corpse.

The giant swung the smoking gun barrel at the man nearest him. "You want to join him?"

"No Veck, I'm with you--always was."

"Sure you were." The big man moved the gun barrel to the next man. "And you?"

"I'm with you, too."

"Glad to hear it," he replied sarcastically. "Get your shit together; we're leaving."

The big man holstered his weapon. As he turned to leave, he tripped over the silver case and cursed, "Bloody hell!"

The scientist rose to her knees and yelled, "Be careful with that! You have no idea what's in there."

The big man reached down and slapped the woman across the face with the back of his hand. "Shut it!"

Alex grit his teeth. It was everything he could do to remain still and not go after the big man. He considered himself a man of great compassion, but when confronted with evil, he could kill with ease, without hesitation or remorse.

He learned early on in life that the only way to defeat evil was to meet it head-on, with full, unyielding force. The big man was bursting of such evil, and if given the chance, he wouldn't hesitate to end the monster's life.

The giant hunched over the whimpering scientist. He reached down and effortlessly yanked her to her feet. He snarled and shoved her forward.

He picked the silver case up by the handle and then turned to his men. "Grab Rafferty's rifle and pack. We're taking them with us."

"What do we do with his body?"

The giant grinned. "Leave him for the animals."

3

When the killers hiked off, Alex and Mike stepped out from behind the vegetation. They walked up to the dead body, and Alex used his shoe to press the smoldering cigarette into the wet leaves.

He pondered what he had just witnessed. What stuck out most was that the cigarette man was more frightened of the natives than incurring the wrath of the big guy…and that was saying a lot.

It was best that he and Mike be on the lookout for dangerous natives too. It made him recall the warning Hernando gave them before they left the helicopter, about the area being cursed and people going missing. It appears Hernando's warning had merit.

Before setting out, Alex went through the dead man's pockets in hopes of finding something useful. He found nothing, so they got back on the killer's trail.

Two hours later, it started to rain. What began as mere droplets, turned into a mighty downpour. It became increasingly difficult to navigate the terrain as it became muddier with the incessant rain.

Alex watched the elderly scientist from a distance and found himself admiring the woman's courage. Traversing in the jungle wasn't easy, especially for a lady in her sixties who wasn't physically prepared for it. Yet, despite the declining jungle conditions, she bravely trudged on.

The rain stopped by mid-afternoon and the jungle came alive again. Spider monkeys squealed in the trees and flung themselves to neighboring branches. Unfortunately, the mosquitoes returned. Alex wasn't bothered much by their bites. They were an irritant to be sure, but they were also a danger. The little insects were carriers of disease such as malaria and dengue fever.

As night approached, the killers stopped to make camp. Alex and Mike watched the killers set up motion sensors around the camp; it was obvious the natives still had them worried. After securing the perimeter, they ate a quick meal and then strung up hammocks to trees.

Alex and Mike eased back a safe distance from the camp. From behind a thick tree, Mike whispered, "Now we wait until they fall asleep and then rescue the scientist, right?"

"No," Alex replied. "I want to wait on rescuing the scientist; something much bigger is going on here and I want to find out what it is. I say we follow them to their destination. Once we learn who their boss is and what his plan is, then we rescue her."

Mike nodded in agreement.

With the visible light remaining, they gathered fallen branches and sticks to build a crude platform in the limbs of a Ceiba tree with thick, spreading limbs. It was better to sleep off the wet ground and away from the nocturnal creatures that roamed the forest floor at night.

When they finished building the foundation, they laid a thick layer of palms for padding.

As darkness fell, the two men stretched out on the platform. It had been a busy day. Both ignored hunger pangs and fell right to sleep.

Early the following morning, with steam rising off

the ground, Alex woke to an unusual creaking sound. He opened his eyes and jolted awake into a nightmare! Dead bodies, strung up by their ankles, swayed in the branches around the platform with their limp arms dangling toward the earth.

He kicked Mike.

Mike jerked backward. "What the hell?" He looked upward, and both men stared silently at the display of hanging cadavers. Mike gestured at the hanging bodies. "Who could have done this? I didn't hear a thing."

"Neither did I and that has me worried."

Alex counted six Caucasian males, two Black men, and one Asian female. "My guess is that they're from that archeological expedition that went missing a few weeks ago."

"The ones Hernando told us about?"

Alex nodded. "It must have been the natives the killers talked about."

Mike shook his head in disbelief. "So if natives did this, why didn't they just kill us?"

"Maybe because we're unarmed and pose no threat."

"Or…" Mike countered. "Maybe this is their one and final warning before they kill us."

"It's time to go."

The men didn't waste time. They scampered down the tree. Once on the ground Alex looked up at the dead bodies swaying in the tree. It was a damn spooky sight, alright. Damn spooky. He turned to Mike. "From now on we take turns keeping watch at night."

Mike nodded. "You got that right."

With heightened awareness of their surroundings, they hiked to the killer's camp. When they arrived, they found them packing up to leave. The scientist, apparently too weak to go on, was put upon a stretcher made of bamboo and vines. Veck, the big man, grabbed the silver case. The two other men lifted the stretcher, and they hiked off together.

Questions still plagued Alex. Where were the killers going? And how soon would they arrive? After the previous night, he didn't want to stay in the jungle any longer than he had to.

4

In the Oval Office of the White House, the President of the United States, Thomas Grant, hung up the phone and rubbed his tired eyes. He'd been on the phone for the past forty-five minutes speaking with the Chinese President, Zhou Lichang, and it hadn't been easy.

Tired, he pushed his chair back and got to his feet. Shooting pains stabbed aching knees and he grabbed the desk for support. His arthritis was getting much worse, and the pills he took for pain, didn't help much anymore.

He took a moment to steady himself, to let the burning pain subside. He grew frustrated. It was only a matter of time before the public learned of his condition. Walking had become increasingly difficult, but he refused to allow the public to see him use a cane.

His dear wife Millicent urged him to go public with his condition, but he steadfastly refused. The people wanted a healthy, vibrant President and not some old coot who showed his age. He only had a little time in office left and if he could make it without telling them, he would. Snatching his cane, he used it to hobble around his desk.

Suddenly his office door burst open, and his red-faced Vice President stormed into the room.

Calvin Jeffords was the person he least wanted to

see. He was a young, good looking man with expensive suits who got by on his looks and knowing the right people. The man was an ignorant, self-loving egomaniac, and though he put on a competent face in public, for those who truly knew him, he was anything but. There wasn't a day that went by that President Grant wished he'd never met the man.

"Calvin, what do you want?"

"I hear that you're grounding me; barring me from Air Force Two and forbidding me from all official functions; is this true?"

"You heard correct. Do you know what I've been doing for the last forty-five minutes? I was on the phone with the president of China, Zhou Lichang, apologizing for that stupid remark you made at the state dinner."

"I only said that..."

The president cut him off. "I know what you said. You said that you admired Taiwan's courage and in your opinion, they should do more to stress their independence."

"Yes..."

"For your information China considers Taiwan to be a renegade province and they want it back. Yes, we support Taiwan's independence, but you insulted the man. How stupid can you be?"

"Mr. President, in my defense..."

"Shut up Calvin, there is no defense. From now on you are going to sit on your hands until I'm out of office. Got that?"

"You can't do that to me," the vice president fumed. "If I'm to seek the nomination for president after you leave office. I need to position myself in front of the voters."

"You'll do no such thing!" yelled the president and

the vein on his temple began to throb. "You better get this through your head—you will never become president, and I will personally see to that."

"Just because of a few little incidents?"

"A few little incidents?" the president shouted. "You've sent my foreign relations back years."

"But—I..."

"Calvin, it all stops here."

There was a light rap on the door. "Who is it?" The president barked. His chief of staff, David Lawson sheepishly peeked in the room.

"Oh, David, I'm sorry; please come in."

David Lawson was a tall, good-looking African-American man, highly intelligent, a gregarious man, loved and respected by all, and Calvin Jeffords detested him for it.

The president returned to his desk, and his tone lightened. "Anything new on the plane crash?"

"Too soon to tell. Colonel Don Degendorfer and his team are going over the crash site, but there still is no sign of Dr. Farah or the case."

"No luck with the dogs?"

"No, it's rained hard down there and wiped out all traces of them."

"I see you brought a file; something you want to show me?"

"Yes, sir. I do have one item. The FBI identified the two men who dropped from the helicopter to search for survivors."

"Let's see what you've got."

David Lawson stepped forward and handed the president the folder. The president stared at the folder for a moment, yawned, and then handed it back. "It's been a long night David, why don't you just read it to me."

"Of course, sir," replied the chief of staff. "To begin with, those men are not your typical vacationers. They're ex-Navy SEALs. Says in the report they retired only three weeks ago."

"Didn't take them long to find some action, did it?"

"No sir, it didn't." David opened the folder. "The first man, Alex McCade, age 32, retired with the rank of Lieutenant Commander."

"Alex McCade," the president said aloud, "I've heard that name before."

"It wouldn't surprise me. He has countless reports of heroism in his file. He's been awarded a Bronze Stars, a purple heart with three oak leaf clusters, and a Navy Commendation Medal."

"Very impressive."

"Yes, it is. Our other man is Lieutenant Mike Garrison, with an impressive service record as well. The rest of the report goes into some background detail. I'll leave it with you, in case you'd like to read it further." He closed the report and laid it on the desk.

"Has there been any sign of them?"

"No sir, but Colonel Degendorfer believes they may have gone after Dr. Farah."

The president smiled. "It appears, we may finally have some luck going our way."

"It certainly does."

"Is that all?"

"For now, yes."

"The moment something new arises I want to know immediately."

"Yes, sir," replied the chief of staff. He turned to leave but stopped. He glanced back, and his voice took on a personal tone, "Mr. President, you look tired. You really ought to get some rest."

The president smiled. "Thank you, David, I think I'll do just that."

The vice president eyed the chief of staff and burned a hole in his back as he walked out. When the door closed, the vice president stepped forward to speak, but the president shook his head and pointed at the door. Calvin Jeffords screwed his face tight, huffed, and stormed from the room.

5

In the Belizean jungle, Alex hoped they were finally approaching the killer's destination, but he was wrong. They ended up following the killers for two more miserable days.

On the morning of the fourth day, the men crouched under a tree and ate caterpillars and fat grubs for breakfast. Not the best tasting cuisine, but it was nutritious and kept them alive. While they slurped and chewed the rubbery food, they kept a watchful eye out for the natives.

Since that morning, when they woke to find the hanging bodies in the trees, neither had seen nor heard anything from the natives. Both men felt they were being watched, yet they could offer no proof. Noises in the vegetation caused them to tense up. Was the noise caused by animals or the natives? They couldn't be sure.

The natives had a great psychological advantage over them. Like on the battlefield, not knowing when the enemy would strike was nearly as bad as the attack itself.

Alex usually had a sixth sense about impending danger. In combat, this innate ability had kept him and his men safe on many occasions. This feeling of vulnerability was new to him. He felt like a child being toyed with, and he didn't like it.

After the men finished eating, they got back on the

killer's trail. A few hours into the trek, the killers stopped to rest along a moderately flowing brown colored river. They watched as the two men lowered the stretcher to give the scientist water to drink. The big man sipped water from own his canteen.

When he finished, he consulted a GPS unit. He pointed up river and waved for his men to follow.

The killers soon stopped beside a log bridge made of two felled trees. The big man, called Veck, picked up the scientist up from the stretcher and threw her over his shoulder like a piece of rolled up carpeting. He hiked across the log bridge, and his men with the empty stretcher followed.

When they all arrived on the other side of the river, Veck dropped the scientist onto the stretcher. He waved his men onward, and they disappeared into the jungle on the other side.

Alex and Mike waited to be sure the killers wouldn't double back. After a few minutes, they stepped out of hiding and crossed the log bridge.

Once on the other side of the river, they followed the tracks into the forest and up a gently rising slope. At the top, the killer's tracks ended at the base of a steep hill covered with even taller trees.

Alex glanced to his left and then to his right. The tracks only went one way. He paused a moment and then reached into the brush, parted the vegetation and revealed a long, dark tunnel lined with ancient stone blocks. He sniffed the pungent air inside and glanced back at Mike. "You want to go first?"

Mike smiled. "Wouldn't dream of it. You found it, it's only right that you have the honors."

"I knew you'd say that."

Alex took in deep breaths of fresh air and then

stepped inside. His feet landed in putrid, ankle-deep water and he groaned as the liquid filled his shoes. No going back.

He sloshed forward. As he trudged through the dark tunnel, he tripped on something hidden under the water. He used the wall the regain his balance and his hand came away covered in green slime. He flung the slime off his hand and wiped the remaining ooze on his shorts.

When he reached the end, he brushed aside the foliage and stepped out of the tunnel. He didn't know what he would find, but he certainly did not expect this. Before him lay the remains of an ancient Mayan city.

He felt like he had gone back in time. Centuries of jungle growth climbed over magnificent buildings, courtyards, and statues. Vines swirled around stone pillars and crawled up grand staircases.

In the center was a plaza; most likely once an open area, but now filled with tall trees and upturned stones. Along both sides of the plaza stood ornate one-story structures built on pedestals with central staircases.

Anchoring the left end of the plaza loomed a soaring seven-tiered pyramid, with an ominous stone temple at its summit. Three darkened doorways marked the entrance of the temple.

On top of the temple was a highly decorative roof comb. He could easily imagine a time when Mayan high priests, wearing colorful garments, stood outside those very temple doorways and addressed the throngs of faithful below.

He had accumulated basic knowledge of the Mayan culture from general reading. He recalled that the Maya didn't have one centralized government, but instead had many independent cities scattered throughout the jungle. Unfortunately, these independent city-states were often at war with one another.

Despite an advanced skill in astronomy and mathematics, theirs was a bloodthirsty society. Their gods were many, and one way to please these gods was the offering of human sacrifice. The pyramid was the site of these horrific sacrifices.

Turning to his right, he looked toward the other end of the plaza. There stood the most impressive structure he had seen so far. It was a massive building with three-tiered levels, like that of a wedding cake; the smallest on top, the largest on the bottom.

A ninety foot-wide, intricately carved staircase climbed the center of the building, allowing access to the second and third levels.

The structure was accented with sculpted stone pillars, stone friezes, and a repeating serpent motif. The entire building was so extraordinary that it left no doubt in his mind that this was once the palace of a mighty king.

Alex noticed movement at the palace. He grabbed Mike's arm and pulled him behind the nearest tree. They watched a man walking across the open portico on the second level of the palace.

He was dressed strangely for the jungle. He wore a white Panama hat, a white shirt, a loosened white cravat, white pants, a white belt, and white shoes. He appeared to be a very handsome man, which was a stark contrast to the hideous Veck.

That must be Sebastian, the brains of the outfit, Alex thought. Sebastian was looking to his left. Alex followed his gaze and located the killers who were rapidly approaching the palace.

Using the jungle as cover, the men dashed to within earshot of the palace. They arrived just as the killers arrived at the palace steps.

Veck called out from below. "The plane was right where you said it would be."

"Of course, *mon ami,*" Sebastian replied with a French accent.

Veck separated from his men and climbed the palace steps with the silver case. When he arrived on the second level,

Sebastian reached for the case but yanked his hand away like he'd been bitten by a snake. "You disabled the security device, didn't you?"

"Of course," Veck replied, and he handed the case to him. The big man pointed down the stairs. "I've got a surprise for you."

Sebastian looked. "*Mon dieu!* She survived? Bring her to me at once."

The men hoisted the stretcher and climbed to the second level. Sebastian scanned over Dr. Farah's physical state and seemed pleased. "Bring her inside," he said and ushered them into the palace.

Alex scanned the area. He detected motion sensors mounted in the trees. It occurred to him that Sebastian had to turn off the motion sensors to let the killers through. So, if they wanted to get close to the palace, they had to do it now, before he turned them on again.

Alex waved Mike forward. Keeping low, they sprinted to the palace. Upon reaching the great staircase, they veered right and settled with their backs flat against the wall. No alarms went off. Alex took a relieved breath; so far, so good.

They pushed off the wall and continued the length of the building. They turned left around the corner and crept along the side of the palace. They stopped at a junction box mounted on the wall. Insulated wires from the tree mounted motion sensors snaked along the ground and gathered at the base of the wall.

The group of wires entered the bottom of the junction box. One thick wire exited the top. It ran up the wall and disappeared into a third-story window opening.

Using Mike's pocketknife, Alex pried open the lid of the junction box. He spent the next few minutes rewiring the sensors. He disabled them but made them appear operational. When he finished, he closed the lid and returned the knife to Mike and then continued to the back of the palace.

While the front of the palace was relatively plant-free, the entire back of the palace was covered in vegetation. Only a few window openings had been cleared.

Alex heard indistinct voices coming from a second-story window. He looked up and saw a wide ledge running beneath the second-story window opening; unfortunately, it was some twenty-five feet over his head. He wanted to hear what was being said, but he needed to get up there.

He grasped a fistful of vines growing on the wall, but they tore away in his hands. The vegetation could not hold his weight. He eyed a tree growing beside the wall. No good. The branches were too high to reach.

Then he had an idea.

He stepped back a few paces from the wall and pointed to the second story ledge. Mike caught his meaning. His friend put his back to the wall, leaned over and clasped his hands in front of him.

On the silent count of three, Alex burst forward. He landed his right foot into Mike's cupped hands and was heaved into the air. Alex stretched as high as he could. He was just able to grab the second story ledge with his fingertips.

Then, with the combined strength and agility of a rock climber, he pulled his body up. Once on top of the ledge, he slid his bottom backward until he was directly under the window opening. He listened, as minutes passed in silence.

Fearing they had moved to another room, he took a chance and raised his head. He peered through the black mosquito netting and into the room. He was stunned at what he saw. He expected to find the room filthy from centuries of neglect, but it was spotlessly clean. Even more than that, it was beautifully decorated.

The room was illuminated by Tiffany lamps. Persian rugs lay on the stone floor and expensive French paintings hung on the walls. The room was filled with high-quality furnishings; equal or better than any on Park Avenue apartment in New York City. Who the hell is this guy?

Alex saw Dr. Farah sleeping on a sofa on the other side of the room. The silver case sat on the floor beside her. He heard footsteps and ducked, in time, to avoid being seen by Sebastian and Veck as they entered the room.

The Frenchman said, "I see you came back with half the men you started with. Natives give you trouble?

"They are some real sneaky bastards," Veck replied.

"I see they got Rafferty, too."

Veck laughed. "Nah, we weren't so lucky. I killed him myself and left him for the animals."

"Good, I'm glad. He was such an annoying little pest."

Alex lifted his head. Sebastian was standing near the sleeping scientist on the other side of the room with Veck beside him. Veck turned. "Boss, we have her and the case. When do we leave?"

"As soon as Dr. Valerius arrives with the flash drives, we'll go."

"When is he supposed to get here?"

"Anytime within the next few days, I should think." Sebastian turned. "Ah, here comes Dr. Benga."

A tall, lanky black man with a stethoscope hanging from his neck entered the room and in his hand was a small medical bag. "I hear you have a new patient for me?"

"*Oui,* she is on the sofa."

"Well, let me have a look at her," he said.

Doctor Benga checked her condition. When he finished, he said, "Her vitals are fine, and those cuts and scratches are only superficial, and they won't require stitches. I'll clean her wounds and then get her on an IV and replenish her lost fluids."

"Fine."

"Other than that, I recommend she gets plenty of rest. Will there be anything else?"

"Wake her."

"Wake her? But I just told you she needs her rest."

"I need her awake."

The doctor nodded dutifully.

He opened his medical kit and pulled a small stick of ammonia from his bag. "This should do it." He snapped the stick in the middle to activate the ammonia. The doctor waved it under the woman's nose. She twitched from the burning sensation and swatted the doctor's hand away.

Her eyes flickered open. "Where am I?" she asked weakly.

The Frenchman sat beside her on the couch and took her hand in his. In a soft, fatherly tone he said, "Not to worry my dear, you are in good hands."

"Who are you?"

"My name is Sebastian."

"What am I doing here?"

"I will explain it all in good time, but first I need something from you. I need you to open the case."

"My case? I won't."

"I'm sorry, but you misunderstand. You do not have a choice."

"But I can't," she protested, "I don't even know the combination."

"Do not play games with me doctor; I am well acquainted with your security procedures. All I need is your thumbprint on the scanner, so please..." he said motioning to the case.

"It won't do any good. You need my partner's thumbprint on the scanner at the same time or it won't open."

Veck produced a small container approximately the size of a pack of cigarettes. He opened the container and dumped the contents on the floor. Amid the blue cooling agent was her partners severed the thumb.

"No!" Dr. Farah screamed and turned away.

Sebastian squeezed her hand until it caused considerable pain. "Dr. Farah, I am not a patient man. I will only say this once more. Place your thumb on the scanner or I will order Veck to remove it."

The big man grinned and jerked a long knife from a leather sheath on his belt.

Dr. Farah shivered. "No! Stop. I'll do it...," she sobbed.

Sebastian let go of her hand and used his foot to slide the case close to her.

Dr. Farah sat up, hesitated, and then pressed her thumb to the scanner on top of the case. She turned away as Veck placed Dr. Llewellyn's severed thumb beside it. The two thumbprints registered, the internal lock 'clicked,' and the latches opened.

6

It was late afternoon in the Oval Office. President Grant was busy signing papers at his desk when his secretary knocked on the door. "Mr. President, everyone is waiting for you in the situation room."

"Thank you, Violet."

The president set down the pen, snatched his cane and rolled the chair away from his desk. As he painfully got to his feet, a tall, slender man with a gray beard and fine tailored suit walked into the room.

"Mr. President," he said with a wide grin.

"Charles," replied the president happily.

The former senator strode across the room and gave the president a hug.

"Thanks for coming," said the president.

"I just hope I can be of some assistance."

"I'm sure you will. C'mon, the meeting's about to start."

"Race ya," Senator McDaniel joked.

"You bastard!" replied the president with a laugh. "This is probably the only time in my life you could ever beat me. Even with my bad knees, it would be a close race."

"What do you mean?"

"You are the slowest runner I ever met. Remember the time we went on a panty raid in the girl's dorm? You were the only one caught."

"Yes, but I tripped."

"Did you also trip when we set off firecrackers in the dean's office?"

"You know, I almost got expelled for that one."

The president laughed and slapped the senator's back.

The president and Senator McDaniel arrived at the Situation Room. As soon as they entered the idle chattering stopped.

Seated dutifully around the oval mahogany table was the Secretary of State Joanne Briers, the Secretary of Defense Paul Ashley, the Secretary of Homeland Security Eric Turbeville, National Security Advisor Mary Ann Tuggs, the Military Joint Chiefs, the Directors of FBI, CIA, NSA, the president's chief of staff and senior advisor David Lawson.

Pleasantries were exchanged between the president and his people, but the real attention was directed at the popular former senator from Colorado.

"Senator, how's retirement?" asked one.

The senator stroked his gray beard. "It has its perks. I don't have to shave every day, and I can sleep in as long as I want."

"With that beard, you look like a mountain man," joked another.

The senator waved good-naturedly and took an empty seat at the end of the table.

The president sat down in his chair at the center of the table and leaned his cane against it. As he pulled his chair up to the table, he looked at the empty seat across from him. He turned to his chief of staff. "David, was the vice president informed of the meeting?"

"Yes, sir."

The President shook his head. He took a drink of water and then set down the glass. He looked around the table. "I know all of you are wondering why I dragged Senator McDaniel out of mothballs and brought him to this meeting. Let me start by saying that the senator and I go way back; we were college roommates. I trust him implicitly, and that's not an easy thing for any politician to say.

"When he called the other day complaining that he'd been doing nothing but staring at the walls, I jumped at the chance to bring him on board. He was a champion in the Senate for Dr. Farah's and Dr. Llewellyn's project. He is also one of the very few people who know the intimate details of it. He and David will act as my advisors and personal liaison."

The president folded his hands in front of him. His expression turned serious. "I should start by saying, as of yet, we have had no luck locating Dr. Farah or the case. But we do have new information I think you should know." The president nodded at Colonel Don Degendorfer, the man in charge of the crash site.

Colonel Degendorfer opened a folder, consulted his notes for a moment and then began. "Ladies and gentlemen, after an extensive examination of the wreckage, we now have conclusive proof of what caused the crash.

"We discovered a sophisticated remote guidance chip installed into the flight's computer system. With this chip, it was possible for someone on the ground to take over the controls of the aircraft. Once our plane entered Belizean airspace, our pilots lost all control.

"We also discovered that approximately right

before, during, and after the crash, all those flying in the vicinity had been unable to receive or transmit over their radios. We believe whoever pulled this off was jamming all radio frequencies. This prevented the pilots from reporting their circumstances and their location.

"The culprits wanted to make finding the aircraft as difficult as possible. They accomplished this by disabling the plane's emergency transmitter. If it weren't for our eyewitnesses in the helicopter, it may have taken us weeks, maybe even months to find the plane in that dense rainforest.

"To sum up, this was a well thought out, well-executed plan. Dr. Farah and Dr. Llewellyn's plane was intentionally crashed in a predetermined location where men on the ground were waiting for it.

"They boarded the plane, killed Dr. Llewellyn and two security officers, and then took Dr. Farah and the case. They also cut off Dr. Llewellyn's thumb presumably to open the case. We are dealing with ruthless killers who knew exactly what they were doing. Other than that, the search is ongoing." Colonel Degendorfer closed the folder.

The president nodded his head thoughtfully and said, "Any news of those two former Navy SEALs lowered from the helicopter?"

Colonel Degendorfer shook his head. "No, sir."

Navy Admiral Carr leaned forward in his chair. "Excuse me, but may I ask the names of those SEALs?"

"I have them right here," the FBI director replied. He glanced at his notes, "Um...Alex McCade and Mike Garrison."

Admiral Carr leaned back in his seat and smiled. "McCade and Garrison?"

"You know them?"

"I do, and off the record, I'll never want to play cards with those two again," he said laughing.

"Good men?" asked the president.

"None better."

Senator McDaniel interrupted. "Mr. President, I know these men as well. As you know my daughter, Kimberly, was kidnapped eight years ago by terrorists and it was Commander McCade who led the team to rescue her and Lieutenant Garrison was with him."

"Are you sure it's these same two men?"

"Yes, sir. After I got my daughter back, I made it a point to personally thank all the men involved in her rescue."

National Security Advisor, Mary Ann Tuggs broke in, "That may be all well and good, but have any of you considered that these men might be a part of all this? That they didn't just 'happen' to be in the area but are part of the scheme to steal the project?"

The Admiral shook his head confidently. "Not these two."

The FBI director agreed. "We've checked them out thoroughly and their stories check out. They're legit."

"What if...?"

"Stop," said the President firmly. "From what I've heard we're damn lucky to have these men on our team, so unless there is proof to the contrary, we will consider them on our side."

President Grant turned to the director of the FBI. "What do we have on your end?"

Before the director could speak, the door to the situation room burst open and the vice president came rushing in. "Sorry I'm late," he said and slipped into his chair.

"Glad you could join us," the president said sarcastically.

The president nodded for the FBI director to begin.

The FBI director said, "The guidance microchip that Colonel Degendorfer's team discovered in the wreckage takes time to install. Since the plane made no stops in route, it could only have been accomplished at the island's laboratory facility. Security is extremely tight on the island. We speculated that it was an inside job, and we were right.

"The body of an avionics expert was found dead in a locked storage room. He had been stabbed repeatedly with a knife. We found the knife and got clean prints off it. The fingerprints belong to Special Projects Director, Dr. Paul Valerius. We searched Dr. Valerius's office and discovered he had downloaded highly classified files of the project from his computer."

"Where is he now?" The president asked.

"He escaped the island just before the flight departed and hasn't been seen since."

The president locked onto the man's eyes and said, "Find him."

7

Alex sat under the Mayan palace window and thought about what he heard. Now he had a good sense of what was going on. Somehow Sebastian forced the executive jet down where his men were waiting for it.

Their sole purpose was to steal the case. Alex still didn't know what was in the case, but it had to be important for them to go to all that trouble to get it. The scientist was not expected to survive the crash, but she did. Having her alive was a fortunate bonus.

He slid to the end of the ledge, swung his body around and dropped to the ground. He spotted Mike waving to him from behind a crumbling courtyard wall and he joined him.

Behind the wall, Mike said, "So, what'd you hear?"

Alex told him everything he heard inside the palace room.

"He really cut that guy's thumb off? There was so much blood on that plane I didn't notice. So, what's the plan?"

"What makes you think I have a plan?"

"You always have a plan."

"Alright, I have a plan. I want you to go back to the crash site and bring back help."

"Go back? Why? We should both stay and rescue

the scientist."

"She's in no shape to hike out of here. Not yet, anyway. I need you to go back. It's important that someone else knows what's going on here. If we both stay, we take the chance of being captured and that information dies with us."

"Think someone will still be at the crash site?"

"If the scientist and the case are as important as I think they are; they'll still be searching for them."

"What will you do while I'm gone?"

"I'll sit tight and make sure they don't go anywhere until you bring back the cavalry."

"Okay, I'll do it on one condition. Since I'm the one doing all the hard work, and you, more than likely, will just be sitting on your lazy ass while I'm gone--you owe me a big seafood dinner and all the beer I can drink when we get back home."

"You cheap-ass. I always end up paying anyway, and you know it."

"Yeah, but next time you can't complain about it."

"Alright, it's a deal," Alex replied.

Mike got to his feet. He slapped Alex on the shoulder and headed back the way they had come.

Now alone, Alex got to his feet. With a couple of hours left before nightfall, it was time to do a little reconnaissance. The more he learned of his surroundings, the better off he'd be.

He spent the next hour hiking around the outskirts of the Mayan jungle city, noting the number of armed men, the different buildings and possible escape routes. He was making his way back to his original position behind the palace wall when he heard footsteps.

He ducked behind a tree and watched as four men

headed single file down a jungle trail. The man in the lead had an AK-47 rifle, while the three men following carried wooden crates. Alex allowed them to get ahead of him and then he followed.

A short distance down the trail the men passed through an arched opening in a ten-foot high stone wall draped heavily in jungle plants.

As Alex approached, he saw human skulls visible within the vegetation. Hundreds of them lined up side by side. Vines slipped eerily through eye sockets, over cheekbones, and between the gaping jaws.

He went through the opening in the wall and continued along the trail. A short distance ahead the path led onto the field of an ancient Mayan ball court. Under the bright glow of modern floodlights, Sebastian's men loaded the wooden crates into a sleek, black helicopter.

Alex visually examined the ball court. The court was in the shape of the letter 'I' with high, slanted stone walls on both sides. Mounted high on the walls, two stone rings where ancient players once attempted to pass a hard rubber ball through.

Some scholars believe the games had been played to the death. That wall full of skulls now made sense. It must be some kind of gruesome trophy that displayed the heads of losing team members.

He scanned the area and noted that on each corner of the field were thick, steel supports that rose high into the trees. He looked up. On top of these vertical supports was a webbing of steel beams that spanned the field. It was a retractable roof.

Atop the roof was an artificial rainforest canopy to hide the field from above. This retractable roof would allow Sebastian's helicopter to come and go as it pleased while keeping the city a secret. It was clear a lot of trouble and expense went into keeping this location hidden from view.

After the crates had been loaded, the men closed the chopper door and returned to the jungle path they'd come from. The last man stopped at the edge of the field. He opened a small metal box attached to a support pole. He flipped a switch, and the field went dark.

While the men hiked back to the palace, Alex stayed where he was and contemplated this new development. He no longer had to wait for help to arrive. Finding the helicopter changed everything. He would use it to rescue the scientist and fly her out tonight. He smiled. He couldn't wait to see the look on Mike's face when he beat him back to civilization.

When darkness fell, he was hunched behind the crumbling stone wall in the rear of the palace. He had spent the remaining daylight fashioning a long rope from flexible vines.

By midnight, the interior lights of the palace had been off for hours, and Alex saw no activity whatsoever. It was time to make his move.

He dug his fingers into the wet mud and applied it until every inch of his exposed skin was covered. Satisfactorily camouflaged, he slipped the coiled rope over his shoulder and got to his feet.

A howler monkey roared in the distance. He took that as his cue and advanced silently on the palace.

When he reached the rear palace wall, he located a perfect climbing tree. He wrapped his arms around it and shimmied up it like a pacific islander going for coconuts. When he reached the height of the second story, he extended his leg, pushed off the tree, and stepped onto the stone ledge.

Standing on the ledge, with his back pressed against the wall, he remained completely still. All was quiet. Dr.

Farah's room was about forty feet away. He began to move. To keep from falling, he kept his hand in contact with the wall. Treading along a ledge, some twenty-five feet off the ground, was dangerous. One misstep could cause a bad fall, and this was no time to break a leg.

Suddenly, he saw an orange glow from a window a few feet ahead of him and froze. It was a guard leaning out the window as he smoked a cigarette.

Quietly, Alex sidled up to the guard's window. He assumed the sentry would be sleepy and only half interested in what he was doing. From experience, he knew that sentry duty could be very boring. Even the best soldiers constantly had to fight the urge to relax and let their minds wander.

Alex made a fist with his right hand.

The cigarette glowed again.

Alex let go with a powerful back-fist. He made solid contact, and the man dropped with a heavy thud to the floor. He was sure that the man never knew what hit him.

Alex walked by the window and stopped at Dr. Farah's. Inside, he could hear the rhythmic breathing of someone sleeping. He lifted his leg and slipped into the dark room.

He laid the coil of vines lightly on the floor and started moving toward the sound of the sleeping scientist.

He was suddenly blinded by the bright beam of a flashlight. On instinct, he dropped below the beam and was ready to launch, when he realized it was only a frightened woman holding it. And a very beautiful woman at that.

She had a narrow face; high cheekbones, fair skin, with stunning eyes and thick, dark brown hair that fell past her shoulders. The woman appeared to be in her late twenties and wore only panties and a white t-shirt. She looked scared, but she wasn't backing down. There was a fierceness about her. She had a flashlight in one hand and a raised water pitcher in the other.

"Who are you?" she demanded.

"Keep your voice down," Alex whispered. "My name is Alex McCade."

"Wait, you're not one of Sebastian's men are you?"

"That's right, I'm not. I'm here to rescue Dr. Farah."

She lowered the flashlight. "If that's the case I'm coming with you. I'm being held prisoner, too." She held out her hand. "My name is Sophie Marcus."

Alex shook it. "Nice to meet you Sophie."

From the glow of the downturned flashlight, he saw the scientist lying on a cot, asleep. A bag of saline solution hung from a pole beside her bed. The solution was being fed intravenously.

As he reached to wake her, Sophie grabbed his arm. "Don't, the way you look you'll scare her half to death. Let me do it."

Sophie gently shook her shoulder, and said tenderly, "Dr. Farah, its Sophie," She shook her again. "Dr. Farah, wake up."

The scientist mumbled something and slowly opened her eyes. "Is it morning, already?"

"No, we're leaving?"

"Leaving?"

"Yes, a man has come to rescue you."

He stepped forward. "Dr. Farah, excuse the way I look, but my name is Alex McCade, and I've come to get you out of here."

"Oh, thank god," replied the scientist. "Help me up."

Sophie helped her to a sitting position on the bed.

"How are you feeling?" He asked.

"A little better," she replied and rubbed her eyes, "How did you find me?"

"I followed you from the crash site."

"Oh, my word. I never saw or heard you at all."

"We didn't want to ruin the surprise." Alex pulled the needle from her arm and helped her to her feet. "Sophie, help her out the window and wait for me on the ledge."

He retrieved the rope from the floor and looked around for something to tie it too. The room was mostly empty. Then his eyes settled on the cot the scientist was sleeping on. That would do.

He tied one end of the rope to the cot frame and tossed the free end out the window. He climbed out the window and stood on the ledge next to the two women.

He pulled on the rope until the cot rested flat against the inside part of the window frame. Once secure, he handed the rope to Sophie, and whispered, "You first. Tug on the rope when you're on the ground."

She descended the rope. Due to the darkness, he lost sight of her immediately. Moments later, he felt the rope wiggle in his hands.

"Dr. Farah clutched his arm and whispered into his ear, "I'm sorry. I'm afraid I'm too weak to climb down a rope."

"I didn't expect you to," Alex replied and crouched. "Hop on."

Dr. Farah climbed onto his back. She wrapped her arms and legs around him. Then she stiffened. "Wait! I can't leave without my case. That awful man has it."

"Don't worry about it. I'll get you to the helicopter and then I'll come back for it."

With Dr. Farah secure on his back and the rope held tightly in his hands, Alex stepped off the ledge.

8

In the White House Situation Room, President Grant sat forward in his chair. Before he could speak, the National Security Advisor Mary Ann Tuggs gave him an exasperated look. "Mr. President, we know Dr. Farah's project has been stolen, but beyond that, we know very little. This is an extremely important matter, and I believe it's time we were all brought in on it."

"I agree, Mary Ann. That's the reason I called this meeting and why I asked Dr. Toshi Tanimura, the director of the Advanced Weapons Research and Development facility to join us." The president turned to the large monitor on the wall, and the screen lit up.

Dr. Tanimura, a second generation Japanese American, appeared wearing a white shirt and green herringbone patterned tie. He had black hair parted in a perfectly straight line along the side of his head and wore a pair of rounded metal-rimmed glasses.

"Good afternoon, Dr. Tanimura," the president said, "Thank you for joining us. Please enlighten us on the Morpheus Project."

"Certainly," replied Dr. Tanimura. "Dr. Farah and the late Dr. Llewellyn spent the last fifteen years working on the project at our island facility. To say they made gigantic scientific gains is an understatement. They created a weapons system like no other, a weapon that may end war as we know it. Imagine a war with no shots fired. No deaths."

He turned. "Behind me is a diagram of the 'Morpheus Project'. This space-age weapon is a laser rifle which is primarily made from titanium and graphite composites making it surprisingly light and mobile.

"It is a solid-state laser and operates as all lasers do. Molecules are excited by heat which is reflected in mirrors to increase its speed. As the velocity increases, a light is produced. With a pull of the trigger mechanism, this light leaves the barrel as a narrow, highly charged beam of light.

"What makes this laser rifle truly amazing is the addition of a sleep agent. Before light exits the barrel, it passes through the canister containing the sleep agent.

"Basically, molecules of a gasified sleeping agent adhere to the particles of the light beam. These molecules, in essence, hitch a ride with the laser beam as it travels to the target.

"When the laser beam makes contact with a human target, the sleeping agent is absorbed through the skin and enters the bloodstream. Moments later, they are rendered unconscious anywhere from four to six hours with no lasting effects."

Dr. Tanimura leaned forward with his hands on the table. "Now you understand why we named this project after Morpheus, the Greek God of sleep and dreams. Hence the name, the Morpheus Project.

"And depending on the width and strength of the beam, the laser can strike one soldier or an entire division in one shot."

General Hopkins of the Joint Chiefs spoke up, "How is it that the sleeping agent isn't destroyed by the intense heat from the laser?"

"Because Dr. Farah came up with a solution to that very question. She did it by the ingenious use of nanotechnology. Tiny units, one-billionth of a meter in size, are used to coat the gaseous light particles and insulate it from the heat."

Mary Ann looked skeptical, "Are you saying Dr. Farah's transformation process doesn't change the molecular structure of the sleeping agent at all?"

"That's right," he answered. "The molecular structure and potency of the agent remain at 100%."

General Price asked, "What about contamination to the shooter?"

"Good question," Dr. Tanimura replied. "Let me assure you, there is absolutely no contamination to the shooter. Inside the laser is a negative vacuuming system that prevents matter from escaping.

"I would also like to mention that there is an internal cooling system, so the weapon can be fired multiple times in succession without excessive heat buildup."

"What type of power supply is needed to fire the weapon?"

"Actually, very little power is needed. This laser rifle isn't meant to shoot down missiles from the sky; the beam only needs to make 'light contact' with the target. So, to answer your question, any AC/DC source will do. It also comes with a battery pack that can be worn around the waist."

"What about operating the laser in bad weather?" asked the national security advisor.

"The laser uses a highly sophisticated electronic guidance system, which incidentally was designed by the late Dr. Llewellyn. Once the beam locks on target, it stays on target despite the weather conditions."

Dr. Tanimura adjusted his glasses. "I would like to add that the light beam is infrared. The only indication that a person has been hit is a small red dot of light, approximately the size of a pencil eraser. This light will appear briefly at the point of contact and then disappear within a matter of seconds."

With no further questions, the president thanked the esteemed scientist for his time, and the screen went black.

The president scanned the faces around the table. "As you know, the Morpheus Project has been stolen. What you don't know is—there were also canisters of deadly chemical and biological agents in that case, too."

The room erupted with people talking over one another.

The president slapped his palm on the table. "Everyone please calm down."

The room went quiet.

The president's tone was serious. "The chemical and biological agents, in that case, were only to be tested on cattle at the White Sands missile range. When Dr. Farah and Dr. Llewellyn finished those tests, the canisters were to be returned to the laboratory and sealed in the vault."

The president read the horrified faces around the table.

Mary Ann blurted out, "Mr. President, how could you include chemical and biological agents? That seems highly irresponsible."

"I understand your concern, but as president, my number one priority is to protect the citizens of the United States. It is my thinking that if we were attacked with chemical and biological weapons, then I want the ability to retaliate in kind.

"I repeat…the addition of chemical and biological agents for use in the laser rifle was for test purposes only. The emphasis of the laser is and will always be intended for nonlethal use."

"Mr. President, how many of the chemical and biological agents are in the case?" asked the Secretary of Defense.

"Twelve."

Mary Ann Tuggs narrowed her brows. "What kind agents are we talking about?"

"The deadliest kind--smallpox, the black plague, Ebola, sarin gas, mustard gas, and more."

Mary Ann huffed. "And now it's in the hands of some mad man!"

"There is one bright spot, Admiral Carr interjected.

"What can that possibly be?"

"We still have McCade and Garrison on the thief's tail, and I for one will never underestimate what they can do."

"I hope you're right Admiral," replied the president, "because at the moment... they're our only hope."

9

Alex descended the palace wall with Dr. Farah on his back. As he reached the ground, he bent over to ease the scientist off. But as he straightened, he was blasted off his feet by a tremendous blow to his head.

He hit the ground hard. He looked up from the ground and peered into the darkness. He didn't see anyone, but he heard heavy breathing directly in front of him. Fueled by anger and a sore head, he jumped to his feet.

In a burst of energy, he exploded forward. He hit the man with the impact of a linebacker stuffing a running back coming through the line, but it felt like he hit a tree by mistake. The man didn't move. Nonetheless, Alex wrapped his arms around the man's torso and kept his legs pumping.

He managed to drive the man back a few feet before he finally toppled to the ground. Alex landed right on top of him. As he rolled to his knees, he delivered an elbow to the man's head as a parting gift.

Alex didn't want to give him a chance to recover. He blindly grabbed the man's chin in his left hand and calculated where the nose would be. He brought his right fist back to strike--when he was hit by a multitude of flashlight beams.

Using his palm to block the light, he saw that he

was completely surrounded by armed men. Off to the side, he saw Sophie and Dr. Farah being held by men with hands over their mouths.

"Hands up!" demanded a voice from behind one of the flashlights.

Alex, angry at himself for being caught, reluctantly raised his hands in the air. A man rushed forward. He wrenched his arms behind his back and used a rope to tightly bind his wrists.

When the man finished, he stepped away. Only then did Alex see who attacked him. It was Veck. The big man was lying on the ground, and he did not look happy.

The large mass rose from the ground, his grotesque face twisting with fury and the scar under his eye seemed to pulsate with a life of its own. He growled and lumbered toward Alex. The giant stopped two feet from him.

Without warning, he thrust his beastly palm into Alex's windpipe and squeezed. Alex's throat felt like it was caught in a vise. He could not breathe. Then, with his one massive arm, Veck hoisted him completely off the ground. The monster's strength was staggering.

With his oxygen cut off, Alex's face began to turn purple, and he could feel an immense pressure building behind his eyes. He was within seconds of blacking out, when a familiar voice with a French accent shouted, "Drop him."

Veck groaned his displeasure and released his grip.

Alex dropped to the ground and gasped for air. As oxygen refilled his lungs, his vision improved enough to see a pair of white silk slippers standing inches from his face.

With effort, he turned his head and looked up. Sebastian stood above him with his hands firmly set in the pockets of his white silk robe. He looked down with contempt and said, "Who the devil are you?"

Alex coughed, unable to answer.

"Very well," Sebastian said. "Veck, bring him to my room."

Sebastian yelled to a guard, "Take your men and check the sensors. I want to know how he slipped by, and make sure there are no more like him out there."

"Yes sir," the guard replied. He took other men with rifles with him and hurried off.

Veck yanked Alex to his feet and roughly patted him down for weapons. He found none. He grasped the back of Alex's neck and hissed, "When Sebastian is done with you mate--you're all mine."

Alex was marched to the front of the palace, up the stairs, then taken inside. He was brought to Sebastian's room. Veck pushed him into the center of the room and turned the lights up bright.

Sebastian eyed him. "Well, *monsieur*, why don't we start by telling me your name?"

Alex gulped. His throat burned. "Name's Smith," He replied in a raspy voice.

"Smith? How nice. I assume you're an American."

He said nothing.

"Mr. Smith, why don't we stop playing games, hmmm? I want you to tell me your real name and how you got here?"

He said nothing.

Sebastian began to walk in slow circles around him, sizing up his prey. "It's a shame you don't feel like talking." The Frenchman stopped. He nodded to Veck and the big man took his cue.

He circled behind Alex and let go of a vicious

punch to his kidney. A bolt of intense pain shot through his body and he involuntarily dropped to a knee.

Sebastian smiled. "It'll be a lot easier if you simply tell me what I want to know."

Alex bit back the pain and stared defiantly ahead.

The Frenchman turned to the women. "*Mademoiselles*, do either of you know this man?"

Both women shook their heads.

"Did he say whether anyone else was with him?

Both shook their heads again.

Sebastian turned to a guard entering the room. "What about the motion sensors?"

"The sensors were rewired at the junction box. They weren't operational."

"Fix them, *immediatement*!" Those natives may be out there right now just waiting to attack us."

"Yes sir, it's already being taken care of."

Sebastian pointed at his prisoner. "Any more like him out there?"

"Not that we can tell sir, but we'll keep looking."

"Good."

The guard left the room as fast as he entered.

Veck glared at the prisoner with hatred, "The Yank looks like the Special Forces type to me."

Sebastian nodded, "*Oui*, I think you may be right *mon ami*. If that's the case, he is too dangerous to keep. Kill him."

"You can't!" Sophie screamed.

Veck smiled and withdrew a long knife from his sheath. The big man held it for a moment and then pressed the sharp steel blade to Alex's throat.

"Wait," Sebastian said.

Veck's knife hand froze. His eyes lifted, pleading for permission to kill the intruder.

Sebastian shook his head. "Not yet. I'll give him until morning to decide whether he wants to cooperate or not."

The big man snarled, "Give me time alone with him; I'll make him talk."

Sebastian grinned. "When morning comes, and if he still refuses to cooperate, you may do with him as you please. In the meantime, take him and Dr. Marcus to the pyramid for safe keeping…and leave a guard."

Veck appeared shocked. "Dr. Marcus, too? But she belongs to me."

"*Oui, mon ami,* but not until later. I still need her…professionally speaking."

The big man angrily thrust his knife into his sheath. He grabbed Alex by the back of the shirt and lifted him to his feet. Veck kicked him with his huge boot and sent him stumbling toward the door.

Sebastian tightened the sash around his robe, "I want him in good enough condition to answer my questions in the morning."

Veck snarled, "He will be."

Before leaving, Veck grabbed a long, heavy metal flashlight from a box near the door and then waved to an armed guard to accompany him.

The big man led the small group by flashlight. He marched them down the palace stairs and then across the grand plaza.

When they arrived at the base of the pyramid Veck aimed the flashlight up the nearly vertical staircase and began to climb. A firm jab from the guard's rifle persuaded Alex and Sophie to follow.

After a strenuous climb to the top, they paused in front of the temple doorways to catch their breath. Alex expected to see the big man collapse from exhaustion, but to his surprise, he was no more winded than the rest of them. Alex could not help but be impressed...and a little wary.

The brute was incredibly strong, as he exhibited earlier by lifting him completely off the ground and by being so well-conditioned, as he proved by hiking up the pyramid steps. This was one man he did not dare underestimate.

The guard pushed him toward the temple. As Alex went in, he got a good look at the long stone frieze looming above the doorways. The frieze showed images of the ancient Maya taking prisoners, followed by scenes of painful torture, ending in human sacrifice. He hoped those images were not a sign of things to come.

"Go," the guard barked.

Once inside the temple, he saw Veck dropping to knees. The big man removed a stone plug from the middle of the floor. Then, reaching into the shadows, he retrieved a rope with a five-inch metal rod fastened to one end.

He slipped the rod into the hole and gave the rope a securing tug. Rising to his feet, he took the rope in both hands and pulled. A heavy stone slab lifted from the floor, exposing a vaulted staircase that led deep into the dark bowels of the pyramid.

10

Alex was forced into the hole with his hands still tied behind his back, and he carefully descended the stairs with care.

When he arrived at the bottom, he entered a dark inner chamber. The air was cool and stale. Sophie entered the chamber behind him. She stepped up and locked her arm around his. He could feel her shivering.

Veck walked into the chamber and swept his flashlight beam around the room. The walls were smooth, coated with white plaster. Three thick stone pillars supported the ceiling which ran the length of the room.

On the rear wall, Alex saw two 3' x 5' colorful Mayan paintings. Other than hanging spider webs and a small pile of human bones lying in a corner, the chamber was empty.

Without warning, Veck sucker-punched him in the stomach. Alex doubled over and gasped hard for breath.

"Stop it!" Sophie yelled.

Veck raised his big boot and kicked Alex to the floor. "Watch him," he said to the guard.

With Alex out of the way, Veck turned a lustful eye to Sophie. He snatched her in his arms. She tried wiggling free, but he was far too strong.

"Relax love," he said and drove his mouth toward hers. Then he rammed his thick tongue past her tightly pursed lips.

Alex, still gasping for air on the floor, struggled to loosen the rope around his wrists, but it was too tight. Outraged by the treatment of Sophie, he rolled onto his feet.

The guard jabbed the AK-47 barrel into his ribs and said, "Don't even think about it."

Never one to listen to threats, Alex moved quickly. He sharply rotated his upper torso and used his elbow to knock the barrel away from his body. Then, he lunged and head-butted the guard in the face. The man dropped like dead weight to the floor.

In a flash, Alex pivoted on the balls of his feet and catapulted himself at Veck, but he wasn't fast enough. The big man saw him coming. He swung the heavy flashlight, and the metal casing connected solidly with Alex's head. Everything went black.

Sometime later, he awoke lying on the hard stone floor. His mouth was dry and chalky, and his head was throbbing. He wasn't sure how long he'd been out. The chamber was completely dark, and he felt disoriented. He tried to clear his head and rise, but severe dizziness forced him to lie back down. Then he passed out again.

He woke again later. It was still completely dark in the chamber, but at least he was feeling better. Instead of the jackhammer pounding inside his head, it was now only a few bass drums.

He touched the lump on the side of his head with his fingers and winced. It was then he realized with surprise that his hands had been freed from the ropes. He rose to a sitting position. Peering into the darkness, he called out, "Sophie?"

A hand unexpectedly touched his thigh, and he jerked back.

"Sorry to startle you," she said. "How are you feeling?"

He couldn't see her, but from the sound of her voice she was sitting right next to him. "Head's a little sore," he replied, "but other than that I'm okay. The more important question is…how are you?"

"Thanks to you, I'm fine. But I swear, one day I am going to get even with that bastard."

Alex felt the lump on his head again. "That makes two of us."

He scooted backward until he felt the wall behind him. He leaned back to rest. "What happened?"

"You mean after he hit you?"

"Yes."

"The flashlight went out. He tried to fix it but got frustrated. Then, he dropped the flashlight and stormed up the stairs."

"He left you alone, then?"

"Yes."

"Glad to hear the knock on my head did some good; although, in my younger days I may have been able to shake off a hit like that."

"Younger days? How old are you?"

"Thirty-two."

"That's not old," she said with a chuckle.

"From what I've put this body through it is."

Alex leaned forward. "So, what's the story with you and Veck? It appears he has taken quite an interest with you."

"Ugh, it started from the moment I was captured,

Veck stared at me. At first he tried to hide it, but as time went on, he became bolder. When it became too much to bear I complained to Sebastian."

"Did it help?"

"For a little while, but the longer I was here, the more Veck became obsessed. He even began warning others not to look at me because I was his girl."

"Frightening."

"You can say that again. I get the shivers even thinking about it."

"How did you end up in the city?"

"About three weeks ago, I led an archeological team to search for the lost Mayan city of Kan Ajaw K'uhul. The city had been lost for over 500 years and finding it had been my dream since I was a little girl.

"My father used to tell me stories of the infamous jungle city and its mighty king. While most girls dreamed of boys, I dreamed of finding the city. I spent hundreds of hours of research. When I believed I had finally nailed down the location, I put a team together to find it."

"And you found it."

She spat, "Only to learn that someone else found the city six months before me!"

"Sebastian."

She nodded.

"What happened to your team?"

"From the start, we were hounded by natives. Eventually, nine of our members went missing. We tried to call for help, but our satellite phone didn't work. The rest of us thought about turning back, but we decided to keep going.

"Then we found the ancient Mayan city and once we entered the city Sebastian's men pounced on us. They held us for about a week and then killed the rest of my team."

"Why'd Sebastian keep you alive?"

"He said he knew about my reputation as an archeologist and needed my help finding the king's treasure."

"Treasure?"

"The former ruler of this city was a very rich and powerful king. It was said that before his death he hid a vast treasure in the city."

"And Sebastian wants it."

"Yes, and he's plundering all the antiquities he finds."

Alex recalled men loading wooden crates into the helicopter. Those crates must have been filled with the antiquities she was talking about. "Is he planning to keep them for his own collection?"

"Yes and no. He plans on keeping the best pieces for himself and then sell the rest on the black market."

"Does anyone on the outside know the city's been found?"

"Not yet. But just wait. Once the world hears that the lost City of the Serpent King has been found, it will be the biggest thing since King Tut's tomb was discovered in Egypt."

"That big?"

"You bet."

Alex blindly swept his hands in front of him hoping to find the broken flashlight. "You said Veck dropped the flashlight. Do you know where it is? Maybe I can fix it?"

"Way ahead of you," she replied. She turned on the flashlight, and a light beam illuminated a spot on the far wall. "A few loose batteries, that's all."

With effort, Alex rose to his feet. He wobbled slightly and used the wall to steady himself.

"What are you doing?" she asked.

"It's time to go."

"We can't," she replied. "Veck sealed us in and posted a guard up top."

"Maybe there's another way out."

"I'm an archeologist, and I've been down here many times before. There is no other exit."

He held his hand out for the flashlight. "Well, it won't hurt to have another look, will it?"

Sophie handed it to him.

Alex panned the beam around the room. There was no obvious way out, but who didn't watch movies? There was always a secret passage out of these situations. Okay, maybe he watched too many movies as a kid, but it wouldn't hurt to look around.

He slowly walked around the chamber trying to feel any hint of air seeping out the joints in the stone walls. Unfortunately, the joints were tight. Whoever made these walls had been highly skilled. Not even a knife blade could fit between these cracks.

He continued on. Every few feet or so he stopped and used the end of the flashlight to tap against the stones, hoping to find a hollow one.

After making two complete passes around the room he gave up and plopped down next to Sophie. "Nothing."

"Like I told you. I've been down here many times before and I've never found any other way out. But..." she said, rising to her feet, "I did find something extremely valuable. Want to see?"

Alex gave her the flashlight and followed her to the foot of the stairs.

Sophie dropped to her knees. She worked her fingers into a crack and lowered a stone slab to the floor. Reaching inside a hollow cavity, she removed a large book covered in the orange and black spotted pelt of a jaguar. She held out the book for him to see.

"What is this?" he asked.

"This is a very rare Mayan Codex." She carefully opened the front cover of the book. Inside were beautiful drawings and hieroglyphics done in luminous red and black paint. "To date, only four have been found," she said, "Until now, that is. This makes the fifth."

Her eyes sparkled. "At one time, thousands existed, but when the Spanish came and attempted to conquer the Maya, they burned as many as they could find. It was a deliberate act to destroy their culture and turn the Maya into Christians. And what the Spanish couldn't destroy, time and the elements did. To even find a codex is a very rare thing, but to find one in this good of condition is even rarer."

"That's quite a find."

"But that's not all. While the other codices dealt with astronomy, religion, the calendar, and mathematics, this one deals solely with Kan Ajaw K'uhul."

"Who?"

"The great Maya king. You've never heard of him?"

"Can't say that I have."

"Translated, Kan Ajaw K'uhul, means 'The Divine Serpent King'.

"And this is his city?"

"Yes."

Slowly she paged through the book, and he marveled at all the strange and wonderful hieroglyphs inside. "Can you read these?" he asked.

"Yes...well, all but the last three pages."

"Why not those?"

"Because they're filled with glyphs I've never seen before--no one has. But once I get a chance to dig into it, I'm sure I'll be able to decipher them."

He pointed at the back wall. "Since you're the expert what can you tell me about those paintings?"

"Quite a bit actually; give me a second."

Sophie closed the book. She handed Alex the flashlight and then carefully placed the codex inside the cavity under the stairs. She lifted the stone slab and then gave it a bump with her fist to secure it.

Rising, the two proceeded to the rear wall. "Which one would you like to know about first?" she asked.

He aimed the beam at the colorful painting on the left. "Let's start with this one."

"Alright. The man standing is Kan Ajaw K'uhul. Kneeling below him is his wife. Both are participating in a bloodletting ceremony.

"As you can see, his wife is passing a rope with thorns through her tongue, and that woven basket under her chin is filled with paper. The paper catches the dripping blood and will later be burned in a tribute to their gods."

"They really used to do that?"

"They sure did."

He panned the flashlight to the painting on the right. "Okay, now this one."

"This painting depicts Kan Ajaw K'uhul's birth."

"His birth? All I see is a nude man floating above a

line."

"That nude man is the king, and that line represents a crack in the earth from which he is being born. The Maya believed their gods lived within the earth and their kings were born from it."

"So, they considered him a god on earth?"

"Exactly."

"What's he holding in his hand?"

"That is the infamous 'golden scepter.' That scepter was the king's symbol of power. It was said to have been given to him directly by the gods. It's made in the image of a serpent. The shaft is made of hardwood, covered in a thick gold leaf. The head of the serpent is made from solid gold, and its eyes are inset with red rubies."

"Impressive."

"Even more so in person."

"You've seen it?"

"Many times, and I can say without a doubt that it's the most beautiful object I've ever seen in my life."

Alex peered closer at the painting. She was right. If the painting did the scepter any justice, it was spectacular. "Where is it now?"

"It's part of a traveling exhibition and currently on display at the *Museo Nacional De Antropologia* in Mexico City."

"How did the scepter end up in a museum?"

"It's quite an interesting story if you care to hear it."

"I'm listening."

Sophie met his eyes. "In the year 1502 A.D., Spanish Major Alejandro de Aguilar and fifty conquistadors came to this land in search of treasure. When they arrived..."

Sophie abruptly stopped. Alex heard it too and snapped off the flashlight.

They were coming.

11

Alex whispered his plan into Sophie's ear. It was a simple plan which relied on misdirection and precise timing. He slipped off his shirt and handed it to Sophie.

She hurried to left side of the chamber, lay down, faced the wall and pretended to sleep while Alex moved behind a pillar in the center of the room.

He listened intently as two pairs of boots clomped down the stairs. As the footsteps grew louder, he peeked around the pillar and saw two flashlight beams crisscrossing at the bottom of the stairs.

He pulled back as two of Sebastian's men, armed with AK-47's, stepped into the chamber. One guard remained at the foot of the stairs while the other guard approached Sophie lying on the floor.

She had her back toward him with Alex's shirt partially draped over her waist to give the illusion they were lying together. It was not very convincing, but in the dark, a second of doubt and hesitation was what Alex needed.

The guard yelled, "Get up! Sebastian wants to see... hey!"

Alex sprang from behind the pillar and pounced on the guard at the stairs. Alex hit him in the throat with the hard edge of his hand. The guard's first reaction was to gag. His second was to drop his weapon and bring his hands up to his injured throat. Alex caught the falling weapon, turned, and fired the AK-47.

The noise was deafening in the small room. Bullets slammed into the guard's chest, and he danced backward and dropped dead at Sophie's feet.

Alex turned to the injured guard on the stairs. The man had one hand on his throat, and the other struggled to withdraw a machete from his belt. Alex flipped the rifle around, slammed the butt end into his forehead and knocked him unconscious. Alex took the guard's machete and slipped it into his own belt.

Sophie got off the floor looking stunned. She glanced at the dead guard and then to the unconscious guard on the stairs. With wide eyes, she asked, "How can you possibly do something like that? Who the hell are you, some secret agent or something?"

Alex shrugged. "No, I'm just a guy on vacation."

"Some vacation!"

She strode over and handed him his shirt. He slipped it on and then led her up the stairs.

At the top, He eased his head from the hole. Finding the room empty, he climbed out. Sophie followed. Moving forward, he shielded his eyes from the morning sunlight seeping through the temple doorways.

He looked outside expecting to see more of Sebastian's men, but he saw no one. Was it possible no one heard the shots?

"Follow me," he said.

Alex and Sophie ran out of the temple doorway. He led her behind the temple. She looked down the backside covered in jungle vegetation. "How do we get down? There's no stairs back here. Why didn't we take the front steps?"

"Too exposed. They'd easily pick us off with rifles."

"But no one is coming."

"We can't be sure. They may just be waiting until we show ourselves. We're going down this way."

Alex shouldered the strap of the AK-47 and began climbing down. Sophie followed. Tier after tier they lowered themselves until they reached the ground.

Alex put his back to the pyramid wall and swung the AK-47 off his shoulder. He edged along the back wall. He reached the end, peeked around the corner, and--gunfire erupted!

Bullets ricocheted off the pyramid sending shards of stone into the air. He pulled back and did the only sensible thing he could do. He ran in the opposite direction of the gunfire.

Alex and Sophie bust through the foliage, dodged trees, slid passed vines, and jumped over logs. They had a head start, but not by much.

Gunfire erupted again.

Bullets peppered the tree beside them. He grabbed Sophie's hand and angled a hard right. They ran and changed directions often in an effort to throw off their pursuers.

After a short time, they ran onto the grassy field of the Mayan ball court. This was exactly where he wanted to be. With all the changes in direction they'd taken, he was glad to see his internal compass was still working.

They crossed the field and took cover behind a stone wall. Alex brought the AK-47 up to his shoulder. He leaned around the corner and fired at the helicopter.

Sebastian's men skid to a stop. They scrambled behind the trees on the edge of the field so as not to get hit. It wasn't until they saw smoke rising from the helicopter that they realized they weren't the targets he was aiming for.

Alex smiled. This ought to keep them here until Mike arrives with help. When the magazine was empty, he dropped the rifle, and they ran. Three of Sebastian's men stayed to put out the flames, while two continued in pursuit.

As they ran Sophie panted, "Where are we going?"

Alex pointed. "To a tunnel that will lead us out of the city."

She pulled on his arm and dug her heels into the ground. It felt like he was pulling an anchor. Finally, he stopped. "What?"

"We can't go that way. Sebastian's men know about that tunnel, and they'll have men waiting for us. I know another one, this way." Sophie turned.

This time it was Alex who followed.

She guided him through the jungle until they came upon a gathering of colossal stone monoliths rising up from the ground. Green moss and plants covered the old stones which stood twenty feet high and weighed over twenty tons. Etched into the rock were vague images of animals and grotesque human forms.

Sophie led him into the forest of giant stones.

They weaved their way through huge monoliths and exited the other side. She continued to a steep and heavily forested hill. She swept back the vegetation and revealed a tunnel. They hurried inside. It was nearly identical to the tunnel he and Mike passed through.

Sophie and Alex splashed through water and muck. As they neared the end, two of Sebastian's men entered the tunnel. The men raised their rifles to fire, but Alex and Sophie exited out the other end before they could pull the trigger.

They dashed down the slope in the direction of the river. Alex could feel his heart thumping hard in his chest and sweat pouring off him like rainwater.

As they neared the river, they stopped short and crept to the edge of the river. Peering through the vegetation, they saw more of Sebastian's men on the other side searching for them.

Sophie looked worried. "Alex, we're trapped. Sebastian's men are behind us, and there are more in front of us. What do we do?"

Alex cast a look down river. "We're going in. There's a bend some sixty yards down river. Stay under until we pass it."

"But I can't hold my breath that long. I'm not a very strong swimmer."

"Don't worry; the river's moving at a good clip. Just hold your breath and let the current do most of the work."

"But I can't."

Alex heard Sebastian's men coming up behind them. They were close. "You don't have a choice. Either you swim, or you go back to Veck. Which is it?"

She scowled and mouthed the words, "...I hate you."

He dropped to his stomach. Sophie grudgingly did the same. Lying side by side under dense vegetation, they took multiple deep breaths. Then, like alligators, they crawled forward and slipped silently into the water.

Alex held his breath and let his body go with the current. The river water was murky, and he couldn't see more than a few inches in front of his face.

Unfortunately, there was a real possibility of being blindly slammed into a submerged rock or log. But he had no choice. Surfacing at this point was not an option.

Soon he felt a slight pressure difference on the left side of his body as the river moved around the bend. He gave it ten more seconds and then angled upward.

He surfaced, opened his eyes and immediately scanned both sides of the river bank. He was relieved. None of Sebastian's men were in sight.

A few yards away Sophie burst to the surface. She choked and took in deep, huge gulps of air.

He swam to her and steadied her in the water. "You alright?"

"Yes, I think so," she replied.

"Can you swim a while longer? We'll be able to put more distance on them, if we do."

She coughed. "I'll...try."

They kept to the river and swam for another thirty minutes before Sophie had enough. She had tried her best, but in time she could barely keep her head above water. Alex saw this and motioned to shore. The relieved look on her face said it all.

She made it to shore under her own power, but after only a few steps on dry land she crumpled to the ground, rolled onto her back, and cried, "Oh my god, I've never been so tired in my life."

"You did well."

She had no reply but gave him the 'death glare' as if to blame him for making her swim in the first place.

Alex sat on the ground a few feet away and removed his shoes. He drained the water and put them back on. Next, he removed his shirt. As he wrung water from it, Sophie noticed a number of scars on his back and chest. "I guess your body has been through a lot."

He put on his shirt. "Stay here and rest," he said

and then disappeared into the jungle.

She was asleep by the time he returned with a stack of six-foot sections of bamboo. The machete he took from the guard came in handy. He laid the bundle on the riverbank and went back into the jungle. After a few trips, he had all the materials he needed to build a raft.

Twenty-five minutes later, he stood back and looked at his little creation bobbing in the water. It wouldn't win any beauty awards, but at least it would float.

It was time to get moving. He reached down to wake Sophie, but he stopped short. Instead, he spent a few moments looking at her. It was funny. Before, he imagined all female archeologists to be the plain sort, with dirty hair and frumpy clothes. Looking at her now, he realized that he was way off base. Even dirty and wet, she was stunning.

Reluctantly, he nudged her shoulder. "Sophie, it's time to go."

She moaned, "Already?" She rose to a sitting position and rubbed her tired eyes. "Can't we stay a little longer?"

"No, we have to keep moving. It won't take Sebastian's men long to figure out where we went."

He helped her to her feet, but she pulled back. "Alex, I can't swim anymore. I'm exhausted."

"You won't have to," he replied and pointed to the river. "I built us a raft."

Her body slumped in relief. "Oh, thank god."

12

Alex steadied the raft in the water as Sophie stepped on. Next, he climbed on and took a knee. He was pleased the vines holding the bamboo floor remained tight and kept them afloat.

With the use of a long bamboo pole, he pushed away from and maneuvered the raft to the center of the river. Moving with the current, he laid the pole down, leaned back on his hands, and let the sun warm his face.

He immediately felt his tension begin to ease. The more distance they put between themselves and the Mayan jungle city, the better he felt.

He glanced at the passing scenery. He appreciated the beauty of the rainforest; the deep green hues and the solitude.

Sophie put her hand in the water and let the current ripple around her fingers. She appeared deep in thought. After a time, she looked at Alex with a curious expression. "Were you really on vacation when all this started?"

"I was. My friend Mike and I were on our way to a jungle resort. We were traveling by helicopter when we saw Dr. Farah's plane go down. To make a long story short, we found the plane, but there were no survivors, except Dr. Farah.

"What surprised us though, was that the passengers

didn't die on impact. They had been shot in the head at close range."

"By Veck?"

"You guessed it."

"And they took Dr. Farah?"

"She was in trouble, so we followed their tracks. Days later, we ended up in that Mayan city. When we realized what was going on, I sent Mike back to bring help. I stayed to keep an eye on things.

"However, my plans changed when I saw that helicopter parked on the Mayan ball court. I decided to fly Dr. Farah out and that's when I met you. Rock coming."

"What?"

"Rock!" he repeated. He shoved the bamboo pole into the river bottom and pushed the raft out of the way of the oncoming rock. With the path clear of obstacles, he laid the pole down.

"What about the natives?" Alex asked. "Mike and I had a little encounter with them. Are they connected with the city somehow?"

"I believe they are protectors of the city. They cover a wide area and anyone who crosses their invisible borders are captured and put to death."

"How many of Sebastian's men go missing?"

"About one a day a man goes missing."

"What does he do about it?"

"Nothing. He just hires more. I'm sure he doesn't tell the new recruits how dangerous it is and by the time they get here, it's too late. Later, if the men get spooked and refuse to work, he triples their pay, but they usually go missing before they can collect."

"Nice system he's got," Alex replied sarcastically.

He got to thinking about Sebastian. It was clear the man had a dual purpose for the being in the city: plundering treasure and antiquities, as well as using it to hide Dr. Farah and her case. And what better place to hide than in a city that's been lost for over 500 years.

As the raft floated downriver, the two quietly absorbed the tranquil atmosphere of the jungle. After a while, Sophie lifted her head and asked, "Do you think Dr. Farah will be alright?"

Alex nodded. "I'm sure of it. As long as Sebastian needs her she'll be fine."

That answer seemed to settle thoughts in Sophie's mind, but not his. He hated the thought of leaving Dr. Farah behind with those killers. At the moment he was helpless to do anything to save her, but he made a vow. As soon as he got Sophie to safety he'd go back to the city and save her.

Around the next bend the river current picked up speed, and the bamboo raft rocked side-to-side, forward and back. Soon white water began splashing up the sides.

They grabbed the vines wrapped around the bamboo poles to hold during the bumpy ride. Then, in the distance, they heard the low, thundering sound of a waterfall

Alex grabbed the long bamboo pole, stuck it in the water, and pushed hard for shore. He poled again and again, but the river was pulling too hard. He realized it was too late to land the craft on shore.

His best hope was to get the raft within a few feet of the riverbank. Through sheer strength, he managed to push the raft close to shore and yelled, "Sophie, you have to jump."

"What?"

"Jump!"

She got to her feet. She took a breath and then sprang from the raft. She sailed through the air and landed on shore with a few inches to spare. He lost sight of her as she rolled into the bushes. At least she was safe. He couldn't say that about himself.

The raft spun left and then right. He no longer had control of the craft. Suddenly, a swell of water lifted the front of the raft and then it slammed it down. When it straightened out, he felt a shifting under his knees.

The vines holding the raft were loosening. The raft was coming apart. He took a hurried look to shore. The raft was at least ten feet from the riverbank.

It was too far to jump to shore, but he had an idea. Alex got to his feet. He faced the riverbank with the bamboo pole in his hands. With fluidly of movement, he thrust the long bamboo pole into the bottom of the river and, at the same time, flung his body over the water using the pole like a pole-vaulter.

He hurled himself toward shore. For a moment he thought he was going to make it. Then--the pole snapped and he fell into the river.

He hit with a splash and the current carried him away. When he resurfaced, he was surprised to learn he was within an arm's length to shore. He grabbed an exposed tree root. Hand over hand, he climbed up the root and crawled onto the riverbank.

By the time his heart rate was returning to normal, Sophie stepped out from the trees. She offered him a hand and helped him to his feet. "Now what?" she asked.

"We proceed on foot. Once we pass the waterfall, I'll build us another raft."

The plan was set. They headed out and followed the course of the river. A half mile later, they came to another river, merging with the one they had been following. The two merging rivers continued as one, flowing for a hundred yards and before plunging over the waterfall.

They walked onto a narrow rocky point between the two rivers to survey their situation. Sophie plopped herself down on a large rock and looked across the river. "Alex, we can't cross, the current is moving too fast."

Alex scanned the area. He pointed up the connecting river. "Let's head that way until we find a place to cross."

The sound of a branch snapping caused them to turn just as four of Sebastian's grim-faced soldiers materialized from the jungle. Alex instinctively stepped in front of Sophie. His hand went for the machete, but it must have fallen into the river when he jumped.

A man with a hard face and stained yellow teeth stepped in front of the group. He spit a black stream of tobacco juice on the rocks, sneered and said, "You gave us quite a run, but it's over."

"How'd you find us?" Alex asked.

"Wasn't hard. We guessed you'd be following the river and knew once you got to this point you'd be trapped. We took a short cut and here you are." The man lowered his AK-47. "Take off, son. We don't want you. We only want the girl."

"You're not touching her," Alex replied.

The leader grinned. "Think it over friend. You don't have a weapon. We'll just kill you and then take the girl anyway. So, save yourself. Get lost. Can't ask for anything fairer than that, can you?"

Sophie angrily shouted, "You slime can't do anything to me! Sebastian needs me, and Veck will cut off your balls if you touch me!"

The four men snickered.

"Miss, as far as they know you died going over the falls."

Alex grit his teeth. "Leave and go back the way you came. No one is touching her."

The leader wiped tobacco juice running down his chin. "You got it wrong, friend. We ain't going anywhere...but you are."

He lifted his rifle. He put his finger on the trigger, and—his eyes bulged! He screamed, dropped the rifle, and fell to the ground.

A split second later, the rest of Sebastian's men screamed, dropped their weapons, and fell to the ground. They looked like puppets whose strings had been cut. Each man was quivering, screaming in pain, and grabbing at the arrow shafts sticking out the back of their legs.

Alex's eyes lifted.

His heart pounded as he stared into the jungle. Then it happened. The foliage parted and out walked ten fearsome, horrific looking native warriors. Dressed in loincloths, the natives carried primitive weapons: spears with stone points, bows and arrows, and wooden swords edged with sharp chips of obsidian.

They were unlike anything Alex had ever seen before.

The warriors had severely wrinkled brown skin that looked like dried prunes. Each man possessed deeply sloped foreheads that angled backwards with long, stringy black hair. Without a doubt, their most disturbing feature was their bulging, yellow eyes, which had to be at least two times the normal size.

The warriors walked barefoot onto the rocky point and hit Sebastian's men with wooden clubs. Then they tied the hands and feet of the unconscious men. The natives slipped long wooden poles through their bonds, paired off, and hoisted the poles in the air. Sebastian's men now looked like pigs on a spit.

Using stone knives, the natives cut the arrow shafts from the back of their legs, leaving the arrowheads embedded. Alex guessed this made them easier to transport.

Without looking at Alex or Sophie, the natives carried Sebastian's men into the jungle and disappeared. A few of the warriors stayed behind. With warlike expressions, they walked slowly toward them.

Alex had to decide quickly, to allow themselves to be captured and die, or risk going over the falls. He may only be trading one type of death for another but... he spun, grabbed Sophie around the waist, and leapt into the raging river.

They hit the water with a splash, and the fast moving current swept them away from the warriors. Thirty seconds later, water dropped beneath them, and they went over the falls.

13

Alex plunged over one-hundred feet in an avalanche of cascading water. When he hit the river below, the pounding water drove him deep. He was spun, tossed and turned. He was nearly out of oxygen when he was finally able to surface.

As he inhaled air into his lungs, he spun in circles looking for Sophie. He visually looked up and down the river, but she hadn't surfaced. She wasn't a strong swimmer. He was worried.

Terrible mental images began to form in his mind. She may have hit rocks at the bottom of the waterfall, or she may have drowned, and her body carried farther downriver.

Relief swept over him when Sophie surfaced a few yards away. Unfortunately, she coughed, flailed her arms, and went under again.

Using strong arm strokes and powerful leg kicks Alex swam to her. He lifted her to the surface, tucked an arm under her chin, and brought her to shore.

Once on the riverbank, he laid her down. She turned her head and spit up water. She coughed and tried to catch her breath.

Alex asked, "You okay?"

"Yeah, I think so," she replied in a weak voice.

She rose to a sitting position and leaned back against a tree. She glanced back at the waterfall. "I can't believe we survived. I thought we were goners for sure."

"Me too," he replied. He jerked a thumb back at the waterfall. "Any idea who they are?"

"The natives?"

"Yeah."

"Judging by their clothing, weapons, and sloped foreheads, I'd say they're Maya. Centuries ago Mayan mothers used to tie boards to their babies heads in order to slant them back like that. It was considered a mark of beauty."

"I got news for 'em," he chuckled, "it's not."

Sophie laughed. "The thing is…I don't know any group of Maya that still practice the tradition of skull molding. There are Maya that attempt to live in the traditional way.

"For example, the Lacandon Maya still hunt with bows and arrows, and the women still grind corn, but the natives we just saw are definitely not the Lacandon."

Her eyes widened. "They must be a lost tribe!"

"Could be," Alex agreed. "I've read about lost tribes being found every so often." He paused. "Whoever they are, I'd say we found the ones responsible for kidnapping Sebastian's men."

"And my team," she said sadly.

He nodded in sympathy. He spent a few quiet moments thinking about the native's appearance. The wrinkled skin and bulging eyes. "Sophie, what could cause them to look like that?"

"Some sort of jungle illness, perhaps. But nothing I know of."

Alex nodded. "I was also wondering why they didn't

just kill Sebastian's men and be done with it? Why go to all the trouble of taking them prisoner?"

"If I'm right and these natives are members of a lost tribe, then they'd be following the ancient ways…and the taking of prisoners was a vital part of the Mayan culture."

"Why?"

"To make blood sacrifices to their gods."

"Human sacrifice?"

"Yes. They believe blood offerings are essential in nourishing and pleasing their gods. If the gods are happy, then the people believed they would be provided with good crops, good hunting, etc.

"But a more disturbing fact is that the ancient Maya had been known to keep prisoners alive for up to a year or more in a constant state of pain and humiliation before using them in their ceremonies."

"And after that?"

"When the time was right, each man was stretched backwards over a stone tablet and held down. A Mayan priest would say prayers, and then he'd plunge a sharp knife deeply into the chest. The still beating heart would be ripped from the body and held up for his people to see.

"Then, the priest would place the heart in a bowl, and the victim's arms and legs would be cut off, and eaten later as a part of a ceremony."

A sudden chill went through his body. He got to his feet. "We need to get going. Hopefully, those natives will assume we died going over the falls, but if they get a notion to come looking for us, I don't want to be anywhere near here."

He offered his hand, and she took it. Once on her feet, she swayed unsteadily.

"Sure you're okay?"

"I'm fine, let's go."

For the rest of the day, they trekked swiftly along the edge of the river, trying to put as much distance as possible between themselves and the native warriors.

As early evening approached, they came upon a suitable campsite located on a small hill above the river. "We need to build a shelter, and find something to eat before nightfall," Alex said.

"I'll build the shelter," Sophie replied.

"Alright, then I'll find us some food."

He left Sophie on the hill to build the shelter and hiked down to the river. He was tired of eating bugs and had his eye on catching fish for dinner.

He hiked along the riverbank and found a stick to make a spear; it was long, straight and sturdy. He sharpened one end by rubbing it vigorously on a rock. Then he used a small, sharp rock to make notches in the end; this way the fish wouldn't slip off.

When the spear was ready, he waded waist-deep into the river. He slid the tip into the water and waited.

At dusk, cicadas buzzed throughout the jungle. It was getting late, and Alex took what fish he caught and climbed the hill. Sophie was applying the last of the palm fronds to the outside of the lean-to when she saw him approaching.

Her eyes went immediately to the fish skewered on the end of his spear. "Fish!" she yelped with delight.

"Yep, we're eating good tonight."

Alex collected stones and placed them in a circle for a fire pit. Next, he gathered a pile of wood and set them inside it. He struck a rock against the back of his belt buckle to create sparks. The sparks touched the kindling, and with small puffs of air, he blew the small flames into bigger ones. He added more sticks to the fire, and soon the fire was blazing.

As the sun set over the forest, Sophie warmed herself by the crackling fire. She watched as Alex wrapped the fish in green palm leaves. He buried the wrapped fish under burning embers and waited.

A short time later, he removed the charred palms from the fire. He opened the palms, and the smell of perfectly baked fish made his mouth water. Together they ravenously devoured the fish and licked the bones clean.

"That was delicious," Sophie said. She patted her stomach and then looked into his eyes. "You know, I was thinking. I really don't know anything about you."

"Not much to know," he replied. He hated talking about himself. He never found himself to be that interesting.

After seconds of awkward silence, she tried again. "I can see by your wedding ring that you're married. Tell me about her."

Alex paused. He usually lied when someone asked about his wedding ring. But somehow it was different with her. "I'm not married...not anymore. My wife died 5 years ago." He looked down at his ring. "I suppose I just didn't want to take it off."

"You still have a deep connection with her, don't you?"

Alex nodded.

"I get it. I think that's a beautiful thing. She must have been a very special woman."

"She was."

"If you don't mind me asking, how'd she die?"

"Cancer."

"I'm so sorry. That must have been awful."

He nodded.

She leaned forward. "Okay, let's change the subject, shall we? Where did you grow up?"

"I grew up in a small town south of Seattle. After high school, I went to the University of Washington. After graduation, I enlisted in the Navy and became a SEAL. I retired a few weeks ago."

"You were a commando?"

"Yup."

"Well, that certainly explains a lot," she said with a chuckle. "But you're still young. Why did you retire?"

"It was time. I'd been wounded before, and it never bothered me; I just figured it was just part of the job. But, about two months ago, I was having shrapnel removed from my leg, and it hit me. I'm 32 years old, maybe it's time to let the younger guys take over and do something a little less risky with my life."

"I can't say I blame you. Although, it doesn't seem you've slowed down much."

"I guess some habits die hard. Your turn."

"Not so fast. Tell me about your parents?"

"My mom was Japanese, and my Dad was American. Both are deceased."

"I'm sorry; any brothers or sisters?"

"Only child I'm afraid, but my best friend is like a brother to me."

"Who's that?"

"Mike Garrison. We grew up together. I told you about him. He was the one with me when we followed Dr. Farah to the city."

"What's he like?"

"Mike? He's six feet tall, with blond hair and bright blue eyes that women adore. He's laid-back, quite vain, and a very smooth operator, if you know what I mean?"

"So if I ever meet him I might want to be on my guard?"

"That would be wise," he said with humor in his voice. "Now it's your turn."

"Okay, I'm the oldest in my family. I have two younger sisters and a younger brother. I live alone in a small, rickety old house on a couple of acres outside the city of Hickory Creek, Texas. Although, I'm rarely home as I spend most of my time on archeological digs here in the jungle."

He made a sweeping hand gesture. "So, this is home for you, then."

"It is, but I'm not usually running for my life," she said with a laugh.

"What else?"

"Let's see...oh, I've written 3 books about the ancient Maya, and my last dig was filmed by National Geographic for an upcoming television special."

"You hit the big time then."

"You bet."

"So, how did you become interested in archeology?"

"I can thank my father for that; he's a retired archeologist; well, semi-retired anyway. It seems archeologists can never sit long enough to retire and that's the same with my father. I was 10 years old when he took me on my first archeological dig, and from then on I couldn't imagine spending my life any other way."

The two gazed into the dying light of the fire. After

a time, she rose to her feet. "We have a big day tomorrow. We should probably get some sleep."

Alex agreed. He joined Sophie under the lean-to.

He lay next to Sophie, he closed his eyes and listened to the cacophony of night creatures; the croaking frogs, the rustling of leaves and the strangely hypnotic sound of insects filling the night air.

As he listened, his mind drifted back to the fierce warriors they'd encountered earlier. He had never seen anything like them and hoped he never would again.

14

Early the next morning, Alex woke and rose to a sitting position. He immediately thought of Dr. Farah. He had made a vow, and he meant to keep it. But if he was going to save Dr. Farah he had to do so quickly, before she was removed from the jungle city.

He figured he had two options. Option one: he and Sophie could follow the river until they reached civilization, but that might take weeks.

Option two: they could light a signal fire to attract a rescue team. This was the fastest, but also the riskiest. The smoke signal might also attract the native's attention as well.

He left Sophie sleeping in the lean-to and hiked down to the river to have a look around. The moment he arrived he saw footprints—lots of them.

The native warriors knew they were alive. He set out and carefully followed the tracks downriver. A mile later, with no sign of the natives, he turned and headed back.

When he returned, he used his shoes and palm fronds to erase all the footprints. No sense in worrying Sophie, he thought. Once he finished, he found a spot along the river to make the signal fire; a spot where the smoke could rise unimpeded through the trees.

He collected firewood until the pile was as high as his waist. Then he went in search of green palms. When he returned, he started the fire using the same method as the night before. When the fire was blazing, he picked up an armful of green palms and dropped them on top of the fire.

Standing back, he watched as a thick, grayish-white smoke billow up through the gap in the trees. He smiled. Someone ought to see that.

Sophie appeared. "Good morning," she said in a happy sing-song voice.

"Good morning," he replied. "Get enough sleep?"

"Could have used more, but I smelled the smoke and knew you were up to something. With the natives around, are you sure lighting a fire is a good idea?"

"It'll be fine" he replied.

"Need a hand?" she asked.

"We could use more firewood."

Together they went in search of more wood. Once they had enough wood to keep the fire going for hours, they took a break and sat on a fallen tree.

As they gazed at the smoking fire, they felt small drops of rain on their heads. Within a few seconds--it was a complete downpour. They scurried under a nearby tree, but it did little to keep them dry.

Alex was about to suggest running for the lean-to when he heard a faint thundering in the distance. It grew louder. Soon the sound was unmistakable.

"It's a helicopter," Sophie said. She threw herself into Alex's arms, yelling, "We're saved! We're saved!"

A large black helicopter appeared above the trees. The door opened and a man with a pair of binoculars leaned out. Sophie waved. The man in the chopper waved back.

He disappeared into the chopper and reappeared with a harness attached to a cable. Then he motioned to someone inside, and the harness began its descent.

When the harness arrived, Alex held it out. "Ladies first."

Sophie ecstatically stepped forward. He helped her into the harness, adjusted the leg straps, and looked up. "You're good to go. Remember to use your hands to clear the branches on your way up."

"I will," she replied and then stared at him strangely.

"What? Harness too tight?"

"No, it's perfect," she said, and her eyes began to fill with tears. "Thank you. I'll never forget what you've done."

"Glad to help," he said, and immediately wished he had said something more clever.

She reached out and surprised him by kissing him lightly on the lips.

He lowered his head. "I suppose we better not keep them waiting."

"No, I guess not," she replied modestly.

Alex looked up and waved at the man in the chopper and Sophie began to rise.

He watched her ascend through the trees and into the open sky. It didn't take more than a minute, and the harness was on its way down for him. Alex secured himself in it and gave the man in the chopper a wave. He felt a jerk, and his feet left the ground.

He was on his way up. About fifty feet off the ground, he jerked back when two arrows slammed into the tree beside him. A fraction of a second later, another arrow hit a thick branch in front of his chest.

Native warriors were circling around the fire below. He couldn't hear what they were yelling, over the noise of the chopper, but they waved their fists and looked angry.

The natives lifted their bows again. He couldn't afford to be hit by even one. The tips of the arrows were probably poisoned, where even a scratch could be fatal.

Alex drew his arms and legs in to make as small a target as possible. The natives stretched their strings and then let their arrows fly. One arrow grazed the harness. Other arrows hit trees and branches near him.

The natives were fitting more arrows into their bows as Alex exited the top of the trees, unscathed and thankful to be alive. He laid his head back and let the rain wash down on his face. Too close. Much too close.

When Alex arrived at the chopper, he stiffened. He expected the chopper to be filled with rescue personnel, but instead, he found it packed with eight, big, hard-looking men with thick necks and rippling muscles.

Each had their faces painted and wore jungle fatigues, camouflaged assault vests, and held an assortment of weapons. At first glance, he assumed they were Sebastian's men.

Then a smiling, familiar face stepped from the cockpit. "Hi buddy!" Mike chirped.

15

Inside the chopper, a stout man with a pronounced square jaw stepped up. "Commander McCade?"

"Yes, sir."

The man offered his hand. "I've heard a lot about you. I'm Major Buzz Brozik of Delta One."

He shook it. "Nice to meet you Major; thanks for the lift."

"My pleasure. You commanded SEAL Team 3?"

"Until a few weeks ago."

"I had heard you boys retired. Of course, ever since we picked up Lieutenant Garrison, he hasn't stopped talking about your SEAL exploits."

Alex laughed, "He tends to go on a bit, doesn't he?"

"You can say that again," the Major replied with a smile.

Sophie sidled next to Alex with a green woolen blanket pulled around her shoulders. He offered the introduction, "Major, this is Dr. Sophie Marcus."

The Major smiled, "I've already had the pleasure."

"I haven't," replied Mike. "Where in the world did you find her?"

Before Alex could answer, Mike took Sophie's hand in his. In a low, almost purring tone, he said, "Hello, I'm

Mike." He delicately kissed the back of her hand and then slowly lifted his eyes to hers. "You are a very beautiful woman."

"Thank you. And you're as smooth as Alex says you are."

"Thank you." Then with a sly smile, he flipped over her hand and kissed the back of his own.

Sophie giggled.

"Alright, enough already," Alex said grinning. He turned to the Major. "I assume you know about the missing scientist and her case?"

"We do."

"If we hurry, we still have a chance to recover both."

"Mike told us about the city. How many men would you say are there?"

"Twenty at least; all equipped with AK-47's."

"How far from the city are we?"

"Maybe an hour and a half by air."

"Think you can you find it again?"

"Definitely."

"Good. Put the pilot on course, and then I'd appreciate you briefing us on what we can expect to find once we get there."

"Will do," Alex replied, and he walked into the cockpit.

When he returned, he found Sophie drinking from a bottle of water and the team's medic cleaning her cuts and scratches.

Major Brozik had assembled the men in a semi-circle. Upon seeing Alex, he addressed them. "Alright, listen up. We're proceeding to a lost Mayan City; our mission: to rescue Dr. Farah and secure the titanium case." He gestured to Alex. "If you don't know already, this is Alex McCade; former commander of SEAL team 3."

The stern-faced commandos nodded respectfully.

"And, of course, you've already had the pleasure of meeting Lieutenant Mike Garrison who'll be happy to relive his success in the SEALs whether you want to hear them or not."

The men booed.

Mike smiled proudly.

The Major continued, "Commander McCade has thorough knowledge of the city, and therefore, will brief us on what we can expect to find once we get there." He turned to Alex. "They're all yours."

The Major handed him a black marker, and he proceeded to draw a diagram of the city on the bare metal floor of the chopper. He went on to explain the layout of the city, enemy placements, best points of entry and exits, and the location of the motion sensors around the palace.

He spoke for over fifteen minutes. A session of questions and answers followed. He ended with a final piece of advice.

"There are a group of natives who won't like us in their neighborhood. Dr. Marcus believes they may be part of a lost tribe who follow the ancient ways and beliefs, including the taking of prisoners for human sacrifice.

"To tell you the truth, they are strange looking. I don't know if their condition was caused by a tropical disease or what. Their skin is severely wrinkled and they have huge, bulging, yellow eyes. They wear primitive clothing, and use primitive weapons, but believe me when I say, they are very, very dangerous."

"Thank you, commander," Major Brozik said. "Gentlemen we have about an hour to go. Rest up."

Mike approached Alex. "Those natives must be the ones who left us those dead bodies in the trees."

Alex nodded.

The Major put a friendly hand on Alex's shoulder. "Why don't you have our medic take a look at your wounds? Then grab a bite to eat and get a drink. You're going to need your strength if you're leading us back to the city."

"I don't need the medic, but I could sure use a bite to eat."

Sophie and Alex were given MRE's, the military's pre-prepared food that comes in pouches, and clean bottled drinking water.

After they devoured the prepackaged food, Major Brozik approached. "Feeling better?"

"Yes, thank you, Major," Sophie replied.

Alex said, "I never thought I'd be eating this again, but I really appreciate it."

"You're welcome." Major Brozik dug a small black case out of his pocket and tossed it to Alex. "Time to 'cammie-up.' Remember how?"

"I'll manage," Alex replied.

He opened the case and looked into the small mirror adhered to the inside lid. He dipped his fingers into the paint and applied the green, black and brown colors as he had done a thousand times before.

The aim was to break up lines on the face, to blend into the surrounding environment and hide any skin that could reflect light and draw the enemy's attention. When he finished, he snapped the case shut and tossed it to

Mike.

After Mike applied the face paint, he returned the case to the Major.

Major Brozik gave them a once over. "Now you boys look as pretty as the rest of us." He gave Mike and Alex each a throat microphone and cordless earpiece. "We carry a couple extra in case of malfunctions," he said. "Now you'll be able to communicate with the rest of the team."

He paused, thought about it for a moment, and then unbuckled his side holster. He handed it to Alex and said, "Since you're the one leading to the city I don't think you should go in empty-handed."

"Thanks, Major," Alex replied. He belted the holster around his waist and adjusted the thigh strap. He withdrew the Browning .45 caliber pistol from the holster and was pleased; the pistol felt well balanced in his hand.

"Don't lose it," the Major said, "it's part of the family."

"I'll treat it as my own," he replied.

Mike said, "Major, got anything for me?"

"Think we can trust you with a firearm?" the Major teased.

"Of course. In fact, I remember the time when..."

The Major threw up his hands. "Stop, already. No more stories. I'll give you a weapon if you promise to keep that damn trap of yours shut."

"It's a deal," Mike replied happily.

The Major removed a pistol from his ankle holster. "It's my backup; see that you don't lose it."

"Right, thanks."

From the cockpit came a strained voice. "Major, it's

raining harder; I could use another set of eyes up here."

Major Brozik nodded to Alex. "See what you can do."

Alex went into the cockpit and plopped into the seat next to the pilot. Rain pounded on the outside of the windshield. He put on a headset, turned to the pilot. "How can I help?"

"I can follow the river by my instruments," replied the pilot, "But there's no way I'll be able to spot that log bridge of yours."

"Okay, you fly; I'll look for the bridge. Do you have binoculars?"

"Under your seat."

Alex reached under his seat and pulled out a pair of binoculars. He put the lens to his eyes and looked down at the rainforest. Much of the river was hidden by heavy overhanging tree cover and the driving rain obscured the other parts. Finding that bridge from the air, in a rainstorm, wasn't going to be easy.

Over the next half hour, he strained to keep his eyes open; afraid to blink for fear he might miss the bridge. He had to find it, or all hopes of finding the Mayan City and rescuing Dr. Farah was lost.

The longer he looked for the bridge, the deeper his doubts became. Had they traveled far enough upriver? Not enough? Did they already fly past the bridge and miss it entirely? There was no telling.

Suddenly—the log bridge appeared between gaps in the trees. Alex pointed excitedly. "That's it! Down there." He instructed the pilot to immediately veer left. Then he flung off his headset and hurried to the back of the aircraft.

"Major, we'll be over the drop zone in less than a minute."

"The Major wheeled to his men, "Alright ladies, its go-time."

A quarter mile from the river, the helicopter pilot decreased speed, lowered and hovered over the rainforest canopy. A sharp nod from Major Brozik caused a commando to rip open the door.

Another dragged a heavy, metal-shaped wedge to the door. He attached the line to it, and with a grunt, he heaved the 'Tree Buster,' out the door. The metal weight plunged through the trees creating a hole all the way to the jungle floor.

The men put on thick welder's gloves to prevent rope burns and then lined up at the door with weapons strapped to their backs.

The Major looked at the rainforest below and yelled, "Move out!"

In rapid succession, one man after the other grabbed the rope and left the chopper.

Alex's turn was coming. As he approached the door, Sophie rushed to him. She kissed him on the cheek and said, "Be careful."

He gave her one last look, grabbed the rope, and left the aircraft.

He slid down the rope straight through the hole in the trees. As he neared the ground, he pressed his hands around the rope to brake. He slowed and landed softly on the wet jungle floor.

He stepped away from the rope, tossed the heavy gloves aside, and met the other commandos at the base of a wide tree.

Major Brozik was the last down. After he landed, he approached the group. As he stripped off his gloves, he turned to Alex and smiled. "Nice to get a kiss from a beautiful woman before going out on a mission."

Alex smiled. "That's standard operating procedure in the SEALs."

Mike nodded along enthusiastically.

"Right," the Major said grinning, "Now, how about leading us to this city of yours?"

"Yes, sir."

16

At the Randal Highlands Elementary School in Washington, D.C., President Grant sat comfortably in a folding chair with a children's book in his hands. He smiled at the first graders assembled in a semi-circle on the rug in front of him. He turned the page.

The story he was reading to them was from Aesop's Fables, The Tortoise and the Hare. He was at the point in the story where the big race was about to begin.

Today was all part of his plan to draw attention to his 'Education First' program, and the media was eating it up. The men and women from the TV news channels piled into the room and kept their cameras rolling.

Chief of Staff, David Lawson was listening to the president's story when his cell phone vibrated on his hip. Not wanting to interrupt, he quietly stepped into the hallway to take the call.

Returning a few minutes later, he approached the president and whispered in his ear. "Mr. President, can I have a word with you? It's important."

"Yes, just a moment." The president finished the sentence he was reading and marked the page. He closed the book.

Rising to his feet, he said, "I'm sorry children, but I must speak with my friend. I'll be back shortly to finish the story." The president tucked the book under his arm. He went into the hallway and closed the door behind him.

"David, what's this all about?"

"A DELTA team picked up the two former Navy SEALs in the jungle."

"They did?"

"Yes, and they also picked up an Archeologist who had been reported missing."

"What about Dr. Farah and the weapon?"

"Nothing yet sir, but I'm told she's alive and apparently being held in some ancient Mayan city in the Guatemalan jungle. Our two SEALs are leading the DELTA team to the city as we speak."

"Damn, this is great news," the president said with excitement. "It appears Admiral Carr and Senator McDaniel were right in trusting these men."

"Yes sir, it does."

The president beamed. There was a very good chance that Dr. Farah and the weapon could be rescued before any of this ever leaked to the press. But...? He stopped and took a deep breath to temper his excitement.

Experience had taught him cruelly that when events looked their brightest...things often could and would go wrong. "Thank you, David. Let me know the moment you hear anything new."

"Yes sir," David replied and turned to walk away.

"Aren't you staying to hear the rest of the story? If you leave, you'll never find out who wins the race."

David laughed. "The suspense is killing me, but I've got a few phone calls to make. Be sure to let me know who wins, won't you?"

The president smiled. "I'll do that."

President Grant faced the classroom door. He straightened his shirt, adjusted his tie, and then opened the door. He held the book up triumphantly as he entered the room. The children cheered upon his return.

He chuckled to himself. Who said he didn't know how to make an entrance.

17

In the face of heavy rain, Alex took point and guided the commandos through the wet jungle. When they reached the river, he led them across the log bridge.

Once on the other side, they went up the rising slope and stopped at the base of the steep, forested hill. Alex peeled back the wet vegetation and revealed the tunnel.

Alex would not let anyone enter. If Sebastian's men heard their chopper, then he was certain they'd pick this spot to conduct an ambush. Why? Because this is the exact spot he'd choose.

A tunnel has two ways out. Block one end and there is only one way out. Then it's easy pickings. Toss in a couple of hand grenades or pick them off one by one as they exit. Alex withdrew his pistol, pushed it forward and entered the tunnel alone.

He sloshed through the watery passageway and made his way to the far end. He stopped at the exit and listened for anything unusual. The only sound was the pattering of rain on the leaves. He peeked out the tunnel and scanned the jungle. Seeing nothing, he cautiously stepped out.

He conducted a brief search of the area before concluding it was safe to let the others come through. He lowered his head inside the tunnel and gave a short whistle. He concealed himself behind a tree and was ready to lay down fire if need be.

He watched the commandos exit the tunnel and was amused at their reactions upon seeing the city. It must have been exactly how he and Mike looked when they saw it for the first time.

Once outside the tunnel, the men regrouped, and Alex led them into the city. He stopped behind an old building that bordered the plaza.

Major Brozik leaned around the corner and pressed binoculars to his eyes and scanned the area. He saw no sign of Sebastian's men. With a hand signal, he sent his sniper into his assigned position.

With another hand signal he sent a two-man team to the ball court to secure Sebastian's helicopter in the event it had been repaired.

During a downpour like this, the Major assumed the majority of Sebastian's men would be inside the palace. But as a precaution, he sent a two-man team to make a quick search of the outlying buildings.

After twenty minutes, all but the sniper returned. The two-man team reported finding no one in the outlying buildings. The other team reported finding Sebastian's helicopter in the ball court and deemed it not airworthy.

The Major pressed his throat mic. "ECHO, what's your status?"

The sniper, sitting high in a tree facing the front of the palace, said, "I see movement inside the palace; second level; only shadows though."

"Can you identify?"

"No sir, but there's got to be five or six of them."

"ECHO, keep your eyes open—we're going in."

"Copy that, RED Leader."

The Major turned to Alex and Mike. "Sorry gents, but you'll have to sit this one out."

Mike moaned, but Alex cut in. "No problem, Major".

"Glad you understand."

The Major waved his hand, and he and the rest of the commando's moved out.

Mike folded his arms across his chest and leaned heavily against the moss-covered building. "This stinks. Why do they get to have all the fun?"

Alex laughed. "This, coming from you? You would have been the first one to bitch if some outsiders came in and messed with our team."

"I know...but it still stinks."

Alex grinned. "The Major didn't want us to get involved, but he didn't say we couldn't move in for a closer look, now did he?"

Mike perked up. "Oh buddy, how right you are."

Using the jungle as cover, Alex and Mike moved closer to the action. From their new location, they watched a DELTA commando fire silenced rounds into the junction box on the side wall of the palace. With the motion sensors disabled, the commandos moved up to the palace.

The men lined up on either side of the palace staircase. Two men wheeled around and aimed their weapons to provide cover, while four men ran up the stairs.

On the second story, two men peeled off and provided cover for the other two who continued to the third level. When all men were in position, the Major whispered in his microphone, "ECHO, anything?"

The sniper in the tree, with his finger on the trigger and eye to the scope, replied, "Negative. No movement."

Major Brozik, like all leaders, hated to go in blindly but Dr. Farah and the case were too important to wait any longer. He pressed his throat mic—"Go!"

Acting as one, the commandos pulled pins on the flash-bang grenades and tossed them inside. Deafening blasts and blinding flashes of light followed. In the confusion, the commando's charged through the smoky doorways.

Alex and Mike heard shouting and caught glimpses of the commando's passing by open windows. The commandos plan was to go room by room to search out the enemy.

Alex expected Sebastian's men to fire their weapons in response, but they didn't. It was strange. There was no pushback whatsoever.

Calls began coming in over the radio.

"Red Leader, CHARLIE Team--third level clear."

"Red Leader, ALPHA Team--first level clear."

"Copy that," replied the Major, "second level clear." The Major called his sniper. "ECHO, anything?"

"Negative, Red Leader."

"BRAVO Team--you?"

"Negative," replied the lone commando stationed behind the palace to prevent anyone from escaping out the back.

The rain had slowed to a trickle when the Major ordered all teams to rendezvous in front of the palace steps.

Alex eyed the Major, "What happened?"

"Looks like your friends beat us to them," he replied.

"My friends?"

"The natives. We found blood, as well as, discarded AK-47 rifles with fully loaded magazines. The natives must have hit them hard and fast because no one got off a shot."

"What about Dr. Farah, or the case?"

"No sign of them."

"What about the movement your sniper reported seeing?"

The Major rubbed his chin. "My guess is a few natives were still inside, but they ran off before we got into position."

Alex felt like he'd been hit in the stomach. He made a promise to rescue Dr. Farah, and he failed.

The Major turned, "Zilkowski, Lund, Peterson--find her. We have to get the scientist and the case back ASAP."

The three commandos nodded and hurried away.

Commandos Dixon and Traeger approached the Major. "Sir, we found something interesting on the third level."

The Major nodded and followed the men to the third level.

Alex and Mike climbed the stairs and entered the second story of the palace. Alex wanted to see the scene with his own eyes.

Inside, Alex immediately saw drops of blood in the hallway. Not enough blood to indicate death, but enough to indicate immobilization. Apparently, the natives wanted their captives alive.

Alex picked up an AK-47. He checked the magazine. Sure enough, it was fully loaded. He looked around, trying to understand how they did it.

The natives moved like ghosts and were as deadly as rattlesnakes, but how did they get by the motion sensors without alerting Sebastian's men? And how did they leave the palace without being seen by the commandos?

Alex and Mike entered Sebastian's room. The once immaculate room was a mess. There was a broken table, overturned chairs, and spots of blood--clear signs of a struggle. They walked out of the room and went to Dr. Farah's room. Her cot was broken, and they found a few spots of blood on the door frame.

A call came over the radio from Major Brozik. Alex put his hand to his ear to listen. "Commander McCade, I need you to have a look-see up on the third level to see what you make of it."

"Roger that. I'm on my way."

"Let me know what you find," Mike said. "I want to stay and look around."

Alex went outside and climbed the stone staircase until he reached the third level. He went through the doorway and walked down a dark hallway. As he turned right, into a room lit by flashlights, he was surprised by a blast of cool air. Cool air, in the jungle. It didn't make sense. Then it did.

The air-conditioned room was full of computers, radar screens, and other pieces of electronic equipment; exactly the type of equipment one would find in a small, flight control room. The cool, dry room was essential in keeping the equipment working properly.

Alex nodded. "So, that's how he did it."

"Did what?"

He pointed. "Sebastian tracked Dr. Farah's plane on that radar screen. When the aircraft came into range, he took over the controls and forced it to crash into the jungle, right where his men were waiting for it."

Alex reached and flipped a wall switch. The room illuminated with bright light. On the floor he noticed a thick electrical cable coming out the back of the machines and snaking out a side door. "Keeping this room cool and these machines running requires a lot of power. I wonder where the power is coming from?"

The Major turned. "Dixon, Traeger, follow the cables. Find out where this power is coming from."

"Yes sir," the men replied.

Five minutes later, Major Brozik addressed his men at the base of the palace steps. "I just called in our chopper and a criminal forensics team. While that team is gathering evidence, we will provide the security. In the meantime, pair-off, I want all of you out searching for the scientist. Understood?"

"Yes sir," came a unanimous response.

Commando's Dixon and Traeger ran up.

The Major turned. "What did you find?"

"The cables lead to a concrete bunker fifty yards away. Inside are four industrial size diesel powered generators; big enough to power a small town."

"Very good." The Major turned to Alex. "I've got choppers coming in and I need that roof over the field opened."

"I'll have Mike do it."

Mike's eyes widened. "Me? I don't know how to open it."

"It's easy. There's a small metal box mounted on a support post located on the corner of the field. Inside are switches. One of those should open the roof."

"Ok, but what are you doing?"

"I've got an errand to run."

18

Major Brozik and Mike hiked down the jungle path to the Mayan ball court. When they arrived, Mike located the metal box.

He waited until he heard the chopper approaching and then he flipped the switch. Metal groaned, and the roof began to open. The DELTA chopper lowered onto the field, right next to Sebastian's disabled chopper.

The pilot cut the engine and Sophie opened the side door. She stepped out, under the slowing rotors and hurried to Mike.

"What happened? Where's Dr. Farah?" she shouted over the sound of the chopper."

"By the time we got here, everyone was gone."

"The natives?"

"Yes, but Major Brozik has men out in the jungle looking for her."

"How about Sebastian and Veck?"

"Gone too."

She looked around. "Where's Alex?"

Mike hitched a thumb over his shoulder. "He said he had to run an errand."

"An errand? You mean--he's out there alone? With the natives?"

Major Brozik overheard her concern and smiled. "I wouldn't worry about him, miss; he is definitely one man who can take care of himself."

"I know, but…"

She began pacing back and forth. After ten anxious minutes, she spotted Alex strolling carefree down the jungle path. Her face lit up, and she ran to him. She wrapped her arms around him and the tighter she squeezed, the wider his smile grew.

"Miss me, did you?" he said.

"I was so worried. I thought the natives got you."

"Me? Never. I've got something for you. Hold out your hands."

She pulled back. "What?"

Alex brought his arms forward and handed her a gift.

"The codex!" she screamed. "Oh, Alex--thank you!" She took the old Mayan book and pressed it against her chest. "This means so much to me. Thank you."

A call came over the radio headset Major Brozik was wearing. "Major, it's Zilkowski. No sign of the natives. No footprints, no anything. We can't find a trace. It's like they disappeared."

"Well, keep looking. We have to find her, and the missing case."

The Major walked to the helicopter. He returned a few minutes later and addressed Alex, Mike, and Sophie. "I spoke to command. When the forensics team arrives, you'll take their chopper out of here."

"We can leave?" Sophie asked.

"Yes, miss. The chopper will take you to an airport in Guatemala City. From there, you'll transfer to a plane that will take you back to the States."

"That's wonderful," she replied.

"However...before you're allowed to go home, the FBI will want to debrief you."

"Where?" Alex asked.

"Fort Bliss."

"Fort Bliss? That's in Texas!" Sophie exclaimed. She flew into the Major's arms and planted a big kiss on his cheek. "Thank you, Major."

The Major appeared to be more than a little embarrassed by the show of affection.

Alex smiled. "She's from Texas."

"I see. Well, you're welcome miss," he said. "Um...and after the debriefing, you will be provided transportation to your homes."

Fifty-five minutes later the forensics chopper arrived. The aircraft landed, and the doors opened. A six-member team, carrying a variety of cases, stepped out.

A tall man with neatly trimmed mustache approached the Major. "Major Brozik? I'm Peter Graham. Mind showing me to the palace?"

"In a minute." He turned to Alex. "You three can go aboard now."

Alex and Mike pulled the radio receivers from their ears and the throat mikes around their throats. The former SEALs gave them to the Major. Alex unbuckled the holster, "Thanks for the loaner," he said and handed it to him.

"Don't mention it."

Mike gave back the pistol he was carrying. "Thanks".

They all shook hands.

"Have a good trip back." The Major said.

The Major abruptly turned. He put his hand to his ear to listen to an incoming radio message. His face became serious. "Find them!" he yelled.

"What happened?" Alex asked.

The Major said, "Two of my men were just reported missing. They're part of the group searching for Dr. Farah. One minute they were there, the next--gone. No one heard or saw a thing."

"Sorry to hear that," Alex replied, and he meant it.

The Major slapped Alex on the shoulder. "Get going. I'll handle it from here. Have a good trip back."

The three stepped inside the helicopter. Alex and Sophie introduced themselves to the pilot and then walked to the rear. Mike, on the other hand, plopped into the empty seat beside the pilot.

Alex looked at the pilot and grinned. The poor bastard didn't know what he's in for; he'd have to listen to Mike jabber the entire way. He wasn't sure if the man was up to it--not many were.

Sophie took a seat in the rear of the chopper. She buckled in tight and cradled the codex in her arms. Alex took a seat across from her and fastened his seatbelt. He leaned his head back.

Then it was like someone pulled a plug and all the energy drained from his body. He closed his eyes and fell asleep before the chopper even left the ground.

19

It was just after midnight when the jet landed at Biggs Airfield. Alex awoke as the pilot taxied off the lighted runway. The pilot parked the aircraft in front of a large hangar.

Alex yawned and looked out the window. Parked under a light pole was a military jeep. Behind the wheel of the jeep was a man dressed in military BDU's, battle dress uniform. He was a young, solidly built man with a military-style haircut.

Alex, Mike, and Sophie exited the plane and the man from the jeep was there to greet them. "Good evening," he said. "My name is Sergeant Hall. I'm here to escort you to General Shepard's office. Follow me, please."

Sophie stopped him. "Wait, sergeant. Is there a place where we can get cleaned up and grab a bite to eat first?"

"Sorry ma'am, I have orders to take you to the general's office immediately. After I drop you off, I'll see if I can dig up something for you to eat."

"Thank you, we'd appreciate that."

The three got into the back seat of the jeep. Sergeant Hall handed them security badges for the base. "Put these on."

They clipped the security badges on their shirts.

Sergeant Hall started the engine and drove them off the airbase. They crossed the road. After clearing security, they entered Fort Bliss. The sergeant drove to the other side of the base and pulled in front of a simple, two-story brick building.

He parked, turned off the vehicle, and escorted them inside. He led them down a long hallway lit by fluorescent lights. At the end of the hall, he stopped in front of a door with a sign that read, General Shepard's Office.

They entered the office. Sergeant Hall walked past the vacant secretary's desk and rapped twice on an inner door. "They're here, sir."

From inside, a man with a gruff voice replied, "Very good, sergeant, show them in."

The sergeant opened the door and led the three inside.

A stocky man with silver hair and an unlit cigar clenched in his teeth was standing in front of a wide, wooden desk. Despite the man's advanced age, he appeared fit enough to wrestle a bear and win.

"I'm General Sheppard," he said with a voice like gravel. "Looks like you three have been to hell and back."

"That's exactly how we feel sir," Alex replied.

General Sheppard gestured to the three men on his right. "I want to introduce you to the Director of the FBI, James Meyers."

"Must be important if the Director of the FBI showed up," Alex said.

"It is. The men next to him are President Grant's Chief of Staff, David Lawson, and Senator Charles McDaniel."

The senator stepped forward. With a wide smile, he extended his hand. "Commander McCade. Lieutenant Garrison--this is a real pleasure," he said pumping each of their hands. "I couldn't believe my ears when I heard you two were involved in this."

Alex hardly recognized him because of the gray beard. "It's good to see you again senator. I'm sorry we didn't save Dr. Farah or recover the case," Alex replied.

"Well, I'm damn sure you did more than any other men could possibly do."

The senator turned and spoke to the others in the room, "Not many people know this, but years ago my daughter was kidnapped by a terrorist group, and it was none other than Commander McCade here, who led a Navy SEAL team to rescue her. Lieutenant Garrison was among them and I owe them both more than I can ever say."

"How's your daughter doing, Senator?" Alex asked.

"Very well, thank you. She's twenty-one-years-old now. She's doing well in college and has a steady boyfriend; nice fellow."

Alex motioned to Sophie. "Senator, this is Dr. Sophie Marcus."

"Nice to meet you, young lady," he replied, "although, I must admit I am no longer a senator; I retired over a year ago. After spending forty years in the Senate I thought it was time to slow down and do some fishing."

Alex was curious. "I hope you don't mind my asking, but if you're retired why are you here?"

The senator smiled. "When I was in the senate, I was privy to certain top secret information concerning Dr. Farah's project. After her project was stolen, the president asked me to come out of retirement to help in its recovery. He believes my insight may do some good."

"Can you tell us what the project is?"

"I'm sorry but to use that tired old line—'it's classified.'"

The FBI director cleared his throat. "Excuse me, but time is short."

"Alright," General Sheppard said biting down on his unlit cigar, "I can take a hint." He shook hands with the FBI director, the senator, and the chief of staff. With a raised eyebrow and a smirk, he said, "I assume you boys can let yourselves out when you've finished?"

"Yes, thank you general," replied the director.

The general nodded to Alex, Mike, and Sophie and then left the room.

When the door closed, the FBI director motioned for the three to have a seat on the metal folding chairs in front of the general's desk. "Please have a seat and we'll get started."

The FBI director leaned against the corner of the general's heavy oak desk. "I want to start by saying that I appreciate you coming in at this late hour. From your appearance, I can tell you've been through a lot, so I promise we won't keep you any longer than necessary. To start, I would like to hear each of your stories, one at a time. Who would like to go first?"

Sophie gave a little wave of her hand. "I'll go. I was the first to run into Sebastian."

"Fine," he said. He clipped a small microphone to her shirt. "We'll be recording this so please speak slowly and clearly." The FBI director turned on the digital video camera. "Please, start from the beginning and don't leave anything out."

The senator and the president's chief of staff sat off to the side and listened intently as Sophie gave her statement. When she finished, a series of questions and answers followed.

Then it was Alex's turn, and the microphone was passed to him. As he was clipping it to his tattered shirt, Sergeant Hall entered the room with a tray of sandwiches and coffee.

"Thank you, sergeant," the FBI director said, "please set it over there."

Sophie went and put a sandwich on a paper plate. She picked up a cup full of black coffee and brought them to Alex. Between bites Alex gave a thoroughly detailed report.

He started from the time he saw Dr. Farah's jet crash into the jungle, until the moment that he, Mike and Sophie stepped into the generals' office. This was followed by more questions and answers.

When Alex had finished, he passed the microphone to Mike, and the process began again.

When all three had given their statements, the FBI director turned off the camera. "I have one more thing to ask of you and then you're free to go. Please follow me."

Alex, Mike, and Sophie followed the FBI director into the adjoining room. The room was smaller than the general's office, but just as sparsely decorated.

Seated at a desk in front of a large computer screen was a heavy-set woman in a blue patterned dress. She had dark shoulder length hair that curled up at the bottom and oversized, round glasses that made her look like a giant bug.

"This is Ms. Warner," the director said. "She's an artist who works closely with the FBI. With your help, she will create a facial composite of Sebastian and Veck. Like you said, we don't know if they are alive...but we need to learn their identities as part of our investigation."

Ms. Warner smiled warmly and motioned to have a seat. Each sat with a clear view of the screen. "Let's begin with Sebastian," she said, "We'll start with the overall shape of the face." With a few clicks of the keyboard, she had a screen with an array of face shapes. "Which one would you say best describes his look?"

"That one," Alex said pointing at the long, thin shaped face.

"Alright," said Ms. Warner with a click of the mouse. They spent the next fifteen minutes choosing the right cheekbones, skin color, age, eyes, hair, eyebrows, lips, and nose. After a little tweaking of the image, Ms. Warner slid back her chair back. "Is this how he looks?"

"Yes, it's perfect," replied Alex. The others agreed.

Ms. Warner saved the composite of Sebastian to a file on the computer. "Now let's work on the other man. We'll start again on the shape of the face."

By the time they finished the image of Veck was enough to make Alex want to punch the screen and make Sophie feel like vomiting.

"I'd say by the looks on your faces we have our man," Ms. Warner said.

The FBI artist positioned the composites side by side on the computer screen, and then she hit the 'print' key. She snatched the sheet of paper as it came out of the printer. She went into the general's office with it.

Moments later, she returned with the FBI director, the senator, and the president's chief of staff.

The director held up the sheet of paper with the facial composites on it. "Are you absolutely sure these are the men?"

"Positive," Alex said.

He turned to Ms. Warner. "Alright, get these out right away."

"Yes sir," she replied.

"Are we finished here?" Alex asked.

"Yes, you are. However, I must remind you that everything you have seen, or heard must remain confidential. This is a matter of national security." All three nodded in agreement. "Good. I'll inform Sergeant Hall you are ready to leave."

"Where do we go from here?" Sophie asked.

"We have accommodations for you here on the base. In the morning, Sergeant Hall will give you your airline tickets and then take you to the airport to catch your flights home.

"If you have any further questions, please direct them to the Sergeant." With that, the director turned on his heels and left the room.

Senator McDaniel approached Alex. "Commander, here's my card. If there's anything you need, please don't hesitate to call. You can reach me at that number any time of the day or night. I'm never away from my phone."

Alex slid the card into his pocket. "Thanks, Senator, but call me Alex. I'm a civilian now."

"Alex, it is then," he said smiling. He glanced at his watch. "I'd love to stay and buy you and your friends a drink, but I need to get back to Washington right away."

"Another time, then."

"Let's plan on it," replied the senator.

The senator left the room, and the president's chief of staff stepped up in his place. "On behalf of the President of the United States I would like to thank you. You can be sure that when I get back to Washington, I will inform him of your extraordinary efforts."

"Thank you, sir," Alex replied.

The chief of staff pulled his business card from his pocket and handed it to Alex. "Should you remember anything else that may prove useful, don't hesitate to call. Have a good trip home."

"Mr. Lawson?" said Sophie. "Do you think I could use the general's phone? I'd like to call my parents and let them know I'm alright."

"I don't think the general would mind. Dial 9 for an outside line," he replied and left the room.

Mike looked at Alex. "Speaking of phone calls, we need to call the jungle resort."

"Go ahead. While you're at it call Hernando and ask him to send our duffle bags home."

"Is vacation over?"

"I've had enough of the jungle, how about you?"

"I'm done."

Alex left the general's office and strolled outside to wait. He breathed in the cool night air. He felt a presence behind him and wheeled around. Senator McDaniel stepped out from the shadows. "Still want to know what's in the case? Let's walk."

They strolled down a dimly lit sidewalk in front of the administration buildings. Alex spoke as they walked. "I thought the project was top secret?"

"It is, but given your tremendous service to this country, not to mention that you just spent days risking your life to rescue Dr. Farah and the case, I believe you have a right to know. Good enough?"

"Good enough," Alex replied.

The senator continued. "Inside that case is a revolutionary weapon that Dr. Farah and her partner Dr.

Llewellyn spent the better part of fifteen years perfecting. The venture went by the code name: the 'Morpheus Project'.

The two scientists were on their way to White Sands Missile Range in New Mexico to perform final tests on the weapon when their plane was intercepted by this Sebastian fellow."

Alex listened intently as the senator went on to explain the details of the weapon. When the senator finished, Alex was speechless. This was far worse than he imagined. One shot of the smallpox virus in Manhattan at rush hour would wipe out half the city, and the pandemonium that would ensue would kill even more. Millions of people would die.

He was almost sorry he asked about the contents of the case, because it made his failure to obtain it and save Dr. Farah even more gut-wrenching.

The senator added, "Now you know why it is so important we find the weapon. It's far too dangerous to leave it unaccounted for."

Alex met the senator's eyes. "If I can help in any way, let me know."

The senator slapped him on the back. "Alex my boy, that's commendable, but you've done enough. Let us handle it from here."

A tall chain-link fence marked the end of the walkway. They turned around and headed back. The trip back was marked by silence.

When they arrived in front of the general's building, Alex stopped and shook the senator's hand. "Thanks for confiding in me senator."

"You're welcome. Take care."

Alex walked to the jeep thinking about what the senator had told him. It left him with a real uneasy feeling.

Mike and Sophie were sitting in the back of the jeep when he arrived. "Was that the senator?" Mike asked.

"Yeah," Alex replied.

"What did he want?"

He thought fast. "He wanted to know about fishing in the Seattle area." Alex hopped into the front seat of the jeep and changed the subject. "Mike, did you get a hold of the resort and Hernando?"

"Yeah, I cancelled what was left of our reservation at the resort. Then, I called Hernando. He was glad to hear that we're okay and agreed to send our bags to Seattle the first chance he gets."

"Good." Alex turned to Sophie. "Did you get a hold of your parents?"

"Yes, and when they heard my voice, they were completely speechless. I told them I was fine and that I'll explain everything when I come home tomorrow."

Alex stiffened. His mind whirled. His face lost all expression.

"Alex, what's wrong?" She asked.

Alex didn't say a thing; couldn't say a thing. His stomach churned. What was wrong with him? Then it hit him. The thought of Sophie leaving tomorrow flipped a switch in his brain.

Suddenly, he realized he wanted to see her again. This feeling caught him completely by surprise. He was conflicted. As absurd as it sounded…if he asked to see her again, was he somehow cheating on the memory of his deceased wife?

"Alex? Are you okay?"

It had been a long and difficult five years since the death of his wife, and he knew he had trouble letting go.

Come on man--do it, he thought. Logically he knew he wanted to see Sophie again, so why was asking her out so hard?

He could wade through the deepest, smelliest swamps, go for days without food or drink, fight the enemy in hand to hand combat, but to ask her out seemed so overwhelmingly difficult.

"Alex?"

"Um…" He gulped hard, but his throat was dry. It felt like he swallowed a handful of sand. He coughed into his fist and then tried again. "Um…after you see your family…I was wondering if you wanted to come up to Seattle for the Memorial Day weekend. I was thinking we could spend some more time together."

She appeared shocked, then pleased. She smiled and said, "Yes, I would love to come."

20

Four days later, with a newspaper tucked under his arm, Alex opened the door of a local coffee shop in the heart of Seattle. As the door swung open, an old-fashioned bell rang.

He walked to the counter and ordered what he always did; a hot cup of black coffee. The shop itself was not the fancy chain store type, but rather a mom and pop coffee shop that had been open since the early 1950s.

The ambiance was plain and grimy. The tables had cigarette burns, probably there since the place opened. The coffee shop had definitely seen better days, but the coffee was superb.

He glanced around. There were only two other people in the shop. A teenager tapping a laptop keyboard and a businesswoman texting on her cellphone.

He paid the man for the coffee and headed to his favorite table by the window. He set the cup down and unfolded the newspaper. He was eager to see how the Seattle Mariners fared in last night's baseball game.

He had just found the sports section when the door opened and the bell clanged. Alex raised his eyes and saw Mike walking in. His friend spotted him and came directly to his table.

Mike took a chair and sat across from him. He glanced at the sports section and said, "The Mariners lost last night. We got routed, 10-1."

"Well, thanks for ruining the surprise," Alex replied. "So, are you going to get a coffee or just watch me read the paper?"

"Neither. Uncle Gus wants to meet us for lunch. He has some investment opportunities to run by us."

It had been a few years since Alex had seen Mike's Uncle Gus. He had been a father figure to Alex after his dad passed away. The man was good-natured and funny. Alex liked him. He was also a hell of a financial guru.

He ran his own financial investment firm out of a high-rise office building in downtown Seattle. His clients were some of the most wealthy, most famous people in the world. He had movie stars, software CEO's, foreign royalty, sports legends, and more, among his clientele.

During their college years, Uncle Gus had gotten he and Mike in on the ground floor of a computer software company. Some ten years later, both were financially set for life. If Uncle Gus was willing to share more advice, he was certainly willing to listen.

"When does he want to meet?"

"Now."

"A little short notice, don't you think?" Alex replied.

"Well, he's a busy man."

Alex took one last sip of coffee and got to his feet. "Who drives?"

Mike held up his keys. "I'll drive."

The lunch meeting was set to take place at the rotating restaurant on top of the Seattle Space Needle, a structure that resembled a giant alien spacecraft sitting upon three long poles. The iconic restaurant was built in 1962, just in time for the Seattle's World's Fair. At the time, it was the tallest structure west of the Mississippi.

The food was good, but Alex suspected that wasn't the reason the restaurant was chosen. Uncle Gus was friends with the manager and knew he could get a free meal. The man was not only a financial genius he was also very thrifty, which is one reason he was so good at managing people's money. He didn't waste a dime.

They left the coffee shop in Mike's car. When they arrived, he parked on the street a block away. They walked up the front walk of the Space Needle and then took the elevator up to the restaurant.

Alex stepped from the elevator and felt the floor slowly moving under his feet. He knew from previous visits that the restaurant rotated a complete circle about every 45 minutes.

He looked out the windows circling the entire restaurant. The view was impressive. In one sitting, a person could see downtown Seattle, the Cascade and Olympic mountain ranges, Elliot Bay, Mount Rainier, and more.

They spotted Uncle Gus. He was hard to miss. He was a large man who loved food and didn't care for exercise. He always said--he made his living with his brain, not his body. He had a full face and meaty jowls that jiggled when he laughed.

The top of his head was bald except for strands of gray hair he fashioned into the classic comb-over style. Alex always wondered if Mike was adopted. The two men appeared to share none of the same genes.

Uncle Gus waved them to his table by the window. Whether he was at the office or at home, he always wore a white shirt with rolled up sleeves, a faded yellow tie loose around his neck, and dark slacks. Alex couldn't recall him ever wearing anything else. Today was no different.

"Alex, how have you been?" he bellowed.

"Fine. And you?"

"Never better," he replied.

Alex and Mike took a seat opposite him.

Uncle Gus leaned forward. "Mike tells me you two had quite an adventure in the jungle recently."

Alex grinned. "We did. It got a little hairy, but we survived."

The uncle laughed. "You boys always do."

Mike smiled, and like a little brother tattling on the other, he said, "Uncle Gus, I've got news. Alex has a woman flying in to visit him Memorial Day weekend."

The uncle looked at Alex. "Good, it's about time you jumped back into the market. You don't want to be alone all your life, do you? What's she like?"

Alex was about to answer when Mike jumped in. "She's beautiful, smart and get this…he met her while we were in the jungle."

"The jungle?"

"It's a long story," Alex replied sheepishly.

"Well, I'm happy for you, son."

The waiter came to the table, and Alex was happy for the interruption. He ordered the wild king salmon sandwich, Mike ordered the crab melt, and Uncle Gus ordered the Caesar salad with grilled Jidori chicken.

When the food arrived, they ate and engaged in small talk. After lunch, the talk of business began. Uncle Gus wiped his mouth with his napkin. "You boys got out of the Navy, what? A month ago?"

The men nodded.

"Do you have anything planned?"

"Not yet," Alex answered.

Uncle Gus said, "I know the both of you like you are my own sons. You may not need the money, but I know you'll go crazy without something to keep yourselves occupied. Am I right? Of course, I am. So, I have two opportunities for you.

Number one: how would you like to do a little gold mining in Alaska? It's a little side project I've been meaning to get to. I bought some land years ago in Alaska with the intention of mining it. It's something I always wanted to do, but time slipped away, and now I'm too old to do it myself." He rubbed his large belly and added, "And just a little bit out of shape.

"My plan is to start small and then grow big. I will incur all the operating expenses of the gold mine. I will supply all the equipment, bulldozers, loaders, a wash-plate, generators, water pumps, whatever is needed. You, on the other hand, will do all the work."

"What's the split once we find the gold?" Mike asked.

"I am willing to do a 50/50 split. If you were anyone other than my favorite nephew and the son I never had, the split would be quite different. If you need to hire additional workers, you'll take it out of your split. When the project grows bigger in size, we may see a need to renegotiate."

"But we don't have any gold mining experience," Mike replied.

"Don't worry about that. I hired an expert who knows what he's doing. He'll teach you."

"Who pays him?"

"I'll take on his salary the first year. By the second year, you shouldn't need him."

"Seems more than fair," Mike said. "When do you want to start?"

"It's too late to get this up and running for this year. In Alaska, the ground is frozen for most of the year, so it's a tight window. The gold mining season usually runs June through September, giving us roughly 125 days to dig. I'm aiming to start the operation next year. It'll give you time to think about whether you want to be involved or not."

Uncle Gus called the waiter over and asked for the dessert menu. He ordered alone. As they waited for the dessert to arrive, Mike said, "You said you had two opportunities for us to consider."

"That's right. On to opportunity number two: This one is solely an investment opportunity. Friends of mine in Los Angeles are looking for investors for a movie they're producing."

"You told us that investing in movies is too risky."

"It is, but not when its stars Vivian Grey."

"Vivian Grey," Mike repeated. "Wow."

The whole world knew the name and face of Vivian Grey. She was perhaps the most famous actress in the world. She was 28 years old, gorgeous and had starred in twelve feature films. She had been on hundreds of magazine covers and was the spokesperson for a line of cosmetics and upscale perfume. She was America's sweetheart. Everyone loved her.

"What's the movie about?" Mike asked.

"It's a love story set in Scotland."

"Do we get to meet her?"

"I think I could arrange that, after all, she is a client of mine."

Mike's mouth dropped open. "A client of yours? And this is the first I'm hearing of it?"

Uncle Gus smiled. "I know how you get, that's why

I never told you."

Alex laughed. He had a point.

Dessert arrived.

Uncle Gus dug into his cake as they discussed the financial aspects of the movie investment. A rather large financial sum was needed, but with every Vivian Grey movie came a big budget, a large amount of expenses, and a huge profit.

After dessert, it was time to go. They thanked Uncle Gus for the opportunities. Uncle Gus told them to think about it and get back to him within a few weeks.

Alex and Mike got up from the table and walked to the elevator. As they waited for the elevator, Alex turned around and noticed Uncle Gus ordering another dessert. Alex smiled. The man lived large and ate large.

Mike drove Alex back to the coffee shop. Full from lunch, Alex didn't go inside, but instead walked to his pickup truck he parked on the street. He still had five minutes left on the meter.

On the drive home, he thought of Sophie. He pulled out his cell phone and dialed.

She answered.

"Sophie, this is Alex."

"Alex, how are you?"

"I'm fine, how are you?"

"Tired. It's been go-go-go since I got back. I've talked to the police on multiple occasions, filled out reports and spoke with some family members of the expedition. It's been awful. Most of the ones I lost were my friends."

"It sounds like a tough week." Alex heard a commotion in the background. "What's that?"

"The media. They've been camped on my doorstep

since yesterday. They each want an exclusive story about what happened in the jungle. I'm just not ready for that."

"Want to come to Seattle early and get away from all that?"

"I'd love to, but I can't just yet. I have to meet with one more family on Saturday night. Okay if I fly up Sunday morning?"

"Sure. I'll change your flight reservation to Sunday morning. Then I'll text you back with the details."

"Okay, but Alex, promise me one thing. It's been so stressful here. While I'm there, I want nothing but rest and relaxation."

"You got it."

21

The Memorial Day weekend was finally here. Alex parked his truck in the covered parking at the Seattle/Tacoma International Airport.

He walked inside and found it packed with holiday travelers. He glanced at the arrival monitor. Sophie's flight had just landed. He double-checked the gate and then proceeded to wait for her outside the secured area.

As he scanned the faces of the passengers, looking for Sophie, he anxiously played with the wedding ring on his finger. Mike hounded him to take it off, but he just couldn't, not yet. One step at a time, he thought. This was the first woman that interested him since his wife died and he was filled with apprehension.

He spotted her in the middle of the pack. She was wearing a silky blue blouse, a black ankle-length skirt with a wide black belt, and black leather boots. She exited the secured area and spotted him. She smiled and gave a little wave. His heart jumped.

She angled through the mass of people, and said, "Quite the busy place you have here."

"Holiday weekend," he replied. "How was your flight?"

"It must have been good because I slept the entire way here. It's the first good sleep I've had all week."

"Now you can relax. Like I promised…nothing but rest and relaxation while you're here."

"Thank you."

She raised a black leather case in her hand. "Oh, by the way, I was so busy I didn't have time to work on the Mayan codex. I hope you don't mind I brought it along."

"Not at all."

They walked to baggage claim. After collecting her luggage, they went out of the terminal and over the sky bridge to the parking lot.

Alex found his blue 1991 Chevy Silverado pickup truck. It wasn't much to look at, with dents, scratches, and a dashboard held together by duct tape, but it was a good runner.

He placed her luggage in the back bed. Sophie got in through the passenger door and put the case containing the codex on her lap. Alex got behind the wheel and started the engine. He put it in gear and drove from the parking garage.

Once on the I-5 freeway, he headed north toward the city of Seattle. Sophie glanced at the blue sky and then to the tall evergreen trees lining the side of the freeway. She faced west and got a good view of the snow-capped peaks of the Olympic Mountain Range.

"Everyone talks about the clouds and rain in Seattle, but they rarely mention how beautiful it is here."

"Best place in the world," Alex replied.

Reaching the city, Alex took the downtown exit. Next, he drove down a steep hill toward the waterfront. At the stop light, he took a right turn and drove north along a busy thoroughfare. Small American flags marking the Memorial Day weekend waved outside stores, coffee shops, and restaurants.

At Fairview Avenue North he went right and continued along the east side of Lake Union. A half mile up the road, Alex slowed and pulled into a gravel parking lot facing the lake. He placed the truck in park and said, "This is it."

Sophie stared at the multitude of houseboats floating in the water.

"You live on a houseboat? You never told me you live on a houseboat."

"Sophie--I live on a houseboat."

Alex got out of the truck. He reached into the bed and removed her luggage. The two walked down a short flight of stairs and proceeded along a lengthy wooden dock.

She scanned the houseboats on either side. None of them looked alike. "Which one is yours?"

"That one," he said pointing to a modest, one story houseboat at the end of the dock. It had gray clapboard siding with gunmetal blue trim. He paid a premium for the houseboat when he purchased it, but it was worth every penny. The houseboat faced the middle of the lake and had incredible views.

He unlocked the backdoor with a key. They entered, and he turned off the security system. He flipped on the kitchen light, and said, "Welcome to my humble abode."

The kitchen was dated with dark wooden cupboards and almond colored appliances. In the center of the kitchen was a small table with two chairs. "The house isn't all that big, but it's home."

"It's marvelous," she said looking around. "What does it float on?"

"It floats on thirty Polystyrene barrels."

"Can you feel it move?"

"Sometimes during storms, or high winds."

"Right this way," he said and continued through the kitchen. He stopped in the living room and set down her luggage.

Sophie strolled around the living room and liked what she saw. A worn leather couch faced a large stone fireplace; over the thick, oak mantel hung an authentic Civil War musket. To the left of the fireplace was the TV. An antique armoire stood against one wall and on the opposite wall stood two large bookcases.

She went to the bookcases and read from some of the titles. "Napoleon, Rommel, Caesar. I see you like history." Then, she noticed a brightly colored book, 'Flowers of the Northwest.' She turned. "It's nice to see a man who likes flowers."

"Um...yeah," he replied sheepishly. He didn't feel the need to mention that the book belonged to his deceased wife, and he'd never opened it. He could tell her what plants to eat in the wilderness in order to survive, but he knew very little about flowers.

"Come on, I'll show you the rest of the house."

He led her down the hallway. He pointed out the bathroom and then his bedroom at the end of the hall. She peeked in. It was basic, but that's just how he liked it. His bed was in the center of the room. To the left was a desk with a laptop computer and to the right a dresser.

He guided her to the only other room in the house. He slid open the sliding shoji screen door. It was a simple room decorated in the Japanese style. The floor was covered with tatami mats and Japanese block prints hung on the wall.

"This is beautiful," she said.

"My mom was Japanese, and we had a room like this in our house when I was little," he said.

"Where in Japan was she from?"

"A city called Sapporo. It's on the northern island of Hokkaido."

"Have you been there?"

"Many times," he replied. "I used to go with my mom every summer to visit relatives…that is, before she died."

"Do you speak the language?"

"I do, but not as well as I used to."

"When's the last time you were there?"

"When I was eleven."

"Have you been back since?"

"No, but I was thinking of taking a trip back sometime and try to reconnect with my relatives." He closed the shoji screen door and brought her back to the living room.

She glanced around the room.

"Looking for something?" he asked.

"I don't know; I guess I expected to see some photos of your late wife."

Alex grimaced. "That's Mike's doing. He snuck in here last night and took down her photos."

"He didn't have to do that," she replied. "I think it's beautiful you keep her memory alive. What did she look like?"

"You really want to know?"

"I do."

Alex left the room and returned with a small metal box. He opened it. Inside, he had personal mementos of his late wife.

He took out a photo and handed it to Sophie. The photo was of his wife holding up a large salmon beside a lake. "It's in Alaska. We were on our honeymoon," he said.

"She's beautiful."

"Yes, she was," he replied.

She chuckled. "You really went fishing in Alaska on your honeymoon?"

Alex shrugged and smiled. "It was her idea."

She gave him back the photo. He placed it in the box, closed the lid and then brought the box to his bedroom. He returned to the living room and said, "The tour isn't over. I've got one more thing to show you." He whisked back the front window curtains and sunlight poured into the room.

"Wow, what an incredible view," she said.

"It's even better out there."

He opened the door, and they walked onto the wide outside deck facing the lake.

She eyed the panoramic view of the Seattle skyline and its tall, iconic Space Needle. "It's beautiful."

Alex pointed. "Directly across the lake is Queen Anne hill," he said, "and at the north end of the lake is Gas Works Park; a popular spot for picnickers and kite flyers.

"What's that metal monstrosity on the right side of the park?"

"That's the remains of the old Gas Processing plant. After the plant shut down, the city turned the site into a park and left some of the machinery behind. Maybe we can go there for a picnic tomorrow?"

"I'd like that."

She lowered her vision and looked to the right side and then to the left side of the deck. "Wait a second. You have a speedboat and a seaplane?"

"Doesn't everybody?"

"No-o-o..." she said laughing.

He loved to hear her laugh.

Alex nodded toward the plane. "Since you slept on your flight, how about I take you up and show you what you missed?"

"Sounds great."

Sophie went inside and changed her clothes. She put on a pair of jeans, a t-shirt, and sneakers. She came back outside and found Alex waiting for her by the plane.

He helped her into the 1955 De Havilland Beaver seaplane. He didn't mention it, but he recently refinished the entire plane himself.

Casting off the lines, he boarded the aircraft and started the engine. The engine hummed soundly, and the propellers whirled. He taxied the aircraft to the north end of the lake, turned the plane around and faced in a southerly direction.

Without a tower regulating traffic, he scanned the water and air for traffic. When it was safe, he gave the plane the throttle. The engine roared and the seaplane shot forward.

As the speed increased the plane lifted higher in the water and soon it was skipping across the surface. Reaching takeoff speed, Alex pulled back on the yoke, and the aircraft lifted effortlessly in the air.

He gained altitude and then banked the aircraft until he was flying in a northerly direction.

He pointed out the left side window. "That's the Olympic Mountain range over there," he said. "And down to the right, is the University of Washington campus. That big body of water to the right is Lake Washington."

Alex craned his neck and looked back over his right shoulder. "And that snowcapped mountain behind us is Mount Rainer. The mountain is 14, 410 feet tall."

"Have you ever climbed it?"

"No, not me. I may do a lot of things, but mountain climbing for fun isn't one of them."

He cruised up to the San Juan Islands and showed her the scenic beauty the Pacific Northwest had to offer.

Two hours later, he returned to the Seattle area. He flew over the Puget Sound and pointed out the large white ferries transporting people and vehicles across the water. "People live on the islands, and they use the ferries to go back and forth to the mainland."

He banked the plane and flew along Alki Beach which gave Sophie a full view of the city in the distance. A short time later, Alex set up his approach for landing.

He came in from the north and landed the seaplane on the smooth water of Lake Union. He taxied the aircraft to the houseboat and cut the engine.

Sophie was beaming. "Alex that was incredible!"

"We can go up again tomorrow, if you'd like?"

"I'd love to."

22

As Alex and Sophie stepped out of the plane, his cell phone rang. "Hello? Yeah, she's here," he said. "Okay, I'll ask her." He lowered the phone. "Want to meet Mike for dinner?"

"Sure, that'd be great."

He returned the phone to his ear. "She said okay...but only if she's forced to."

She grabbed for the phone. "I didn't say that Mike!"

Alex grinned. "See you in twenty minutes," he said and hung up.

She playfully hit him in the arm. "You stinker, that's not what I said."

He smiled.

The two went inside the houseboat and grabbed their coats. The sun was beginning to sink below the horizon, and the temperature was dropping. It was a chilly 58 degrees, a far cry from the hot and humid jungle temperatures.

Alex grabbed a key off the hook and met Sophie at the door. "Do you like seafood?" he asked.

"Love it."

"Well, this place has the best seafood in town." Alex moved past her.

"Where are you going? Aren't we taking the truck?"

"The restaurant is on the other side of the lake. We'll take the boat."

"A plane ride, and now a boat ride? I'm getting to like this."

They went outside and got into the speedboat. He attempted to start the engine, but it coughed, sputtered, and wouldn't start. "I've been having trouble with this thing lately," he said. He tried again.

After the fourth attempt, the engine started. He put the boat in gear, pulled away from the deck, and increased speed. As the boat sliced through the water, Alex tossed friendly waves to passing boaters.

Sophie waved too. "Do you know them?"

"No, but you'll find that Seattle has some of the friendliest people around."

On the other side of the lake, he eased the boat along the restaurant's dock. He cut the engine and secured the line to the post. He and Sophie got out of the boat and walked up to the restaurant.

The rear deck was full of people sitting around tables, chatting and having drinks under the warm glow of the umbrella style heating lamps.

They entered the restaurant through the back door and found the inside of the restaurant crowded, too. Amid the sound of people talking and the clanging dishes and silverware, they proceeded to the front of the restaurant.

Alex spoke to the young lady taking names. He glanced at the waiting list, and Mike's name was third from the bottom. He looked at Sophie. "This could take a while."

He led her into the bar which, no surprise, was

crowded. Among the mobs of people, he spotted Mike chatting up the attractive new female bartender. They waded through the crowd and Sophie tapped Mike on the shoulder.

He turned, set his beer down, and hugged Sophie. "Great to see you again."

"You too. Mike, don't believe what Alex said earlier. I'm really glad to see you."

"I didn't believe him for a second. C'mon have a drink," Mike said.

He turned and introduced them to Tawny, the new bartender. She was a tall, blond haired girl with long legs, blue eyes, and swelling breasts. Mike said, "Tawny, two beers for my friends please."

The female bartender winked at Mike and then went off to fill the order.

Mike raised his eyebrow at Alex. "Not bad, huh?"

"What happened to Desiree, our last bartender?"

"Poor thing moved back to California."

"California? You broke her heart didn't you?"

Mike gave him a guilty grin.

"Every time you break up with a girl they move away."

"I know, but this time it's different."

"You say that every time. Why don't you leave this one alone? I'm sure management would appreciate it."

"Too late," he replied and held up a coaster with the bartender's name and phone number on it.

When the beers arrived, Mike turned to Alex. "Alright big guy, pay the woman, and don't forget to add in a generous tip."

"Me?"

"Do I need to remind you of our little agreement in the jungle? Mike tapped his finger into Alex's chest. "And remember--you can't complain about it."

Alex grumbled. He pulled out his wallet, paid the bartender, and then added a generous tip.

Mike spotted people leaving a table in the corner of the bar, and they quickly pounced on it before anyone else could nab it.

When they were seated around the table, Alex lifted his glass of beer. "A toast…to our making it out of the jungle alive."

The three clinked glasses and drank in unison.

Mike held up his glass for another toast. "And here's to my new sports car, which I just purchased today."

The three clicked glasses again.

While Sophie asked questions about the car, Alex rolled his eyes. Mike was a spender who liked the best of everything: nice clothes, fast cars, jewelry, even an expensive Seattle condo overlooking Elliot Bay. Admittedly, it was irritating to hear about all his latest purchases. But Alex wasn't jealous.

While Mike enjoyed material items, Alex was content with very little. The latest gizmos or fads had never been important to him.

In fact, he preferred older things, things with character. He lived in an old house, had old furniture, and drove an old truck. He had money to buy all new things, but he didn't want to. He didn't see the point. He was perfectly happy with what he had.

"I'd love to see your new car," Sophie said.

"How about after dinner?"

"Sounds good," she replied.

She took a sip of beer, licked the beer foam from her lips, and said, "Well, it's obvious you have been friends a long time. How did you meet?"

Mike jumped in. "I get to tell her."

"No, I'll tell her," Alex replied, "the truth always gets lost when you tell it."

"Does not."

Alex put up his hand. "I'll tell the story. In the middle of fourth grade, my family moved to a small town called Puyallup."

"Puy...?"

"Puyallup. It comes from an Indian word meaning 'Generous, or friendly people.' It's a city about 45 minutes south of here.

"Anyway, it was my first day at the new school. It was time for recess, and all the kids went out to play. I was moving toward the swing set when I was stopped by a kid. He told me that a bully didn't allow anyone on the swing set without his permission."

Mike smiled at Sophie and pointed proudly at himself.

"Of course, I didn't listen and got on anyway. Mike saw me and ordered me off the swing. I wouldn't, so he pushed me--and the fight was on."

"I won the fight," Mike added quickly.

Alex shook his head. "No, I won the fight. Mike has a faulty memory due to the serious pounding I gave him that day."

Sophie grinned, "And to this day you boys still argue about who won the fight?"

"Yes," both responded in unison.

"Incredible."

Alex slid his chair back and rose from the table. "I'll

go see where we are on the list."

Mike watched Alex leave the bar area and then turned to Sophie. "Just to be honest...I won the fight."

Sophie laughed.

Alex returned with the news that their name had only moved up two places. It was going to be a long wait. So, instead of waiting for a table in the restaurant they placed their food orders from the bar.

Over the next few hours, they ate a delicious seafood dinner, followed by drinking, swapping stories and laughing until their bellies ached. It was close to 11 p.m. when Alex settled the bill. It was time to go.

Sophie rose from her chair and nearly fell over. She leaned on the table and slurred, "Bye M-Mike." She held on to Alex's arm for support as they walked out the back door of the restaurant.

Although, the moment her face hit the cool air she began singing. He tried to quiet her, but the more he tried, the louder she sang.

They laughed and made it to the dock without incident. He eased her into the boat, but when she went to sit down, she missed the seat and landed on the bottom.

Giggling, she sat up. "I-I may have had too much to drink."

Alex smiled. "Yes, you may have," he replied and helped her onto the seat.

He was untying the boat rope from the dock when his senses went on high alert. His eyes snapped up. He scanned the area. Someone was watching them from the darkness, he knew it. He always had this special ability to sense danger.

The only time he ever recalled it failing him was in

the jungle when the natives hung the dead bodies in the tree while he and Mike slept. He still didn't understand how he hadn't he heard them. He may have lost his special 'danger indicator' in the jungle, but it was fully functioning now.

He again peered through the darkness and listened for the slightest movement, the lightest sound. He fought the urge to go and investigate, but he didn't want to leave Sophie alone. Instead, he turned the key, but the motor didn't start. He swore under his breath and tried again.

After three attempts, it finally started. As he motored away from the dock, he glanced back. No one appeared to be following. Maybe it was simply some drunk heaving his guts out behind the restaurant, but he doubted it.

When he arrived at the houseboat, he slid alongside the deck and cut the engine. As he tied the boat up, he looked at Sophie who was sound asleep.

He scooped her in his arms, carried her to his bedroom and laid her gently on the bed. Before leaving he covered her with a blanket.

On the way back to the living room he grabbed a blanket and pillow from the hall closet. He tossed the bedding on the couch.

As he slipped out of his pants and shirt, he heard an unusual creaking sound on the outside deck. Someone was out there.

He snuck to the window and lifted the edge of the curtain. He saw no one, but after what he sensed at the restaurant, it was time to investigate. He went to the bookcase and removed a loaded .45 caliber pistol from behind a book.

With the handgun, he padded through the kitchen. He turned off his security alarm, opened the back door and slipped out under a chorus of crickets. Wearing only his boxer underwear, he crept along the wooden walkway that wrapped around the house.

Reaching the far end, he raised the handgun and wheeled around the corner. The deck was empty. He checked inside his plane and boat to make sure no one was hiding. No one was.

He shook his head in disbelief. What the hell was wrong with him? Earlier, at the restaurant he sensed someone watching. Now, he knew someone was on his deck. Or maybe those damn natives threw off his mojo so bad he just didn't have it anymore. At least Sophie didn't witness his foolishness. This was just plain embarrassing.

He walked around the houseboat and entered through the back door. Once inside, he set the alarm. As a safety precaution, he made a thorough search of the house and double checked the door locks and window locks before going to bed.

As he lay down on the couch, he slipped his hand under his pillow and felt the cold steel of his pistol. He might be off his game, but he felt better having the weapon close by.

He pulled the blanket up to his chin. For a long time, he stared at the ceiling and listened for strange sounds. Finally, he closed his eyes and went to sleep.

23

The next morning, Alex was standing over a hot stove when he heard his bedroom door open and then the sound of shuffling feet.

Moments later, Sophie appeared. She slumped against the kitchen doorway and said, "Morning," in a raspy voice.

"Good morning sunshine," Alex replied. "How's the head?"

"A little fuzzy. Sorry about falling asleep on you last night. I'm so embarrassed. I was having so much fun that I lost track of how many drinks I had. Ever since we were nearly killed in the jungle, I've taken on a new attitude of--living life to its fullest!"

"That's a good philosophy...but the key is not to do it all in one night."

"Thanks, I'll remember that."

Alex motioned to the table. "Have a seat. I've got breakfast ready."

She put a hand on her stomach. "Oh, I don't feel much like eating."

"You'll change your mind when you take a bite of my world famous French toast. It'll cure anything."

"Even a hangover?"

"You'll see."

Sophie trudged to the kitchen table and sat heavily in the chair. Alex placed a plate of French toast in front of her. "Coffee?"

"Yes, black please."

"Black? I pictured you for a milk-and-sugar kind of girl."

"When you're away from civilization as much as I am, there isn't always milk and sugar available. So, I just got used to drinking it black."

Alex poured her a cup of black coffee and set it down beside the plate. Sophie poured warm maple syrup on her French toast. She cut it, lifted the fork and took a hesitant bite.

"Now, Dr. Marcus, tell me if that isn't the best French toast you've ever eaten."

She was surprised. "You got me there. This is delicious. What's your secret?"

"I can't tell you."

"What? You have to tell me. Pleasseee...." she said playfully batting her stunning green eyes.

"Okay, okay, stop you broke me. I can't resist the look of a beautiful woman," he replied with a chuckle. "The secret to my famous recipe is finely grated orange rinds, and a splash of Grand Marnier."

"I'm impressed."

"Don't be. To be honest, this is the only thing I know how to make."

Sophie was surprised to find she was suddenly famished. She ate what she had and then took second helpings of the French toast. After breakfast, she felt almost human again. She scooped up the empty dishes and brought them to the sink. "I'll wash; if you dry."

Alex grabbed a kitchen towel. "Sure you're feeling

up to it?"

"You bet. Your world-famous French toast did the trick. I feel much better." As she reached for the dish sponge, she glanced at the oven clock. "Oh no, is that the right time?"

Alex looked. "Yeah, why?"

"We'll do these later." She snatched his hand and pulled him into the living room.

"What's going on?"

"I'm going to be on TV," she exclaimed. "Remember, I told you about the TV special they did about my team? It's on now."

"Your team?"

"Yes, we found a cave in the Yucatan Peninsula that the Maya used to perform their religious ceremonies. The Maya believed that caves were the access points to reach their gods who lived inside the earth and National Geographic was there to film it."

"Then we sure don't want to miss it," Alex replied.

Sophie jumped on the worn leather couch.

Alex grabbed the remote and pointed it at the TV. "What channel?"

"PBS."

Alex turned to the PBS channel and then set the DVR to record the program. He joined Sophie on the couch.

A commercial for floor wax was on. After the commercial, there was an image of a large American flag waving in the breeze and a man with a deep voice said, "As we announced earlier, today's programming will be shown in its entirety, after we present to you the President of the United States and his special Memorial Day salute to our fallen soldiers."

Sophie turned. "Let's watch this. I bet they'll show my program after."

On TV, images taken from a helicopter high above Arlington National Cemetery showed hundreds of perfectly aligned white gravestones with small American flags beside them.

Then, the scene of the gravestones dissolved into a shot of the interior of the white marble Memorial Amphitheater where a crowd had gathered to hear the president speak.

The Secretary of Defense, Paul Ashley was standing at the flag-draped podium. He thanked the people for coming and gave a short speech. When he finished, he turned to the wings and introduced the President of the United States.

President Grant, dressed in a dark pinstripe suit with a red tie, walked solemnly to the podium. He tapped the microphone twice and began. "My fellow Americans, we are here today to honor all those who gave their lives in service of their country. Freedom comes at a price; a very high price. If you need a reminder, I suggest you look at all the white headstones in this cemetery and ..."

Alex didn't need a reminder; he knew the cost of freedom firsthand. Many of his friends had given their lives in service to their country. Every SEAL mission he undertook he risked the same.

He continued watching the president's speech when, unexpectedly, a small red dot of light appeared on the side of the president's neck. It stayed for a moment and then disappeared. Alex stared at the screen; seeing but not believing.

He snatched the remote to the DVR and reversed the recorded program to the exact moment the red dot appeared. He pushed 'pause,' and the president's image froze on the screen. How can this be?

"Alex, what's going on? What's wrong?"

"See that red dot of light on the president's neck?"

"I see it."

Alex dropped the remote and rushed to his bedroom. He snatched the senator's card off the top of his dresser, pulled the cell phone from his pocket, and dialed the senator's private number.

"Hello?"

"Senator, this is Alex McCade."

"Alex, good to hear from you, son. What can I do for you?"

"We have a problem. President Grant was just shot with the laser."

"What?"

"It happened minutes ago at Arlington National Cemetery. While he was giving his speech at the podium, I saw a red dot of light appear and then disappear on the side of his neck."

"And you think it was the laser?"

"I'm sure of it."

The senator paused. "Maybe it was a reflection of light off of one of the TV cameras, or...?"

"Senator, that was no reflection, I'll bet my life on it."

"Okay, I believe you Alex, but I have to tell you, I'm watching the president on TV this very moment and he appears in fine shape. If the president was shot, he'd be unconscious by now, wouldn't he?"

"Not if he was hit with one of those deadly agents you told me about."

"Oh my god, you're right. If this wasn't coming

from you, I'd swear it was a hoax." The senator thought a moment. "Alright, here's what I am going to do: I'll call the president's Chief of Staff David Lawson. He's with the president at the amphitheater. I'll get him to take the president back to the White House immediately."

"Thank you, Senator."

"I'll call you back when I have some news." And the senator hung up.

***

Senator McDaniel pushed the speed dial on his phone.

The chief of staff answered. "Charles, can I call you back? The president's in the middle of his speech."

The senator's tone was serious. "You have to get the president back to the White House immediately."

"Are you crazy? Why?"

"There's a good chance he was just shot with Dr. Farah's laser."

"You must be joking?"

"Would I joke about this?"

"No, no you wouldn't."

"I don't know how, but it happened. You have to get him back to the White House now."

"You know, if you're wrong about this both our heads will roll."

"So be it. Just get him back to the White House and have the President's medical team waiting for him when he arrives. I'll meet you at the White House in twenty minutes." The senator hung up and took a deep breath. Then he closed his eyes and sunk his head heavily into his hands.

24

Twenty minutes after Senator McDaniel had spoken with the chief of staff, he was standing beside the man inside the White House doorway. A few feet behind them was a team of medical personnel; all anxiously awaiting the president's arrival.

The senator nervously raked his fingers through his thick grey beard. "I hope to God this is all a horrible mistake," he said.

David nodded.

After five more minutes of waiting, the Presidential motorcade appeared. Three black SUV's and the president's armor-plated limousine drove through the East gates.

The vehicles came up the drive and stopped forty paces from the door. A Secret Service agent opened the door. President Grant stepped out and momentarily lost his balance.

"Just his arthritis," David said calmly.

The senator wasn't so sure.

The President regained his balance and then waved good-naturedly at the members of the media who followed him from the memorial service.

The senator watched the president walk slowly toward the door. He wasn't using his cane, but that was normal in public. What had him concerned was that the president was starting to sweat profusely and his face was growing paler by the moment.

A transformation was happening right before his eyes. Members of the medical team attempted to rush by the senator, but he held them back. He knew the president better than anyone. Even in these circumstances, the president would never forgive anyone that made him look weak.

The president bravely trudged on. By the time he made it to the doorway, he looked as white as a ghost. The senator opened the door. The president stepped inside. He took one look at his friend and collapsed into his arms.

The medical team burst into action. They laid the president on a gurney and placed an oxygen mask over his nose and mouth. Traveling as a group, they rushed him down the length of the hall and wheeled him through the open elevator doors. Someone pushed the button and the doors closed.

The elevator descended two hundred feet into the ground and opened inside a secret bunker called the Presidential Emergency Operations Center. It was a tube-like complex built strong enough to withstand a nuclear blast. It contained a state-of-the-art hospital, a secure communications system, and emergency food and water provisions.

The president was wheeled out of the elevator and whisked into a hospital room across the hall. A Secret Service agent was stationed outside the door with orders not to allow anyone inside.

Minutes later, Senator McDaniel and David Lawson arrived in the bunker. Unable to get in the room to see the president, they began pacing in the hallway.

The elevator doors opened again and the first lady rushed out. She saw the senator. "Charles! What's going on? No one will tell me what's wrong with my husband."

"Millicent, please calm down. Tom is very sick; he's inside with his doctors right now."

"Sick? How?" Without waiting for an answer, she brushed past him and went for the door.

"Wait, Millicent, you can't go in there."

The first lady reached for the doorknob, but was stopped by a Secret Service agent. "I'm sorry ma'am; no one is allowed inside."

"But I'm his wife! I need to see him."

The Secret Service agent shook his head. The first lady wheeled around, stamped her foot. "Charles! What is going on?"

"Please Millicent, have a seat, and I'll explain."

The senator guided the first lady to chairs lined against the wall. They sat. Tears began welling up in her eyes, and she said, "Charles, I've known you since you and my husband were roommates at Harvard. Please, tell me the truth. What's wrong with Tom?"

"Alright," he said and took a deep breath. "Tom has been infected with some type of chemical or biological agent."

"What? How?"

"It happened during his speech at the cemetery."

"How is that even possible? He had secret service agents all around him and…."

"We don't know," he lied.

"Do they, at least, know what he's infected with?"

"Not yet, but I'm certain the doctors are doing everything they can."

Tears streamed down her cheeks, and she wailed, "Charles, he's all I have! I-I can't lose him."

The senator pulled out his handkerchief and handed it to the first lady. As she dabbed away her tears, he saw the chief of staff. He stood and said, "Excuse me a moment, Millicent."

The senator walked over to the chief of staff and spoke low, "David, we have to talk." David nodded solemnly, and the two men walked out of listening range of anyone else. "David, you know, the media is going to be all over this."

"I know, I know. I've been thinking how to handle this, and I think I've got it."

"Let's hear it."

"We tell the media that the president has been fighting the flu all week. We say that his personal physician advised him to get bed rest, but the president, being the stubborn man that he is, refused. We say, he wouldn't miss an opportunity to pay tribute to the fallen men and women of the armed forces, and he went to the cemetery anyway."

"And the reason he left in the middle of his speech?"

"He was feeling very ill. He was afraid he was going to vomit on national TV."

"Not terribly creative, but okay."

"At that point, the decision was made to rush him back to the White House."

"And when people say he looked perfectly healthy when he arrived at the cemetery?"

"We'll tell them he was hiding his flu symptoms, just as he's hidden his arthritic knees. The president won't like us spilling the beans on his arthritis, but if we can keep the jackals away for a while, I know he will understand."

"The media will go berserk when they don't see him in the next few days. And you and I both know that whatever he was shot with, there is absolutely no chance for survival."

"In a few days, we'll say the president's condition worsened. I hate to say this, but when the president dies, we'll say he died from pneumonia. The man's seventy-years old; people will believe it."

"Not bad, but if that's the story you're going with you'd better get everyone on the same page before anything leaks out."

"Right," David said. He turned to walk away.

"Wait," the senator said, "I'll go with you. There are a few details I need to attend to, as well."

The senator walked back to the first lady. "Millicent, I need to go. Will you be okay?"

"Yes," she said with a heavy sigh, "under the circumstances..."

"If there's anything I can do, call me."

The first lady put on a brave face and nodded. Senator McDaniel patted her tenderly on the shoulder and then walked to the elevator with David.

As he reached for the elevator button, the doors suddenly opened. Standing inside was the Vice President, Calvin Jeffords. The man glared at the two of them and then scrunched his nose as if their stench was too much to take.

Without saying a word, Calvin pushed by the two men and headed straight for the first lady.

David sneered and jerked his thumb at him. "Our next President; God help us."

25

The vice president gave his obligatory sympathy to the first lady and then got out of the bunker as fast as he could. He returned to the west wing with a grave look.

He strode into his ceremonial office and barked, "Diane, I'm calling an emergency meeting. I want everyone in the Situation Room within the hour."

"Yes, sir."

Calvin proceeded to his private office and closed the door. The stern, overly concerned look he'd worn from the bunker swiftly softened into a joyous smile. He waved his arms in delight and began dancing across the room.

At his desk, he yanked open the bottom drawer and removed a half bottle of scotch and a glass. He laughed giddily as he poured the liquor into a glass. His lifelong dream of becoming President of the United States was coming true and--no one could stop him.

The vice president plopped into his high-back leather chair. He leaned back, threw his legs on top of his desk, and took a sip of the liquid.

Everything was falling into place, and the feeling of power was unparalleled by anything he had ever felt before, his wedding, the birth of his children—everything! In a short time, he would be the most powerful man in the free world.

He was confident the country was ready to be rid of that old geezer, Thomas Grant, and have the office filled with a much younger, much better man. And despite what his colleagues in Washington think of him, he knew the public loved him.

For years the public regarded he and his wife Heather as the golden couple, young, extremely rich, and gorgeous. In fact, the media often portrayed them as a young version of John and Jacqueline Kennedy, which was a perception that he and his wife always encouraged. His dutiful wife, while barely adequate in private, was a valuable political asset.

Sipping more of the scotch, he laid his head back and took a moment to reflect on his childhood dream. Everything he had ever done in his life had been geared toward achieving his goal of becoming the president of the United States.

His heart swelled knowing that his deceased father, the much beloved Senator Holton Jeffords, would be so proud of him. Calvin had grown up seeing firsthand how his father drew his friends in close and obliterated his enemies. This was how one seized power, and most importantly, held on to it.

Soon, it would be his chance to exact revenge on that blasted Chief of Staff David Lawson. The man clearly didn't know his place. He was an incessant irritant, with a know-it-all attitude, who constantly contradicted him in front of the president. The man was a bug begging to be squashed, and he was going to enjoy doing the squashing.

In a day or so, he would phone a reporter he used over the years to leak administration secrets and inform him of the president's severe illness, and most importantly his impending death.

After that bombshell hit the papers, he would swoop in to reassure a rattled nation that there was nothing to fear. He, Calvin Jeffords, was in charge and the country was safely in his hands.

A thought suddenly occurred to him. It would be important how he appeared on camera. Opening the top drawer of his desk, he removed a small handheld mirror. He gazed into it and practiced different looks and degrees of sadness.

It was important to look affected by the news, yet to appear confident and in control. He knew he could have been a great actor if he had wanted to be.

He practiced the look until he had it just right and then he slid the mirror back in the drawer.

Calvin looked at his watch. The emergency meeting he called, would convene within the hour. He rubbed his palms together with a measure of excitement. He couldn't wait to see the looks on their faces when he told them of his plan.

26

Alex stood outside on the deck of his houseboat. The Seattle sky had become overcast, and he welcomed it. He found the grayness had a calming effect on him, which is what he needed at the moment.

As he gazed across the water, he mulled over what he'd witnessed on TV. It was the dawn of a new era. An era of even more horrible ways to kill people. He wasn't surprised though; forms of chemical and biological warfare had been going on probably since time began.

Warriors throughout the ages rubbed arrows in dirt or manure in order to cause infections when their arrows hit their targets.

When castles in Europe were under siege, the enemy outside the walls would often fling diseased animal carcasses, or humans infected with the plague over the walls in hopes of infecting those inside. The only difference between now and then is, today it's gone high-tech.

He heard the door open behind him. Sophie walked across the deck and slid beside him. She seemed to sense his mood and did not speak.

Alex's cell phone rang, and he answered. "Hello?"

"Alex, this is Senator McDaniel."

"Any news?"

"You were right," the senator replied. "The president was shot with the laser."

Alex felt sick to his stomach. "Any idea what he's been infected with?"

"No, but he's doomed anyway. Every one of those chemical and biological agents, in that case, are 100% fatal."

"I see."

"I'll keep you updated on his condition."

"Thanks, Senator." Alex hung up the phone. He slipped the cell phone into his pocket and stared out at the water.

Sophie touched his arm. "Alex, talk to me. Please tell me what's going on."

While he had many secrets from his SEAL missions, ones he would rather die than divulge, this was different. Sophie was as much a part of this as he was. Most importantly though, he knew he could trust her. He turned and said, "This has to remain between us."

She used her index finger to cross her heart.

"At Fort Bliss, while you and Mike were making phone calls, I met Senator McDaniel outside. We took a walk, and he told me what was in Dr. Farah's case."

"He did? What did he say?"

"He said the case contained a highly classified secret project Dr. Farah and her late partner had created. The project went by the name, 'The Morpheus Project.' The project is a laser rifle capable of delivering an incapacitating agent through its light beam. And that dot of light you saw on the president's neck was from the laser."

"So the president was shot with sleeping gas?"

"Worse. While the project started out using an

incapacitating agent, it didn't stop there. It actually moved well beyond what Dr. Farah intended. Now that laser weapon is capable of delivering deadly chemical and biological agents."

"Oh, my god! Do they know what he was infected with?"

"Not yet, but whatever it is--he only has a few days to live."

"That's awful," she replied and then paused. "but why shoot the president?"

"Probably to test its effectiveness and make a statement. There's no man better protected than the president of the United States. If the president can be shot with the laser–anyone can."

"So, if the laser is out there, does that mean Sebastian and Veck are alive?"

It's possible, but I doubt it. It's more likely that another version of the weapon exists or that Sebastian passed off the weapon to someone before they were attacked. I prefer to think that Sebastian and Veck are being tortured by the natives at this very moment.

"I like that thought, too. But if they are alive, Dr. Farah might be, too."

Alex nodded, but he didn't hold out much hope.

27

After what happened to the president, Alex and Sophie's spirits were deflated and they decided to spend the day at home.

Sophie took the opportunity to go inside and work on the Mayan Codex, while Alex thought it was time to get that boat motor of his working properly.

He opened the motor housing. As he reached for a wrench, he noticed a large speedboat with twin motors coming across the lake. It was unusual to see such a large, powerful boat on such a small lake.

He continued to watch the vessel slow and then anchor fifty yards from his deck. It appeared to be an elderly couple out for a day of fishing.

Alex watched the man sweetly bait his wife's hook and then help her drop the line into the water. Without realizing it, he was beginning to envy them. They had one another and their lives appeared so serene, so simple, and so unaffected by what was going on in the world. It would be wonderful to have that kind of inner peace, he thought.

Alex got back to work.

Forty-five minutes later, the motor was fixed. Satisfied, he walked into the houseboat, rubbing his greasy hands on a rag. He went into the kitchen where

Sophie was sitting at the table with the open codex. She was busy, madly jotting down notes; words had been circled, others words crossed out. Arrows pointed to symbols. Mayan names underlined. He couldn't make any sense of it.

He went to the sink, washed his hands and dried them off with a hand towel. He took out his cell phone and took a photo of Sophie, but she was so absorbed in her work she didn't notice. He laughed. That woman had some serious concentration skills.

He walked behind her and asked, "How's it going?"

She thrust a finger in the air. When she finished writing her last thought, she set the pencil down and looked up. "Sorry, what was that?"

"How's it going?"

"I'm getting close," she said excitedly.

"What do you have so far?"

She pointed at a page in the ancient book. "These glyphs here, tell of the king's vast treasure hidden somewhere in the city, which means the rumors of the treasure are true.

"But it's these glyphs over here," she said pointing at the next page, "that speaks of one very special item the king valued far above all others."

"Any idea what it could be?"

"Not yet, but I'm getting very close to figuring it out."

"Well, how about I throw some steaks on the grill while you keep working?"

"Perfect, I'm starved."

Alex pulled two juicy steaks out of the refrigerator. He set them on a plate and added spices. He carried the plate outside and set them on the table.

After the grill was at the proper temperature, he laid the meat on the hot cooking grid and closed the lid. He glanced at the lake and was surprised to see the elderly couple still fishing. Must have found a good spot, he thought.

He called out, "How's the fishing?"

The old man waved, and then he reached down and lifted a stringer full of fish from the lake.

Inside the houseboat--Sophie screamed!

Alex raced for the door. But before he got there, the door burst open and Sophie ran out waving a piece of paper in her hand. "I did it! I did it!" she screamed.

She tried to slow herself down. "I deciphered the last glyphs. You won't believe..." she said gasping, "...what the king's most valuable possession is?" She put her hands on her knees and tried to catch her breath. The excitement was causing her to hyperventilate.

His cell phone rang. He could hear it ringing from inside the kitchen where he left it. She must have realized the phone call could be news about the president's condition, so she waved to take the call while she calmed down.

Alex hurried into the kitchen. He picked up his cell phone and answered. "Hello, Senator?"

"Senator? No, it's me. Why would the senator call?" Mike asked.

"Um, about the fishing," Alex answered quickly. "What's up?"

"How's our archeologist doing today? She was pretty tipsy by the time we left the restaurant last night." He laughed. "I could hear her singing all the way to my car."

"She woke up in rough shape, but she's doing much

better."

"So, what's going on over there?"

"I finally got around to fixing the boat motor of mine, and Sophie just finished deciphering the codex."

"She did? What does it say?"

"I don't know. She was about to tell me when someone with bad timing called."

Alex glanced outside and was surprised to see the elderly couple in the speedboat had pulled up to his deck. The old man unfolded a map and held it out for Sophie to look at. Something wasn't right. The lake wasn't big enough to require a map.

Sophie leaned over to look, and the old man suddenly grabbed her by the arms and yanked her into the boat. The elderly woman pressed a white rag over her mouth and Sophie went limp.

Alex dropped the phone.

He dashed out of the kitchen, shot across the living room and hurled himself through the screen door; nearly knocking it off its hinges.

The old man raised an automatic weapon and fired. Alex dove to his stomach and the glass windows of the house shattered behind him. The boat engine roared. Alex raised his head as the boat sped away.

Springing to his feet, he ran into the house.

He snatched the boat key and ran back outside. He jumped into his boat, tossed off the line, and started the engine. First try. He was thankful he fixed it.

He jammed the throttle, the engine roared, and the boat shot away from the deck. The two boats raced across the lake, their engines whining and white water splashing up the sides. The old man was increasing his lead.

The elderly couple was heading for Gas Works Park on the north end of the lake. The park was filled with people sitting on blankets, playing Frisbee, and flying kites.

The old man's boat looked like it wouldn't stop. As it neared, people pointed, screamed and began to scatter fearing the boat would crash into the three-foot-high concrete wall barrier separating the land from the water.

At the last second, the old man yanked hard left and reversed engines. A large wave splashed over the concrete wall, and the boat slid softly beside it.

Alex's mouth opened. He'd never seen anything like it, except maybe in some Hollywood movie.

The old man tossed Sophie's unconscious body over his shoulder and stepped out of the boat. The old lady got out too.

Alex swore to himself. He was still too far away. He had to make up the difference somehow. He grabbed two fishing poles and slid them through the steering wheel to keep it locked on course.

With the throttle at full speed, he stepped onto the seat, and then onto the bow of the boat. Perched on the end, he crouched and waited. His timing would have to be perfect.

People on shore, who had begun to recover from the shock of the first boat, stared in disbelief at the next one. Alex's boat was now closing in rapidly. With the engine noise blasting in his ears, he leaned forward on the balls of his feet. He was almost there.

Sixty feet.

Forty feet.

Twenty feet.

Ten feet.

A fraction of a second later, the boat slammed into the wall like a guided missile. There was a tremendous explosion and a giant fireball rose high in the sky.

Alex had launched off the boat just in time. As he flew through the air, he felt the intense heat from the explosion on his back. He landed on the grass and rolled. Uninjured, he got to his feet and continued the pursuit.

The kidnappers crested a small, grassy hill ahead. Most likely they had a car waiting in the parking lot on the other side.

Alex sprinted at full speed. When he reached the top of the hill, he looked down and saw a white cargo van parked below. The van's engine was running and its rear doors were wide open.

The old couple climbed into the back of the van with Sophie. The rear doors shut from the outside. Holding onto the door handle was an enormous bald man. The big man eyed Alex and smiled.

It was Veck.

The monster ran around to the driver's side. He got in and threw the van in gear. The wheels squealed, and the rubber tires smoked.

Alex angled right and used a concrete trash container as a springboard. He jumped onto the top of the moving van as it sped toward the exit. His body splayed across the top and his fingers curled around the edges of van's metal roof.

The van shot out of the exit and took a sharp left turn at full speed. The wheels screeched, and the backend fishtailed.

Alex desperately tried to hold on, but he was thrown off and landed hard into bushes alongside the road. By the time he crawled out, the van was gone.

Slightly injured and mad as hell, he stumbled back

across the street. He swore at himself for being so stupid. He should have listened to his instincts. Last night, he felt someone watching outside the restaurant. Then, he heard a creaking on his deck. Why didn't he go with his gut and take precautions?

He reached to his pocket for his cell phone but remembered he left it in the houseboat with Mike still on the line. He needed to make a call, but not to the police. By the time they responded, Veck would have already changed vehicles twice. There was no way the police could catch a criminal like Veck on such short notice.

No, he was going to handle this his own way; where no rules or laws could get in his way. He clenched both fists until his knuckles cracked. He would get Sophie back, and in the process, he was going to make Veck pay for what he had done.

Alex hobbled back to the parking lot where the van had been parked. He noticed a gray wig lying on the ground; dropped by one of the kidnappers. A part of a disguise, obviously.

He walked onto the grassy area of the park, and, in a non-threatening way, approached a lady with a baby. He asked to use her cellphone. She handed it to him, and he dialed a number he knew by heart.

Mike answered. "Alex, what the hell happened? Was that gunfire I heard?"

"It was, and Sophie was kidnapped right off my deck."

"Who would want to kidnap her?"

"Veck."

"He's alive?"

"I saw him with my own eyes. Pick me up at Gas Works Park, and I'll explain everything."

"Gas Works Park? What are you doing there?"

"Just come."

"Alright, sit tight. I'll be there in a few minutes."

As he waited for his friend to show, Alex kicked at the ground and swore at himself. He promised Sophie nothing but rest and relaxation…and he failed. He failed Dr. Farah, too. He seemed to be doing that a lot lately.

Ten minutes later, under the wailing of police sirens, Mike pulled into the parking lot with his new fiery red convertible. Alex opened the passenger door and got in. "Let's go. I don't want to stick around and answer questions from the police."

Mike nodded and sped out of the parking lot. He headed down the street and said, "So, how did you get to the park anyway?"

"Did you see smoke down by the lake when you drove up?"

"Yeah."

"That's what's left of my boat."

By the time they arrived in front of Alex's houseboat, Mike knew everything. He parked the car and said, "So, we're going after her, right?"

Alex nodded. "Any objections?"

"None. Any idea where he's taking her?"

Alex reached for the door handle. "Not yet, but when I do, I'll call you."

Mike turned off the engine. "Nothing doing, I'm staying. We're doing this together."

Alex expected nothing less from his friend. He and Mike got out of the car and walked down the wooden dock. They continued around the left side of the houseboat to the deck facing the lake.

Mike looked at the shattered windows in their

frames and broken glass scattered on the deck. "Man, how in the world did he miss you?"

"Just lucky I guess."

Thick, black smoke billowed from the grill. Mike opened the lid and stared down at the charred, shriveled meat. "I see you haven't improved your cooking skills any."

The two men went into the houseboat. Mike went straight into the kitchen and helped himself to a cold beer from the fridge.

Alex retrieved his laptop computer from the bedroom and cleared the kitchen table. He set the laptop down and fired it up.

Alex's fingers hovered over the keyboard. "We need to find out the identity of Sebastian, which should lead us to Veck and Sophie.

"What do we know about Sebastian?" Mike asked.

"Not much; he's rich and he's French."

"He also likes fine art and antiquities."

That was a start. Alex hunched over the laptop to begin his search when he was disturbed by a knock on the door. "Who the hell could that be?"

Mike went to the kitchen window and peeked out. "It's the police. Some neighbor probably phoned in about the gunshots.

Alex sighed. "No getting around it. Let them in."

Alex spent the next half hour going over the scene with the police, answering questions, and filling out a report. He tried to hurry them out the door by claiming he didn't know who shot up his windows or why. He didn't want to get the police involved. He only wanted to get back to his laptop and find out the identity of Sebastian.

Finally, with no more information to give, the police took photos and left. Alex got back on the computer. After spending nearly two hours searching for Sebastian, he found absolutely nothing.

Mike went to the refrigerator to get another beer. He came back, twisted the cap off, and said, "I don't get it. Sebastian is supposed to be mega rich. Why can't we find anything on him?"

"It doesn't make sense, does it?"

Alex got back on the laptop. This time he tried to find anything he could about Veck. Thirty minutes later, he threw up his hands. "Nothing."

"These guys know how to cover their tracks," Mike said.

Alex got up from the table. He paced the living room, twisting his wedding ring as he walked. There's got to be a way to find these guys, he thought. It was crucial to learn their identities. It was the only way to save Sophie. How in the world was he going to find them?

Then it hit him. It's possible that the forensics team at the Mayan city had come up with something, fingerprints, scraps of paper, maybe even an address? He had to call Senator McDaniel. As he reached for his cell phone—it rang. Surprised, Alex answered. "Hello?"

"Alex, this is Senator McDaniel."

"I was just about to call you. Veck kidnapped Sophie."

The senator's voice turned serious. "He's alive?

"Yes."

"When?"

"About 3 hours ago."

"Did you contact the police?"

"No, they contacted me," Alex replied. "A neighbor

heard gunshots and reported it. I told the police I knew nothing because I plan on handling this on my own."

"Really?" the senator replied and then paused. "How would you feel about working together on this?"

"How so?"

"Are you available to talk tomorrow?

"I'm available."

"I'll fly in early tomorrow morning. Let's meet somewhere near the airport, somewhere we won't be seen."

"Redondo Beach. It's about ten miles south of the airport," Alex said. "There's a parking lot across the street from the fishing pier. I'll meet you there."

"9 a.m. alright with you?"

"I'll be there."

179

28

Thousands of miles away in the small principality of Monaco, a black Mercedes-Benz EC145 Eurocopter, one of the most expensive civilian helicopters in the world, lifted off the ground and headed out to sea.

Sebastian relaxed in his seat, pleased to be making the final leg of his journey home. He studied his manicured fingernails and then glanced at Doctor Farah sitting across from him.

She snapped her head around to avert his gaze. She hadn't spoken a word since leaving the jungle, but that was alright. Small talk tended to be a colossal waste of time and energy anyway.

All in all, he was pleased with himself. The mission had been a complete success. Admittedly, he hit a few bumps, but in the end, it was nothing he couldn't handle. He had backup plans to his backup plans. For instance, when his helicopter in the jungle had been destroyed, he simply called another one to pick him up.

The only current concern he had was that he hadn't heard from his men since leaving the Mayan city. Not to worry, he thought. The lack of communication was probably due to some radio malfunction. He knew full well how jungle humidity played havoc on machinery.

When Veck returned, he'd send him back to the jungle to get things straightened out. Maybe by then, he'd hear the good news that his men had found the king's treasure.

He glanced at the text message on his cell phone; the one-word text from Veck--'Success,' meaning mission accomplished. He was pleased. Veck shot the president precisely as instructed.

The big man rented a helicopter. He flew up and stayed far behind the 16-mile no-fly zone and the military's fighter jets. The laser was capable of shooting accurately far beyond that, so it was no problem. The only real challenge was to calculate the correct altitude and angle in order to get a clear shot.

Sebastian lifted his eyes. In the distance, he saw his island home.

As the chopper neared, he could see his armed guards with attack dogs patrolling the waterfront, and his luxurious white yacht anchored along the wooden pier.

Inland, standing upon a large manicured lawn was his ancestral home. A beautiful, old French style château with ivy-covered stone walls, pointed turrets, and a steeply sloped, slate roof.

The helicopter reached the island. It soared over the château, flew past the formal garden, and landed on the hill next to the stone block aircraft hangar.

Originally, the stone hangar had been used to stable horses. It was adorned with a slate roof and a tall, pointed, iron weather vane that looked like a six-foot spear. Beside the hanger lay two concrete helicopter pads. An identical helicopter was parked on the pad next to his.

After the chopper landed, the pilot cut the engine. A servant opened the side door.

Sebastian stepped out holding a white cane in one hand and a white fedora hat in the other. Dr. Farah had no choice but to follow.

The two got into the back seat of a white golf cart. The servant drove them down a gravel path to the front entrance of the château. It stopped, and Sebastian and Dr. Farah got out.

As they approached a pair of large, heavy oak doors, they were opened by a woman dressed in a French maid's outfit. She gave a deep curtsy and said, "Welcome back, *Monsieur*."

Sebastian gave a slight nod.

He handed her his hat and cane and stepped inside. Dr. Farah followed into an opulent reception hall. Light from hanging crystal chandeliers reflected off shiny marble floors and artwork from the world's greatest masters hung on the walls.

Next to the grand staircase was a large, ancient statue of a nude male soldier holding a helmet in one hand and a sword in the other.

The maid closed the door. "Pardon Monsieur, but a gentleman visitor is waiting for you in the billiard's room."

"*Merci*," Sebastian replied.

Sebastian led Dr. Farah down a hallway lined with large tapestries and more priceless paintings. He turned into the billiard's room. The room was a paneled in warm oak with stuffed pheasants perched on shelves. In the center sat two large billiard's tables.

Leaning over one of the tables was a thin, balding man with a bad comb-over. The man, approximately sixty-four years of age, was covered in painful looking scratches on his arms, hands, and face. He was just lining up a shot when he heard them enter.

When he looked up the cue stick dropped from his hands. "Oh my god--she's alive?"

Dr. Farah froze. "Dr. Valerius--what are you doing here?"

The special projects director angrily eyed Sebastian. "Why didn't you tell me she survived the crash?"

"It must have slipped my mind," he replied jovially. "Did you bring the files?"

"I brought them," he answered curtly.

"What files?" she asked.

Sebastian smiled. "Copies of your research, of course."

"What? You traitor!" she screamed and ran at the special projects director. "Don't run from me, you weasel," she yelled as he hurried to the opposite side of the pool table.

After two complete circles around the table, the two came to a standoff, Dr. Farah on one side, Dr. Valerius on the other. "Why did you do it?" she demanded.

Breathing hard, he patted the single strands of hair of his comb-over and said, "Come now Isra; don't be so naïve. I did it for the money of course. Sebastian and I are going to sell it for five billion dollars. Can you imagine that type of money? I'll be set for life."

"And copies of my research? Do you plan on selling those too?"

Sebastian interrupted. "No, that information will remain with me."

She stared him down. "So you're planning to sell the weapon outright and then charge your buyer each time he wants additional agents. Is that it?"

"*Oui*, and they will pay me a considerable amount since the laser is worthless without it."

"You mean 'pay us,'" Dr. Valerius corrected.

"*Oui*, I do mean us," Sebastian replied and nodded

genially to Dr. Valerius.

"You won't be able to duplicate the agents on your own," she hissed. "There are key items I never recorded."

"I admit it would have been difficult using my own scientists, but now I have you."

"I'll never help you!"

"We'll see about that."

Sebastian turned to the guard. "Please see Dr. Farah to her room. Dr. Valerius and I have business to discuss."

The guard nodded and removed a struggling Dr. Farah from the room. "We're not finished with this!" she yelled from the hallway.

With the strident screaming fading, Sebastian strolled casually to the bar. "Care for a brandy?"

Dr. Valerius sighed. "I can use one after that little stunt you pulled."

"I thought you'd like that," Sebastian replied. With a smirk, he added, "You know, she almost caught you."

Dr. Valerius stepped out from behind the billiard table and joined Sebastian at the bar. Sebastian poured brandy into two glasses and handed one to his guest. Then he motioned to two chairs in front of a crackling fire. The men sat.

Dr. Valerius eyed Sebastian. "So, why did you want me to meet you here, instead of the jungle city?"

"Because an unexpected visitor showed up and he proved quite troublesome. He tried to rescue Dr. Farah. I presume he would have also taken the laser if given the chance."

"A visitor? In the jungle? How did he find you?"

"You tell me."

184

"Me?" replied Dr. Valerius, "How would I know?"

"You never told anyone our plans? Perhaps, you made a side deal to take the laser for yourself?"

"Sebastian, I swear I would never do that."

"Then, the only logical explanation is that this man arrived at the crash site, and followed Veck and his men to the city."

"That would take some doing, wouldn't it?"

"Quite right. It was clear to me from the beginning that he was no ordinary man. At the time he refused to tell me his name, but after he escaped, Veck persuaded Dr. Farah to give it to us. She told us his name is Alex McCade."

"Never heard of him."

"No reason why you should. After a little digging, I found that *Monsieur* McCade is a former Navy SEAL Commander, and a highly decorated one."

"Was anyone with him?"

"Not that we know of."

Sebastian took a slow sip of his brandy and let it soak into his soft pallet before swallowing. He lowered his glass. "I would like to see the files now."

Dr. Valerius, with the aid of his armrests, rose from his chair. He dug in his pants pocket and withdrew two computer flash drives. He handed them to Sebastian.

The billionaire took the flash drives and walked to the intercom mounted on the wall. He pressed the button. "Send Dr. Gunnerson to me."

Shortly thereafter, a man with stark white hair came into the room carrying a laptop computer. Sebastian introduced the two men, and he handed Dr. Gunnerson the flash drives. "Set up over there."

Dr. Gunnerson went to the bar and opened the

laptop computer on the counter. For the next ten minutes the man examined the contents of the flash drives, and then without saying a word he closed the computer, nodded to Sebastian, and left the room.

Sebastian held up his glass. "To a job well done, *mon ami.*"

Dr. Valerius raised his glass and took a sip. Lowering his glass, he found Sebastian staring at him. "What?" he asked nervously.

"Did you have any trouble getting the files?"

"Not at all; no one ever suspected me. How about you? Did you have any trouble crashing Dr. Farah's plane?"

"None whatsoever; the equipment worked perfectly." He paused. "Tell me...what did you do about the man after he installed the guidance chip on Dr. Farah's plane?"

Dr. Valerius puffed out his chest and smiled proudly. "He was no longer of value to me--so I killed him."

"Ah, very good. I see we think along the same lines."

"We do?"

"*Oui,* getting rid of people who are no longer of value to us."

Dr. Valerius nodded enthusiastically. "And since you don't need Dr. Farah you're going to kill her, right?"

"Oh, no, no, *mon ami.* The laser is a very complicated piece of technology and should it break down...?"

Dr. Valerius grinned. "Right, that's what I'm for."

"No, that's what you *were* for."

The blood suddenly drained from his face. "What

do you mean?"

"It's a pity, but since she survived the crash--you are no longer of value to me."

"But I did everything you asked! You wouldn't have the laser or the files if it wasn't for me."

"That's true, and I do thank you for your contribution."

"You can't--" Dr. Valerius's words stuck in his throat upon seeing two of Sebastian's muscular goons step into the room.

"Please take Dr. Valerius away and dispose of him."

"It'll be a pleasure," grunted a guard.

The two burly guards strode across the room. The special projects director shook uncontrollably as they lifted him from his seat. The glass of brandy slipped from his grip and spilled on the chair.

Sebastian merely gazed at the wet stain. "Don't worry; I'll have one of the maids clean it up."

As the guards dragged him from the room he wailed, "You can't do this to me!"

Sebastian slowly sipped his brandy and smiled. "Oh yes--I can."

29

After a restless night, Alex and Mike woke early. With time to kill before their meeting with the senator, they swept up the broken glass from the shattered windows.

Then Alex made a phone call and arranged to have someone replace them. They drank coffee until eight-fifteen and then left in Alex's truck.

Forty minutes later, they arrived at the waterfront in Redondo. They pulled into the empty parking lot across the street from the fishing pier. Alex parked the truck near a complex of condominiums, and they waited.

A short time later, a black stretch limousine pulled into the lot.

"There he is," Mike said.

Alex opened the truck door. "Stay here."

As Alex approached the vehicle, the limousine driver stepped out of the vehicle and opened the rear door. Sitting in the backseat was Senator McDaniel. Alex still found it difficult getting used to him with a beard.

"Good morning Alex, have a seat."

Alex slipped into the limousine and took a seat across from the senator. The door closed.

The senator held up a thermos. "Coffee?"

"No thanks, I've already had plenty."

The senator set down the thermos. "Sorry to hear about Sophie."

Alex nodded. "How's the president?"

"Not good. The doctors say he's been infected with Ricin."

Alex knew about Ricin, a deadly toxin made from the byproduct of castor beans.

"The doctors say he will live another three to five days at the most."

"I'm sorry to hear that. He's a good man."

The senator nodded sadly. "I've known him practically all my life."

Alex needed to get back on track. He leaned forward. "You said the FBI knows the identities of Veck and Sebastian."

"Yes, the techs were able to lift clean fingerprints from the Mayan city. The FBI ran the prints through Interpol and they came up with matches. They also compared the photo's in the database to the facial composites you and your friends came up with. They were an exact match."

"Who are they? I couldn't find anything about them on the internet."

"I'd be surprised if you did. Sebastian is a man who likes to play in the shadows. He uses different aliases and buys companies using shell corporations He also employs a small team of computer experts to keep him off the radar, to wipe away any mention of him.

"The less people know about him, the more secure he feels. Everything is done on the sly. That's why I'm surprised he used his real name in the jungle."

"He never expected me to escape, that's why. So who is he?"

The senator reached into his suit pocket and removed a piece of paper. He slipped on a pair of half-moon reading glasses.

He read from the paper. "Sebastian is none other than Sebastian Theriault, a billionaire and French citizen by birth. He has worldwide business interests including, oil wells off the coast of Mexico; a fifty percent stake in a diamond mine in Africa, and a very profitable ship building company in Norway. The list goes on.

"He's known to be a man with an insatiable passion for making money. By all accounts, he is a cruel and ruthless employer. He is highly intelligent. He speaks six languages fluently and lives on his own private island off the coast of Monaco."

"Illegal activity?"

"None that we can prove. All businesses seem legitimate as far as we can tell; however, there are some recent rumors of him dealing in illegal arms sales, but again it can't be proven."

"Arms dealer. You think he plans to sell the laser weapon?"

"I do, and can you imagine the kind of price that laser will go for on the open market?"

"Billions, at least."

The senator nodded.

"What do you have on Veck?" Alex asked.

"Veck? Well, he's a different animal altogether." The senator lowered his eyes to the paper. "Thomas Veck, a British citizen and career criminal. In his youth, he was the leader of a notorious street gang in Liverpool.

"After years of being in and out of prison he went to work for Sebastian, though no one knows how they met. Mr. Veck has been suspected of numerous crimes and murders around the world but...he has never been convicted."

"Let me guess; no one's around to testify when it comes to court."

The senator looked up. "Yes, that seems to be the case."

"Does the FBI know if Sebastian is currently on that island of his?"

"He was spotted there yesterday by satellite, and I suspect Veck will be joining him shortly; from all reports, they are never apart for very long."

"Veck will have Sophie with him," Alex said. "I assume there is no official plan to go after them."

"You are correct. When the president was shot, the vice president took over his duties. His first order of business was to call an emergency meeting. During that meeting, he made it clear that no action will be taken against Sebastian. Suffice it to say, the vice president is the ultimate coward who only thinks of himself and his own political future."

"That explains most politicians in Washington, doesn't it?"

The senator laughed. "Yes it does, but this man takes it to a whole new and disturbing level. We believe the vice president is afraid that if he goes after Sebastian, he'll be next on his hit list.

"It's no secret that Calvin Jeffords has spent his entire waking life with the goal of becoming President of the United States, and he will do nothing to jeopardize that."

"So, he would put his own safety ahead of his country and the safety of the world?"

"In a word--yes."

The senator took a sip of coffee. "Once the vice

president announced his decision the room erupted. Arguments ensued, but the vice president wouldn't be swayed. He remained firm, which is something I've rarely seen him do. Fear will do that to a coward."

Alex despised self-centered people; people who would gladly sacrifice everyone else in order to save themselves. People who could talk a good game, but when it came down to actually showing the guts to make a difficult decision or to put themselves in harm's way, they ducked their heads and ran for cover. Alex would just as soon put bullets in their heads rather than talking to them.

The senator continued. "After the meeting, I was pulled aside by certain high-ranking members, members who wish to remain anonymous. They asked me to secretly find a way to go after Sebastian, secure the laser, and rescue Dr. Farah."

"Why you?"

"I'm no longer an official part of the government, so I have deniability. Also, I maintained many contacts I cultivated during my years in the Senate, and I can still put those contacts to use.

"You may not know this, but during my career, I was known as the man who got things done; apparently, certain people have not forgotten that."

"But going against the Vice President's wishes; some might consider that treasonous."

The senator's brows furrowed. "Yes, but I'll be damned if I'm going to let that sniveling-ass coward destroy this country. Can you imagine if that weapon is used against the United States? Alex, action must be taken now, and we don't have much time. Yesterday, the NSA intercepted a phone call from Sebastian's island.

"We learned he already has a buyer for the laser. We

don't know who it is, but a meeting is scheduled on the island two days from now. You must move quickly, before the laser is removed from the island, or we may lose it forever."

"Two days doesn't give me much time."

"I know, but if anyone can pull this off--you can. I should also mention that Sebastian will assume you acted on your own to save Sophie, and not on behalf of the U.S. government. And should you be caught, we will have no choice but to deny we knew anything about you or of your actions."

"Understood."

"I want you to plan and execute it. We'll provide everything you need to get the job done. I want you to bring the laser weapon, Dr. Farah and Sophie back to us." The senator smiled. "And as an added incentive, feel free to dispose of Sebastian and Veck any way you like."

Alex returned the smile. "That'll be a pleasure."

The senator slapped Alex's knee. "Good boy, I knew I could count on you. You should also know, the president's chief of staff, David Lawson will be assisting me. Any questions?"

"No, but I'm going to need all the intel you've got."

"I'll have someone stop by your home this afternoon with all the intelligence data we've gathered. Once you've developed a plan, let us know what you'll need, and we'll make sure you get it."

Alex opened the car door and got out.

The senator leaned over. "You may be interested to learn that the FBI has located Dr. Valerius."

"Dr. Valerius? I heard that name before. Who is he?"

"He was the special projects director at Dr. Farah's

lab. He was also working with Sebastian."

Alex snapped his fingers. "That's where I heard it. In the jungle, I overheard Sebastian say he was waiting for a Dr. Valerius to bring him the flash drives."

"A fisherman found him face down in the Mediterranean with his arms and legs tied."

"It doesn't pay to work with Sebastian, does it?"

"No, it doesn't."

"Goodbye, Senator."

Alex returned to his truck. He opened the door and slid in behind the wheel. Mike was sleeping, and he gave him a shove. "Wake up."

"W-what?" Mike muttered and rubbed his tired eyes. Sitting up in his seat, he asked, "Um...so how'd it go?"

Alex started the engine. "I'll tell you everything on the way home, and I'll start with Dr. Farah's laser."

Mike's eyes widened. "Laser? What laser?"

30

Later in the day, Alex and Mike sat in the kitchen of the houseboat drinking coffee and listening to the radio when the host abruptly stopped mid-sentence. "I'm sorry ladies and gentlemen, but I've just been handed a news bulletin."

"Turn it up," Mike said.

Alex turned up the volume.

"An anonymous source inside the White House has just reported that President Grant is dying from Ricin poisoning. How did it happen? No one is certain, but our own Carol Montgomery is now live at the White House with the vice president."

"This is Carol Montgomery at the White House. I am with Vice President, Calvin Jeffords, who has agreed to speak with me about the president's condition. Mr. Vice President, straight to the point. Has the president been infected with Ricin poisoning?"

"Carol, I am sorry to say that the president has indeed been stricken with Ricin poisoning. We're not sure how it happened, but everything is being done to help him and capture those responsible."

"I understand the president is in isolation."

"Yes, for his benefit as well as those around him. Let me assure you that his doctors are doing everything possible to save the president's life. I also want to assure the American public that during this time of crisis the government is operating smoothly under my watch. I would also like to say... Blah, blah, blah."

Alex turned off the radio.

"I wonder how that bit of news got out," Mike muttered.

"From what the senator told me about the vice president, it wouldn't surprise me if he leaked the story himself."

There was a light knock at the door. Alex pulled the .45 caliber Colt semi-automatic pistol from his waistband. Since the kidnapping the day before; he wasn't going anywhere unarmed.

He strode to the kitchen window and peered out the blinds. Standing at his back door was a neatly groomed man, with sandy brown hair, dark sunglasses, and a dark blue windbreaker.

"Who is it?" Alex shouted through the door.

"The senator sent me."

Alex hid the pistol behind his back and opened the door.

"Alex McCade?"

Alex nodded and motioned for the man to come inside.

The man in the dark sunglasses walked into the kitchen and set his briefcase on the dining table. While leaning a long tube against it he faced Mike. "Who is he?"

"It's alright," Alex replied, "he's with me."

He opened the briefcase, pulled out a stack of 8 X 10 black and white photos and spun them to face Alex and Mike.

"This is a frontal view of Sebastian's island," he said. The man hardly allowed them time to look at the photo, when he replaced it with another. "And this is an aerial view of the island."

He pointed out a large yacht tied to a wooden pier. "This is Sebastian's yacht, 'The Charlemagne.'"

He moved his finger inland, up the gravel drive to an ancient French château with turrets and a steeply pitched roof. "The château was built in 1243 by King Louis IX of France. After the king's death, the château fell into the hands of Sebastian's ancestors and has remained there ever since."

"Nice place," Mike said.

"Directly behind the château are the formal gardens. To the left of the gardens, is an Olympic size swimming pool and cabana area. To the right of the gardens are the tennis courts. Behind the formal gardens is a tree-covered hill. At the top of the hill is a hangar and two concrete helicopter pads."

"Looks like a vineyard behind the hangar," Alex said.

"It is. Sebastian grows his own grapes and makes his own wine. You can't see it, but back in the trees, there is a stone building the king used for storing grain. Twenty years ago Sebastian converted the building into a winery. The rest of the island is nothing but trees and rocks."

"What about the inside layout of the château?" Alex asked.

From his briefcase, the man removed interior plans of the building. "The château consists of three floors with a total of thirty-five rooms. This includes eleven guest rooms, fourteen bathrooms, and twenty-two fireplaces.

"On the main floor, you'll find the reception hall, the music room, a billiards room, a study, an art gallery, a library, and a medieval banquet hall. His security operations center is at the end of this hall.

"On the second floor are the guest rooms, and the third floor is where Sebastian's private quarters are located. He has a full-time staff of twenty-five that live on the premises. This number includes gardeners, maintenance workers, chefs, maids and more. They reside in the basement, along with the kitchen, laundry facilities, a workshop, and a small recreation center for the employees."

The man reached for the long tube he brought with him. He popped the lid off one end, tilted it, and shook out a large roll of paper. He unrolled the paper on top of the table. Alex and Mike used their coffee mugs to hold down the curling edges.

"This is a satellite photo taken of the island yesterday." He pointed to the roof. "Right here, along the center ridgeline is a recessed walkway. The walkway was originally built for the King's lookouts and Sebastian uses it for the same purpose. He keeps two men up there at all times. The walkway itself is five feet deep, by twenty feet wide, and runs the entire length of the building."

The man shifted his gaze to Alex and then to Mike. "As far as security is concerned, he has armed guards with dogs patrolling the island, and according to purchasing records, he has the best electronic security devices money can buy.

"This includes mounted cameras, infrared trip wires, thermal sensors, and underwater sonar that can spot anything larger than a lobster coming near the island."

Mike shot a look at Alex. "It's not going to be easy."

The man pulled a pen and a small piece of paper out of his windbreaker. He scribbled a number on it and handed it to Alex. "Call me at this number when you know what you need."

"Fine, what about travel documents?" Alex asked.

"You will be provided all the documents you need at the time of departure."

Without another word, the man spun on his heels, opened the back door and left.

Mike smirked. "Well, there goes a little ball of sunshine."

Alex locked the door and looked out the window. He watched the man walk briskly to the end of the dock. A car with tinted windows pulled up. The man got in and the car drove off.

Alex walked across the kitchen and poured himself a cup of hot coffee. He cradled the cup in his hands and mulled over the information the man in the sunglasses provided.

After a few minutes, he looked up and found Mike staring at him. "What?"

"I know that look," Mike said.

"What look?"

"You have a plan in mind, don't you?"

"It's risky..."

"That's never stopped us before."

31

The following day Alex and Mike boarded an early commercial flight to London. After landing at London's Heathrow airport, they transferred to a flight bound for the southeast coast of France.

At 8:05 a.m. local time they arrived at the Nice-Cote d'Azur International Airport

After claiming their luggage and making their way through customs and immigration, they proceeded outside the terminal to wait for their contact.

Minutes later, an old, black sedan pulled up to the curb. The window lowered, and a man with a scruffy beard and a lit cigarette hanging out the corner of his mouth, said, "Starsky and Hutch?"

Mike snickered. He had chosen the code names from two characters of a 1970's TV series. He alone thought it was funny.

The driver got out and opened the trunk. Alex and Mike set their luggage inside and closed it. The two men got into the back seat. The interior reeked of smoke and Alex quickly lowered the window to let in the fresh air. The driver got behind the wheel, put the car in drive and pulled away from the curb.

Once on the main road, the driver glanced into the rearview mirror. "My name is Marcel," he said with a French accent. "If there is anything you need during your stay let me know."

"Is everything set for tonight?" Alex asked.

"It is."

"Where are we going now?"

"I'm taking you to a hotel. You look tired."

Alex couldn't argue with that. He barely slept since leaving Seattle. He had always prided himself on being able to sleep anywhere: the jungle, a rice paddy, in a tree, but he had never been seated next to a screaming baby in a plane before. It was excruciating. A little sleep would definitely do him some good.

Twenty-five minutes later, the small principality of Monaco appeared in the distance. The city was built on rugged and hilly terrain overlooking the beautiful Mediterranean Sea. What had once been a Greek colony, and later a Roman colony was now a land dotted with modern villas, tall apartment buildings and luxury hotels.

The city, renowned for its famous casinos and exciting night life was, per capita, the wealthiest nation on earth, and a tax haven for the mega rich.

Marcel drove into the heart of Monaco passing Mercedes, Bentley's and other high-priced cars along the way. He went to a section of town called La Condamine. He turned onto a quiet street and stopped in front of a pink building. The sign read, Hotel de France.

He faced Alex and handed him a large manila envelope. "Inside are false ID's and matching credit cards." He glanced at his watch. "I'll pick you up this evening at five o'clock. There's something I want you to see."

The two men got out of the vehicle. They removed their luggage from the trunk, closed the lid and Marcel drove off. The two men walked into the hotel and checked into their rooms.

At 5 p.m. sharp, a rejuvenated Alex and Mike walked out of the hotel. They found Marcel's beat up black sedan parked at the curb. Both men got into the back seat and Marcel drove off without saying a word.

They had been on the road for less than five minutes when Marcel pulled off to the side of the road. He shut off the engine. He slung the strap of a camera with a telephoto lens around his neck and then he opened the door and got out.

Alex and Mike looked at each other. They shrugged and got out, too.

Marcel walked to the back of the vehicle. He opened the trunk and took out two metal cases. He handed one case to Alex and the other to Mike. "Follow me," he said and crossed the busy street. The two men followed.

On the other side of the street, Marcel continued around a building and stopped on the edge of a hill overlooking the Port of Monaco where expensive white yachts moored. Marcel nodded to Alex's case. "Open it."

Alex set the case on the ground and opened the latches. He lifted the lid and found two pairs of binoculars inside. He handed one pair to Mike and took the other for himself.

Alex faced the harbor and scanned the rows of luxurious white yachts below. "What are we looking for?" he asked.

Marcel pointed. "Right there."

Alex could see a large yacht with the name 'The Charlemagne' written in gilded gold lettering. "That's Sebastian's yacht," he said. "What's it doing here?"

"Waiting for our mystery buyer," Marcel replied. He glanced at his watch. "He should be here any minute."

"Any idea who he is?"

"Not yet, but we'll know soon enough."

The three men waited.

Ten minutes passed.

Then twenty.

Alex was beginning to doubt the buyer was ever going to show. He watched the Frenchman drop another cigarette butt onto the growing pile at his feet. Marcel was reaching for a fresh cigarette when he stopped and pointed below. "This could be him now."

Alex raised the binoculars again. A black limousine was coming their way. The limousine stopped in front of 'The Charlemagne.' The limousine driver, a big, burly Asian man wearing dark sun glasses got out. Presumably a bodyguard.

He nodded to someone in the backseat. A much smaller man exited the limousine. The man appeared to be in his mid-fifties and was immaculately dressed in a black suit with a red silk tie.

"I know him," whispered Marcel, "that's Cheng Wei."

"Who's Cheng Wei?"

Marcel began snapping photos of the man with his telephoto lens. "He's a high-ranking Chinese government official; bad news. The horror he has inflicted upon his own people is reprehensible."

"He looks like the respectable banker type to me," Mike said.

"Hardly; the man is a ruthless barbarian. He once headed the famed Chinese gang, The Black Dragons, but now he holds a high position in the Chinese government. The man is a heartless thug and wouldn't hesitate gouging your eyes out with his bare hands if given the chance."

The Chinese man reached inside the limousine and extracted a briefcase. The large driver/bodyguard, with one suitcase in his hand, escorted Cheng Wei to the ship. The Major of the vessel, a tall man dressed in a starched white uniform and cap, greeted him as he approached.

An even larger man appeared on the deck of the ship. He was Caucasian and leaned heavily against the ship's railing to observe the visitors.

"Guess who I see?" Mike said.

Alex saw him, too. It was Veck. Intense anger raged inside him, and he squeezed the binoculars. He wanted somehow to magically reach through the lens and strangle the bastard with his bare hands.

"Think Sophie is with him?" Mike asked.

Alex scanned the ship. "I don't see her. She might be on the ship, or she may already be on the island."

The Asian limousine driver/bodyguard handed the luggage to Veck. After Cheng Wei boarded the yacht, the driver/bodyguard returned to the limousine and drove away.

The men on the hill watched the crew of 'The Charlemagne' prepare to leave. The Major went to the wheelhouse, and the crew pulled up the boarding ramp and untied the ropes. Cheng Wei stood on deck as the yacht pulled out of the harbor.

"Marcel, got anything more powerful?" Alex asked.

Marcel opened the second case. He removed a powerful telescope and set it on a tripod. Alex moved in behind it.

Looking through the lens, Alex followed the yacht across the open water. The Chinese official, with a drink in hand, strolled to the front of the ship, apparently to get a better view of Sebastian's island in the distance.

Alex swung the telescope to the island. He turned

the knob and adjusted the focus. Now he could see armed guards patrolling the waterfront. He could also see the 13th-century château behind it.

It didn't take long for the yacht to cover the fifteen miles. Alex watched the Major ease the large vessel along the dock. When it stopped, men on the dock tied it off, and the gangplank lowered into place.

Veck carried a suitcase and escorted Cheng Wei off the ship to a white golf cart. When the men had taken their seats, the driver pulled away from the dock and headed up the gravel drive toward the château.

Alex zoomed in on the château. He refocused in time to see Sebastian open the large double oak entry doors of the château.

When the golf cart arrived, Sebastian stepped out. He strode forward and greeted the Chinese official like an old friend.

Alex grit his teeth. Enjoy yourself now, fella's, because tonight it's all coming to an end.

32

At the château, Cheng Wei followed Sebastian through the mighty oak doors. Stepping inside, he marveled at the grandeur of the reception hall; the high ceilings, the gleaming marble floors, and the exceptional artwork.

"I am impressed," Wei said in perfect English. "I have heard many wonderful things about your home and it is nothing less than magnificent."

"*Merci*," replied Sebastian with pride.

The Chinese official was drawn to the life-size statue of a nude male warrior beside the grand marble staircase. Wei stepped closer and inspected the perfectly carved male figure wearing only a helmet and holding a sword. "This is extraordinary."

"Fifth-century; found near the ruins of Ephesus Turkey."

"Superb."

"I see you appreciate the arts," Sebastian replied. "Allow me to give you a tour of my home. I believe you will find many items to your liking."

Sebastian spent the next forty-five minutes guiding Cheng Wei room by room and pointing out some of the most amazing art pieces that had ever been assembled by a private collector. He also showed Wei his most recent additions, artifacts taken from the Mayan city of Kan Ajaw K'uhul. Sebastian ended the tour back in the reception hall.

Cheng Wei shook his host's hand. "I thank you. Never have I seen a more impressive collection."

"*Merci*," Sebastian replied. "I imagine you must be tired after your long journey. Veck will show you to your room. Let's meet again in the Medieval Hall for a late dinner… say, 10:30 p.m."

Wei nodded graciously and followed Veck up the stairs.

At 10:29 p.m. Sebastian stopped outside the medieval hall and stared into a large antique mirror. He was dressed immaculately in a white shirt, white evening jacket, white pants, and white dress shoes.

At his age, he was pleased. Most considered him a very handsome man, and he tended to agree. At precisely 10:30 p.m., Sebastian entered the cavernous Medieval Hall, a room that boasted an eighty-foot-high timbered ceiling and walls decorated with large tapestries, antique armor, and ancient weapons.

Sebastian strolled to the three enormous fireplaces at the left end of the hall. Each fireplace was tall enough for a grown man to stand in and burning logs thicker than his waist. As he warmed his hands in front of the flames, he took out his pocket watch.

It was 10:32, Cheng Wei was late. Normally, he would not tolerate such tardiness, even from a guest, but he was feeling too good to let anything ruin his evening. He stood to make a great deal of money from the sale of the laser and, as always, he was at his happiest when it came to making money.

He, like his ancestors, had an insatiable passion for making money. At one time, the fortune accumulated by his ancestor's rivaled the great kings of Europe. That is, until his father got a hold of it. His father nearly squandered away the whole fortune through foolish drinking, gambling and womanizing.

At the age of fifteen, Sebastian decided he had to do something before his entire inheritance was gone. One night, after one of his father's drinking binges, he passed out on the couch.

When everyone was asleep, Sebastian snuck up to the couch and used a pillow to smother him. After killing his father, he went back to his bedroom and slept like a baby. The maid found his dead father the next morning. Sebastian was never suspected.

At age sixteen, he murdered his mother by poisoning her tea. She was a cranky old witch, who was always complaining about something. He was glad to be rid of her.

The maid found his mother in bed the next morning. Sebastian told the police that he saw the maid poison his mother's tea. He said that when he tried to stop the maid, a large woman, she overpowered him and locked him in a closet.

Based on his testimony, the maid was found guilty of murder. When a life-sentence was handed down, the look of horror on her face was priceless. To this day, he still laughed about it.

On his eighteenth birthday, he was given complete control over his inheritance. His first task was to rebuild the fortune lost by his father. It took some doing, but in ten years' time, he not only equaled it, he had far surpassed it.

Today, at fifty-six years of age, he was ranked number thirty-eight on the Forbes 500 richest men in the world list. Despite his ranking, he was not satisfied. His goal was to reach number one, and as always, he would let nothing stand in his way.

Cheng Wei entered the hall.

Biting back his annoyance, Sebastian said, "Good evening, Wei. I trust you rested well."

"Very well, thank you."

Sebastian gestured to a long oak table with a red silk runner. The table was surrounded by thirty red upholstered chairs. "Shall we dine?" he said.

Servants wearing white waistcoats pulled the chairs out and then pushed them in when they sat.

Sebastian noticed his guest glancing around the hall and said, "You may be interested to know that this château has been in my family for generations and many significant historical figures have dined at this very table. King Henry VI of England dined here in 1416 as did Napoleon Bonaparte in 1815."

"I feel honored," replied Cheng Wei.

"Today your name will be included on that list."

This comment made the Chinese official beam.

A servant set down appetizer plates in front of them while another servant poured cold champagne into crystal flutes.

Wei sipped the champagne. "Delicious."

"I thought you would approve."

Wei set down his glass. "Sebastian, I don't wish to be rude, but when will we discuss our business with the laser? My country is very anxious to have the transaction completed."

"Are your people prepared to wire the money into my Swiss bank account?"

"Five billion dollars is waiting to be wired at this very moment."

"Very good."

"Although...," Wei added with slight hesitation, "I must mention that a few of my comrades feel the price is too high."

"I think not," replied Sebastian evenly. "Considering today's cost of high-tech weaponry, and the fact that the laser is the only one of its kind in the world, I would say it is very reasonably priced. However, *mon ami*, if our deal no longer suits you, I have many other buyers who would find that price quite acceptable."

"No, no," Wei backtracked, "I am sorry I mentioned it. We have the money and are ready to proceed with the deal at your convenience."

"Fine, and once the money is in my account the laser will be yours. Then China will be the most powerful nation on the planet."

Wei said, "I'm a bit surprised you are not keeping the laser for yourself."

"No, no," Sebastian replied. "My sole interest lies in making money. I will gladly leave the 'world domination' thing to you and your people. Now, as we agreed, four canisters of the chemical and biological agents will go with the laser."

"Yes."

"But after that, each canister will cost fifty million dollars."

"Fifty million dollars—each?"

"That's my price," replied Sebastian calmly. "Don't look so shocked, *mon ami*. Once China controls the world, that price will be but a drop in the bucket."

Cheng Wei nodded, but still looked uneasy.

A servant cleared the empty appetizer plates and replaced them with the main course. Sebastian smelled the delicious aroma rising from the roast duck covered in cherry sauce. "Please," he said and nodded toward Wei's plate. "After dessert, we will retire to the library and conclude our business over brandy and cigars."

Cheng Wei smiled.

The two men began to eat their dinner, completely unaware that at that very moment, a cargo plane was directly toward the island.

33

Traveling high over the Mediterranean Sea, at an altitude of 35,000 feet, Alex and Mike moved toward the ramp in the rear of the empty cargo plane.

They wore black insulated jumpsuits, boots, helmets, goggles and breathing apparatus. When they arrived at the closed ramp, they made a final check of their equipment.

"One minute!" yelled the pilot from the open cockpit door.

At 35,000 feet, the outside temperature was a minus forty-seven degrees below zero, which made insulated jumpsuits and oxygen canisters a must. Each man pulled the goggles down over their eyes and placed the oxygen masks over their nose and mouth.

Alex tightened the Velcro strap holding the Heckler & Koch MP5 compact submachine gun to his chest.

During the mission planning phase, Alex realized the islands only security weakness was by air. Even if Sebastian's security team spotted the plane on radar, the plane was flying at such a high altitude that it looked like a routine cargo flight. Of course, there are inherent risks in doing high altitude jumps, but he saw no other way.

"Thirty seconds!" yelled the pilot. He lowered the ramp and yelled, "Go!"

Without hesitation the two men leaped out of the plane and into the cold, black sky.

Plummeting at speeds of nearly one-hundred and sixty miles an hour, the two men lifted their chins and arched their back in the classic skydiving pose.

Alex eyed the phosphorescent dial of the altimeter strapped to his wrist. He waited until it read 27, 000 feet and then reached across his chest. He pulled the ripcord, and the elliptical chute snapped open in the wind.

He floated down in the darkness and looked for Mike, but he didn't see him. It didn't matter, though. Once they reached the island, they each had specific goals to accomplish before they met up again.

In the distance, the security lights shone brightly from Sebastian's island, like a lighted oasis in the middle of a dark sea. Using the toggles above his shoulder, he turned the chute in the direction of the island and glided toward it.

Alex rode the winds and reached the island fourteen minutes later. Below he could see the harbor and armed men with dogs on leashes. He also spotted guards making rounds in front of the main building.

He glided silently to the left of the château and zeroed in on the landing zone. Now he began his descent.

As he neared the rooftop, he turned on his night vision goggles, and the rooftop lit up under a green glow. He could clearly see the guards standing on either end of the long walkway; their eyes turned toward the sea.

He came in on a soundless, downward glide. His plan was to land between the guards. He slowed his speed. There was no room for error. When he had reached the middle of the roof, he pulled back on both toggles, flared his chute and landed gently on the flat recess.

Without delay, he peeled off the sound suppressed MP5 submachine gun strapped to his chest. He took aim and fired. He wheeled around and fired again. Both guards dropped dead. Alex crouched and listened. No dogs barked and no alarms went off; that was a good sign.

He slipped out of the parachute harness. He gathered in the nylon material and stuffed it under a running water pipe. He removed the rest of his equipment and then shed his insulated suit.

From the rucksack, he removed a disguise. He put on workman's tan coverall's, added a tool belt, a roll of silver duct tape, a tan hat, and a clipboard. He peeled the adhesive backing off a false mustache and slapped it above his lip. The look of a maintenance worker was complete.

He pulled out a Sig Sauer P226 handgun from the rucksack and screwed on a silencer. He stuffed the remainder of his items under the pipe and headed for the roof stairs.

He went down the stairs, taking two at a time. At the bottom, he opened a heavy steel door and found himself inside a small room. It had a service elevator and a door leading to the third floor.

He opened the door and peered into a dimly lit hallway. It was empty. Considering the lateness of the hour, he expected most occupants to be asleep, and he was right. This made his infiltration infinitely easier. To avoid being identified by the interior security cameras, he tugged the brim of his hat low. He used the clipboard to hide the pistol and stepped into the hallway.

He found the central staircase and walked down. When he reached the main floor, he swung a left past a statue of a nude warrior and continued down a long spacious hallway. He scanned the rooms on either side as he went. So far he hadn't seen anyone. Then…up ahead, he heard voices.

Moving silently to the door on the left, he listened. He could hear Sebastian's voice. The man was droning on about his art collection. Alex peeked into the open doorway and saw Sebastian and his guest seated at a long table.

Alex had the urge to shoot both of them on the spot, but that pleasure had to wait. He needed to stick to the plan. He continued to the end of the hall and stopped at the door whose sign read SECURITY.

He reached inside the top of his boot and removed a slender piece of metal. He slid it into the lock. After a few jiggles, he heard a soft click. Raising the pistol, he opened the door and found two guards seated in front of a bank of closed-circuit television monitors.

The guard to his left had his feet propped on the table, paging through a nudie magazine. The guard to his right was playing a game of solitaire on the computer. Neither heard him come in.

Alex closed the door. "Good evening, gentlemen."

The guard with the nudie magazine nearly fell out of his chair. The guard on the computer angrily snapped his head up. When he saw the gun, he put his hands into the air.

"Take your weapons out of your holsters," Alex said. "Two fingers only. Then drop them to the floor and kick them to me."

The guards complied.

Alex tossed the roll of duct tape to the guard on the right. "Tape your buddy to his chair." The guard did as he was told and when he finished, Alex said, "Now do yourself," The guard taped his legs to the chair, and one wrist. Alex taped the other wrist for him.

With both guards immobilized, Alex located the electrical panel. With a flick of a switch, he shut off the lights to the rear grounds.

As expected, the calls began pouring in over the radio. He pressed the pistol barrel into the guard's temple, and said, "Do exactly as I say and you'll live. Try anything funny, and I'll splatter your brains across the room and give your friend a chance. Got it?"

The man nodded quickly.

"Get on the radio and tell them you're aware of the problem. Tell them it's going to take time to get it fixed, so be patient."

Alex rolled the man's chair to the table and slid the microphone in front of him. "Answer them." He pushed the 'speak' button and nodded at the guard to begin.

"Um...all stations...this is security. We are aware of the problem with the lights and we're working on it. It should be corrected shortly, so be patient."

Alex lifted his finger off the button. "Good boy." Then he ripped the microphone cord from the unit and tossed it across the room. "Now, tell me where can I find Sophie and Dr. Farah?"

The guard appeared bewildered. "Sophie?"

"The girl Veck brought back with him."

"Oh, second floor--she's on the second floor, in The Remington Room."

"And Dr. Farah?"

"Two doors down in The Bonaparte Room."

"If you're lying...I'll be back, and it won't be pretty."

The guard shook his head vigorously. "No, no, it's the truth--I swear."

Alex slapped duct tape over their mouths. He

turned off all the monitors and overhead lights. Then he opened the door, locked it from the inside, and left.

He hurried down the hallway, the same way that he'd come. He reached the central staircase and ascended to the second floor without being seen. He scanned the nameplates on the doors until he found 'The Remington Room.' She better be in there, or he was going to pay that guard another visit, and he wouldn't be so nice next time.

He turned the doorknob. It was locked. Using the thin metal strip from his boot, he unlocked the door. He opened it and slipped inside.

The room was dimly lit by a small table lamp. A white lace canopy bed was against the far wall. To his right were an antique armoire and a long dressing mirror. To his left a fireplace. A painting by Remington hung above the mantel, hence the name of the room.

An inner door swung open. Alex dropped to one knee and raised his pistol. Standing within a cloud of billowing steam, a figure of a woman appeared. Her hair was wrapped in a towel and another wrapped around her torso.

"Sophie?"

The woman jerked back in shock and then recognized the voice. "Alex!" She ran and leapt into his arms. "I knew you'd come!"

"Are you okay? Did he hurt you?"

"No, I'm fine," she replied.

He was relieved. "Get dressed. It's time to go."

She hurried to get her clothes on. While she dressed, Alex shed his maintenance man disguise. Now he was wearing black slacks and a black cotton shirt. He met Sophie by the door.

Sophie glanced at his face and smiled. "Are you going to keep that?"

He'd forgotten all about it the fake mustache under his nose. "I was thinking of keeping it. What do you think?"

She shook her head and ripped it off.

Alex grinned. He raised his pistol and opened the door. The hallway was deserted. Together they eased out of the room and quietly shut the door behind them.

Alex turned right and located The Bonaparte Room. The door was locked. He picked the lock and entered. They entered so quietly that Dr. Farah didn't hear them come in. She was sitting in bed deeply engrossed in a scientific journal.

Alex walked close to the bed and whispered, "*Psst*...Dr. Farah."

The scientist jumped, and the magazine flew from her hands. She stared at him wide-eyed with a hand pressed to her heart. "Oh my god, you scared the living daylights out of me."

"Sorry about that, but it's time to go."

She smiled. "Mr. McCade, apparently saving me has become a full-time job for you."

"Call me Alex, and yes it's beginning to seem that way, doesn't it?"

Dr. Farah slid out of bed. She saw Sophie standing by the door and gave a wave. They waited for the scientist to get dressed. When she finished, she met them by the door.

Alex whispered, "Dr. Farah, where is Sebastian's keeping the laser?"

Her mouth dropped open. "You know about the laser?"

"Senator McDaniel told me. He's the one helping us with this rescue."

She fought back the shock and said, "It's in Sebastian's laboratory."

Alex tried to jog his memory, but he didn't remember a laboratory in the layout of the château. "I don't know where it is."

"I'll show you."

Alex cracked open the door. The hallway was empty. Dr. Farah slid past him and led them down the hallway.

On the main floor, they turned right and heard voices coming from the library at the end of the hall. Halfway down, they turned and entered a colossal art gallery with masterpiece paintings in heavy gilded frames hanging on the wall.

At the far end of the room hung a large woven tapestry. It was a medieval scene, with women holding fruit baskets, men on horses, and a castle in the background. She pulled the corner of the tapestry back and revealed an old staircase that spiraled deep into the floor.

They descended stone steps that had been worn smooth over the centuries. When they reached the bottom, Dr. Farah flipped a switch. Overhead lights strung along the ceiling illuminated a damp, ancient passageway. It was eerie.

Alex imagined at one time this may have been the way to a dungeon or torture chamber.

They hurried along the cobblestone flooring. At the end of the passage, they came to a modern, stainless steel security door.

Dr. Farah punched numbers into the coded keypad. She hit 'enter' but the door did not open. She tried again and again, but after three failed attempts, she slammed her hand against the door in frustration. "I can't get in. Sebastian must have changed the code."

"Stand back," Alex said.

He lifted his pant leg and ripped off a plastic packet taped to his lower calf. He removed a block of a gray, putty-like substance and stripped off the adhesive backing.

He slapped the C-4 plastic explosive on the side of the door and inserted a miniature, match-size electronic initiator. Pulling a small electronic box from his pocket, he flipped a switch which produced a flashing red light. "Move back."

The women stepped back some twenty paces, and Alex joined them. He stared at the small box in his hand. When the flashing red light turned a steady green, he pushed the button.

A loud explosion rocked the tunnel; filling it with clouds of swirling dust. Alex hoped they didn't hear the explosion upstairs.

When the dust settled, he was met with disappointment. The door had only partially blown open. It was stronger than he anticipated. He grabbed the top left edge and muscled the twisted metal downward. He kept pulling, pushing, and prying until the gap was just wide enough to squeeze through.

Alex went through the gap first. Dr. Farah went next, followed by Sophie. Once inside the laboratory, Dr. Farah turned on the overhead lights.

The laboratory was immaculate. The walls and ceiling had been painted a bright white. Atop the spotlessly clean tables sat beakers, test tubes and a whole assortment of state-of-the-art scientific equipment.

Dr. Farah pointed to a side room. "The laser is in

there."

The three hurried into the room. Alex saw the silver titanium case. The lid was open, and the laser rested inside.

Dr. Farah snatched two flash drives off the desk and tossed them into the case. "Copies of my research," she said. She closed the lid and snapped the latches.

Alex reached for the case. "I'll take it."

34

Meanwhile inside the library, Sebastian and Cheng Wei enjoyed brandy and cigars in front of a crackling fire. As Wei took a sip of brandy, he noticed framed charcoal prints hanging on the wall.

Wei got up from his chair and strolled over to the prints and said, "Sebastian, I don't believe you included these on your tour. Are these originals?"

"*Oui*," replied Sebastian proudly. "Everything I own are originals. Do you recognize them?"

Wei studied them for a moment. "I believe these are sketches by Leonardo De Vinci."

"You have a fine eye; drawn by the master himself."

Wei nodded appreciably and strolled back to his chair and sat.

Sebastian turned to his guest. "Did you happen to see President Grant's Memorial Day speech the other day?"

"I did, and I must say your demonstration of the laser was enough to persuade my colleagues to go ahead with the deal. They were also very pleased with your choice of targets."

"I thought they would be."

Wei smiled. "After the shooting, we had the president's health verified by our own sources in

Washington and they tell me he is very close to death."

"The weapon performed exactly as promised," Sebastian said.

"Yes, it did."

Sebastian leaned forward. "Before we conclude our business, I should mention that if there is any thought of using the laser against me in the future, tell your colleagues not to bother.

"Oh…no doubt your scientists will try to replicate the gasification process, but their attempts will only end in failure. Only I have the knowledge to create the chemical and biological agents used with the laser, and if I die, the secret dies with me. Therefore, your government will have nothing but a giant paperweight on its hands."

"I assure you, we have no intention of using the weapon against you."

"Good."

Wei rubbed his palms together with excitement. "So, when can I see this laser?"

Sebastian turned. "Veck, go to the laboratory and bring me the laser. It's time to show our guest what he is paying for."

The big man nodded and left the room.

35

Alex squeezed out the laboratory door with the pistol in one hand and the oblong titanium laser case in the other. Sophie and Dr. Farah followed.

They hurried along the ancient stone passageway and then climbed the spiral staircase. Upon reaching the top, Alex pushed aside the bottom corner of the tapestry and stepped into the art gallery. Sophie came next, followed by Dr. Farah.

The climb up the stairs was a bit much for aging Dr. Farah and she needed a few moments to catch her breath. Thirty seconds later, she nodded that she was ready to go.

Alex ushered them through a side door of the gallery and into the music room. They passed a white grand piano and marble busts of the world's greatest composers; arriving at French doors at the back of the room, Alex stopped.

He looked out the door's windows to the rear of the estate. He was pleased to see the lights still off. No one found the guards yet. The plan was to leave the château, go through the formal gardens, and then climb up the hill to the hanger. Mike was to meet them in one of Sebastian's helicopters and fly them off the island.

As Alex reached for the door handle, a booming voice said, "Stay where you are and drop the *bloody* gun!"

Alex hesitated. Then he dropped the pistol to the floor. He slowly turned around and saw Veck's hulking figure silhouetted against the hallway light with a pistol aimed directly at his head.

"Kick your weapon to me yank. And don't be cute."

Alex kicked the pistol and it skidded across the floor.

"Now, the case."

Alex set down the case and used his foot to slide it across the slick marble flooring.

Veck picked up the discarded pistol and tucked it into his belt. He grabbed the laser case with his free hand and then nodded his massive bald head toward the hallway behind him. "Move."

At gunpoint, Veck marched Alex, Sophie, and Dr. Farah out of the music room and into the library.

When they entered the billionaire saw Alex and nearly dropped his glass of brandy. "*Mon Dieu!*" he shrieked. "What are you doing here?"

"Just stopped by to say hello," Alex replied with a grin. "But I can see you're busy, so I'll just come back another time."

"Not so fast *monsieur*," Sebastian said composing himself. "In fact, you've come at the perfect time. I am about to show my honored guest how the laser works, and you have just volunteered to assist me."

"I think Veck would be a far better choice, really."

"Oh no, you'll do just fine," replied Sebastian. He gestured. "*Monsieur*, kindly move in front of the fireplace."

When Alex didn't move, Sebastian nodded to Veck.

The big man went to Sophie, and he wrapped his large, sausage size fingers around her throat. "Sorry

Love; nothing personal," he said and squeezed.

Sophie's eyes bulged. Her face burned red and was rapidly turning purple.

"Alright, I get your point," Alex shouted. "Tell the beast to let her go."

"Veck," Sebastian said casually, "let go of Dr. Marcus."

The big man released his grip and Sophie fell to her knees, gasping for air.

Alex walked to the fireplace. Veck shoved him hard against one of the granite pillars that supported the ornate mantel. Using wire normally used to hang paintings, he bound Alex's wrists behind the pillar.

With a sadistic grin, he gave the wire a few extra twists, causing it to cut painfully into Alex's skin.

Sebastian smiled. "Comfortable?"

"Quite," Alex answered through clenched teeth.

Sebastian chuckled. "You'll be interested to know that since our last meeting I have discovered quite a bit about you. You see, I make it a habit to learn all I can about my enemies, which is why I succeed, and other's fail."

Sebastian set his drink down and strolled to Alex. He folded his arms across his chest and said, "Your full name is Alexander Hayato McCade. You were born in Seattle. Your mother's name was Nami. She was from Sapporo, Japan. Your father's name was Steve. He was an American born in Forest Lake, Minnesota.

"Both your parents died in a horrific car crash when you were just eleven-years-old. After their deaths you went to live with your uncle and aunt, however, that didn't go so well, did it?

"Your uncle was a drunk who beat you. In high

school, you turned to alcohol and beating up others to numb the pain. You were failing all your classes. That is...until you met your girlfriend; the future Mrs. McCade.

"This angel of mercy helped you work through your problems and is responsible for turning your life around. Then you married her.

"Upon graduating from the University of Washington, you enlisted into the United States Navy, where you joined the SEALs and rose to the rank of Commander.

"Years later your perfect little life came crashing down when your dearly beloved wife died of cancer. *Tisk-tisk*...it's a shame. And I see you still wear your wedding ring. Such devotion," he said mockingly.

He waited for a reaction from Alex but got none.

"About a month ago, you retired from the Navy. Now you are tied to my fireplace and are within minutes of dying. Have I missed anything?"

"Yeah, you forgot to mention I was in the cub scouts when I was ten."

"Shame on me."

Sebastian turned his back on Alex and approached his guest. "Wei, I'd like to introduce you to Dr. Isra Farah."

Cheng Wei leered at the olive skin, dark-haired scientist with pleasure. "So, this is the infamous Dr. Farah," he said. "May I say, what an honor it is to meet such a brilliant scientist as yourself."

Dr. Farah frowned.

"She isn't exactly pleased with our arrangement," replied Sebastian, "Are you dear?"

"No, I am not."

"In any event *Mademoiselle*, please set up the laser."

Dr. Farah huffed. "And if I refuse?"

"Then you will join *Monsieur* McCade at the fireplace."

Dr. Farah glanced to Alex for guidance. He nodded for her to proceed. He was well aware of what would happen to her if she refused.

With great apprehension, Dr. Farah opened the laser case. She set up the tripod and placed the laser on top of it. She tightened the screws and then pulled the retractable cord from the stock of the weapon and held it up.

"There's an outlet to your right," Sebastian said.

Dr. Farah dragged the loose cord to the wall socket and plugged it in.

"Now, turn it on."

She walked back to the weapon and flipped the switch. The laser began to emit a soft hum.

While the laser was warming up, Alex gave fleeting glances to the door. C'mon Mike, where are you? Once his friend realized they hadn't shown up at the rendezvous site, he would come looking for them. The question is--would he get here in time? Alex wasn't so sure.

He had to stall. His mind raced for ways to delay. He searched for something to say, and then he blurted out, "I heard they found Dr. Valerius's body."

Sebastian raised a curious brow. "You know about Dr. Valerius, do you? Well, it's a pity, but it turns out the man wasn't a very good swimmer."

"The fisherman who found him said his arms and legs had been tied."

Sebastian chuckled. "I imagine that did make things

slightly more difficult for him."

"Why did you kill him?"

"If you must know, I no longer needed him. He had served his usefulness, and when my business here is complete, I will make sure my other partner shares his fate."

This caught Alex by surprise. "Other partner?"

"*Oui*, in fact, he is a very prominent member of your own government."

"Who is it?"

Sebastian laughed. "No one you need to concern yourself with. Now, be quiet *Monsieur*, I have no desire to converse with you further."

Sebastian strolled to the laser case lying on the table. He reached in and removed a 12x18 inch box containing the canisters of gasified chemical and biological agents. He set the box on the couch and sat beside it. He flipped open the lid and read the typed labels on the small cylinders.

"Which one shall I use?   Hmm...Small Pox? Anthrax, maybe? How about the Ebola Virus? No, no, no," he muttered. "We want something fast acting, don't we?" The man contemplated each horrible agent as lightly as if he was trying to decide which cologne to wear for the evening. "Ah...this should do it," he said, plucking out the small canister of VX gas from the case.

"This will do nicely." He held it up for Wei to see. "VX gas is a deadly nerve agent. Once infected, *Monsieur* McCade will experience vomiting, followed by convulsions, paralysis, respiratory arrest and shortly thereafter--death."

"It's perfect," replied Wei with excitement. "But are you sure we won't be affected?"

"No, no, no," Sebastian assured. "The particles go directly into his bloodstream. It's perfectly safe."

Sebastian inserted the canister of VX gas into the laser's compartment at the base of the barrel. Then, he put his eye against the top mounted scope and aligned the crosshairs to align in the middle of Alex's forehead. "*Monsieur*, are you ready to die a most horrible death?"

"Yep, really looking forward to it," Alex replied.

Sebastian laughed. "So brave yet, so foolish."

Sebastian slid his finger to the trigger and was about to squeeze when he was tapped on the shoulder. He looked back at a smiling Cheng Wei.

"May I?" Wei asked.

Sebastian backed away from the laser. "Of course, where are my manners?"

Wei moved in. With excitement he leaned over the laser, set his eye to the scope and wrapped his finger found the trigger.

"You may fire when ready," Sebastian said.

"No!" Sophie screamed.

With tremendous delight, Cheng Wei pulled the trigger. At the same time, an instantaneous red dot of light appeared in the middle of Alex's forehead. It stayed for a moment and then disappeared.

Cheng Wei looked up with uncertainty. "Did it work?"

"Perfectly." Sebastian glanced at Alex. "How do you feel?"

"Never better," Alex replied.

Sebastian turned to Veck. "Take the women back to their rooms and hurry back—I'm sure you won't want to miss a moment of *Monsieur* McCade's agonizing death."

36

Veck guided the women down the second-floor hallway. He stopped at The Bonaparte room, opened the door and roughly shoved Dr. Farah inside.

He closed the door and locked it from the outside. Next, he grabbed Sophie by the arm and dragged her to The Remington room.

He opened the door, but before pushing her inside, he pulled her body close to his. With garlicky breath, he whispered, "After your boyfriend dies, we're going to spend some quality time together." Then he slowly licked her cheek with his cow-sized tongue.

She was thrown into the room. She could hear him laughing as he closed the door and locked it from the outside.

She rubbed the streak of wet saliva off her cheek, and with growing rage, she stormed into the bathroom. She picked up a drinking glass from the sink and smashed it against the marble counter. She chose the largest piece of broken glass and wrapped a small washcloth around the bottom to grip it.

Clutching the sharp weapon in her hand, she smiled. "Now, I'm ready Veck. Let's spend some quality time together."

She dropped onto the bed. When Veck came back,

she would let him get close and then jab him in the neck with the glass shard. She was furious. Not just at Veck, but also about what was happening to Alex. He was downstairs dying, and there was nothing she could do about it. She tried to fight it, but tears slowly leaked out the corners of her eyes and flowed down her cheeks.

The doorknob jiggled.

She snapped her head off the pillow. She tightened her grip on the weapon and then lay back pretending to sleep. As the door opened her heart pounded so loud, she thought Veck must surely hear it. No matter, she was ready. She would make that monster pay.

A dark figure slid into the room. "Sophie? Dr. Farah?"

She jolted upright. "Mike?"

"Sophie? Is that you?"

"Yes!" she cried.

Mike turned on a small flashlight and aimed the beam in her direction. "Sophie, you're crying. What's wrong?"

"It's Alex; he was shot with VX gas from the laser."

"When? Where?"

"About ten minutes ago; in the library."

"Is he still alive?"

"I –I... don't know," she choked.

Mike lowered the flashlight beam and spoke firmly. "Sophie, this is what we're going to do. We'll get Dr. Farah, and then we'll rescue Alex, pack up the laser and get the hell off this rock."

Sophie dropped the glass shard and slid off the bed. "I'll show you to Dr. Farah's room."

The two left the room and hurried two doors down to The Bonaparte room. Mike picked the lock and opened the door. Dr. Farah was inside, pacing.

When they entered Dr. Farah turned. "Sophie! My dear, are you alright?"

Sophie gulped hard and then lowered her chin to hide her puffy eyes.

Dr. Farah took Sophie's hands in hers. "Sophie, look at me. I couldn't tell you earlier, but Alex wasn't infected."

"What? What do you mean? I saw it!"

"What you saw was harmless light hitting him-- nothing more."

"I-I... don't understand."

"When I was setting up the laser, I secretly flipped a switch on the bottom of the unit, used to clean out the system. When the trigger was pulled, the VX gas was sucked out the back of the weapon."

Her heart began pumping rapidly. "You mean...he's alive?"

"That's right; although, I can't say the same for Sebastian and his guest."

Sophie hugged Dr. Farah. "Thank you."

"You're welcome," she replied. The scientist peered over Sophie's shoulder. "Now dear, do you suppose you could introduce me to your friend?"

"Oh, I'm sorry. This is Mike Garrison. He came with Alex to rescue us."

Mike smiled. "Hello Doctor, I'd love to stand around and chat, but we'd better get a move on."

Mike cautiously opened the door with Sophie and Dr. Farah behind him. Taking the lead, they all left the room. They reached the main floor, turned right and dashed down the main hallway.

As they neared the library, they heard horrible moaning and retching sounds. They stepped into the library and found Sebastian and Cheng Wei quivering on the floor in pools of their own vomit. The smell was horrendous.

Mike plugged his nose. "Doctor, is it safe to go in there?"

"Yes, only those two got infected. The rest of the gas dissipated and is harmless now."

"Hey, over here," Alex yelled.

Sophie ran to Alex. She hugged him and kissed his face over and over again. "I thought you were dead!" She said.

"Alright, alright." Alex laughed.

Mike casually strolled to his friend. "Well, well. What do we have here?"

Alex sneered. "Nice of you to show up. Where the hell have you been?"

"Where was I?" Mike asked in mocked amazement. "I was in the chopper waiting for you like we planned, but no-o-o... here you are taking it easy; warming yourself by the fire while I'm out doing all the hard work. So typical," he said shaking his head, "so typical."

"Just get me out of this."

Mike moved behind the pillar. He untwisted the wire from around Alex's wrists. Sophie saw his bloody wrists and said, "You're hurt!"

"I'm fine," Alex replied.

He gave her a quick hug and then strode to Dr. Farah who was packing up the laser. "Thanks, doctor," he said.

"You're welcome. I thought it was about time I saved your life for a change."

234

"I'm glad you did."

She closed the lid and flipped the latches. "I'm ready."

Alex picked up the case. Before leaving, he crouched beside Sebastian, looked him directly in the eyes and said, "Sebastian, thank you for your hospitality, I can't remember having a more enjoyable time."

Sebastian tried to speak, but best he could do was to choke up blood on his fine white clothes.

"Oh, and don't bother getting up," Alex added, "we'll show ourselves out."

Alex met the others by the door. He and Mike led the small group through the music room and to the French door leading to the rear grounds. When they got there, Mike flung open the doors, and they hit the lawn running.

With partial moonlight to see by, they ran for the formal gardens. The plan was to get to one of the choppers Mike had prepared.

Within ten feet of entering the garden, Veck stepped out from behind a tall hedge and blocked their way.

Mike raised his pistol to shoot, but Alex grasped his friend's arm and lowered it. "No."

Mike was utterly baffled. "Why not?"

"Because I said so."

The big man stood his ground. He folded his arms across his massive chest and sneered. "That's right mate; him and I have some unfinished business to attend to."

"Alex, don't!" Sophie urged.

Alex handed the laser case to Mike. "Take this and get them to the chopper."

"Are you kidding? Let me shoot him."

"No. Go to the chopper. If I'm not there in five minutes--leave without me."

"Alright, but do I have to wait the full five minutes?"

Dr. Farah turned to Sophie. "I can't understand these two; they behave like little boys."

"I know, I know," she replied.

Mike led the women around Veck. As Sophie passed him, Veck leaned over and flicked his tongue like a snake, and hissed, "Don't go far love, we'll be together again real soon."

Sophie angrily opened her mouth to reply, but Mike pulled her into the garden, and they hurried away.

Standing in the faint moonlight, the two men squared off like western gunfighters in the middle of town. Alex the six-foot two, 198-pound, former Navy SEAL against the six-foot six, 380-pound monster named Veck.

The overconfident big man didn't wait.

He threw a wild arcing punch at Alex's head and he missed. Alex countered. Using his martial arts training, Alex drove a knee into the big man's thigh and another into his ribs. He followed with an elbow to Veck's chin. The big man wobbled backward in shock and pain.

Alex didn't give him a chance to recover. He threw punches at Veck's face and then to his midsection, but this time the monster absorbed the blows.

He caught Alex in his powerful arms and squeezed. The man's strength was unbelievable. Alex couldn't breathe. He didn't have much time. Either he was going to pass out from lack of oxygen, or his spine would snap; maybe both.

Painfully, he managed to get one arm loose. He raised it and jabbed a thumb into Veck's left eye. The beast howled and let go. Alex fell to the ground. He got up quickly, but Veck was quicker.

The enraged animal surprised him with two earth-shattering blows which sent him reeling backward over a low hedge. Alex landed hard.

With great effort, Alex got onto his hands and knees and shook his head clear. He couldn't take many more blows like that; the man's strength was incredible. He had to finish the fight quickly, or not at all.

Wiping blood trickling into his eye, he rose to his feet and launched himself over the hedge.

He feigned with his right hand, and then in a flash, he performed a spinning back-fist to Veck's face and hit him squarely in the nose. Blood splattered across his wide face and bent his nose sideways. Veck shrieked. He looked at Alex in utter disbelief.

Recognizing doubt in the man's eyes, Alex went in for the kill. He went toe to toe with Veck and unloaded a barrage of punches, each harder than the one before. Veck weaved and tried to avoid the onslaught but Alex stayed with him like a heavyweight fighter going for a knockout in the last round.

Shot after shot, he thundered on Veck until finally the big man's knees buckled, his eyes glazed over, and he toppled over like a giant redwood falling in the forest.

Alex stumbled. He dropped to his knees and raised his battered face to the stars. He took in deep breaths of air and smiled. Though his face was bleeding, his lips swollen, and one eye nearly closed shut, he was happy. The pain was good. The fight was over, and he was victorious.

After he caught his breath, he got to his feet. He

looked back at Veck, shocked to find the monster not only could move but that he was sitting upright with a pistol in his hand.

Veck spat blood from his mouth, and then slowly, painfully, lifted his huge torso off the ground. Once on his feet, he wobbled unsteadily and was forced to widen his stance to maintain his balance. The big man aimed the pistol at Alex's head and said, "Time for you to die."

Alex heard the 'thump' of sudden impact. Then the big man's body contorted, his eyes widened, and he let out a high-pitched squeal. The pistol dropped, and his hands weakly covered his groin.

Sophie stood triumphantly behind him. "Take that you bastard!" she shouted.

Alex glanced at Veck rolling back and forth on the ground. She had kicked him hard in the testicles. He raised his eyes to Sophie and grinned. "Remind me never to get on your bad side."

She smiled, but her expression changed upon seeing his battered face. "Alex--you're hurt!"

"Never better," he replied through swollen and bleeding lips. "Come on, let's get to the chopper."

Suddenly, the rear lights turned on and bathed them in bright light. Sebastian's guards wheeled around the corner of the château and opened fire with automatic weapons. Under a torrent of bullets, Alex and Sophie ran into the gardens.

They hurried over a path of crushed rock and dashed by ornate flower beds, park benches, and classic marble sculptures. When they reached the back wall, Alex gave Sophie a boost up and over.

When she was on the other side of the wall, he jumped and grabbed the top ledge. He pulled himself up and over. Once he was on the other side, they scrambled up the tree-covered hill.

Reaching the top, Alex saw Mike waving from inside a helicopter. He and Sophie ran to it. Sophie got in the back of the chopper and sat next to Dr. Farah. Alex jumped into the right front seat next to Mike.

Mike looked at his friend's bloody face and shook his head in disgust. "Well, don't you look beautiful?"

Alex sneered. "Thank you."

"Next time...just let me shoot him, will ya?"

"Fine, just go."

Mike started the helicopter. As the rotors got up speed, bullets began pinging off the outside shell of the chopper. Mike calmly took his hands off the controls and produced a small box.

"What are you doing?" Sophie asked. "Get us out of here."

"Don't worry; I know how to take care of these bad boys." He pushed the button on the box. Simultaneous explosions rocked the island, and huge fireballs lit the night sky. He grinned. "Like I always say...fireworks can brighten up any occasion."

The gunfire stopped.

Using the diversion to his benefit, Mike put his hands back on the controls, and the helicopter lifted off the ground. But after only a few feet in the air, the aircraft jolted and leaned to the right. Alex and Mike exchanged confused looks.

Alex looked out his window. "Did you miss a tie-off or something?"

"No."

Alex cracked open the door and looked down. "You must have...*ah*." His words got choked off by a large hand clutching his throat.

"It's Veck!" Sophie screamed.

Mike went for his pistol, but in trying to control the rising aircraft, he fumbled the weapon and dropped it between the seats.

The big man wedged his large frame inside the doorway. His face, beaten and bloody, looked like something out of a horror movie.

The helicopter was at forty feet and climbing. Mike banked the aircraft left and then right to shake Veck loose, but the monster held on.

Dr. Farah plucked the pistol from between the seats. She leaned back, closed her eyes, and pulled the trigger. An ear-shattering explosion reverberated inside the small space. Unfortunately, the shot when wide and shattered the side window.

Veck pinned Alex to the seat with his massive weight and lunged for the weapon with his free hand. As he swung his arm back and forth, trying to take the pistol from Dr. Farah, Alex managed to pry Veck's fingers off his throat.

Then, using all his strength, he pushed the man's huge body off him. Veck reeled backward but was able to brace himself against the open doorway.

The big man grinned savagely.

Alex returned the grin. Then he drew in both legs and kicked Veck solidly in the chest.

The monster lost his grip. His eyes widened, and he clawed at the open air as he tumbled out of the chopper and disappeared into the night.

Alex yanked the door shut. "Now, get us the hell out of here!"

Mike put the aircraft into a steep bank.

The gunfire resumed.

37

Mike flew the chopper off the island and out to sea under a hail of gunfire. Once free of the island, elation swept through the cabin.

Sophie and Dr. Farah gave each other hugs. Alex slapped Mike on the back. "Looks like we made it."

Mike smiled, but then did a double take on the flight instruments. "Not so fast. We got a problem."

"What's up?"

"The goons on the ground hit our fuel tanks; we're losing fuel--fast."

Sophie looked behind. "That's not all. There's a chopper following us."

Alex snapped his head around. "Where the hell did that come from?" He turned to Mike. "Didn't you disable the other chopper?"

"Sorry, no time. If you remember, I was a little busy saving your ass."

Dr. Farah leaned forward in her seat. "Can we outrun them?"

"No."

Alex put on a headset and adjusted the lip mic. He dialed the prearranged radio frequency. "Falcon, this is Eagle One, do you copy?" He tried again. "Falcon, this is Eagle One, do you copy?"

A crackle came over the radio. "...Falcon here."

"Falcon, we're off the rock, but we've got a big, bad bird on our tail, and we're losing fuel fast. Need assistance."

"Rodger, Eagle One. We've got you on radar, but unfortunately, we're still an hour from your position. Hang tight, we're on our way."

"Roger, Falcon. Eagle One out," Alex replied.

"An hour? We don't have an hour!" Sophie sputtered.

"You're right," Alex replied. He looked at the fuel gauge. "I'd say we have a few minutes at most."

"Making land is out of the question," Mike added. "We'll have to ditch her at sea."

Since Sebastian lived on an island, Alex counted on the aircraft being prepared for overwater emergencies. "Check under your seat's for life vests," Alex shouted.

Sophie reached under her seat and pulled a life vest out of a pouch. "I found one."

"Me too," added Dr. Farah.

"Put them on, but don't inflate them until you get outside."

Alex shed his seatbelt and climbed into the back seat. He reached behind the two women. "Sorry ladies," he said and opened a rear compartment marked RAFT.

He pulled out a bulky package wrapped in thick plastic and heaved it onto his front seat. He tied the raft's lanyard to the frame of his seat.

The helicopter began making erratic movements. Mike did his best to maintain control. "We don't have much time," he warned.

"Bring her in close," replied Alex.

Mike slowed to a hover. He lowered the helicopter to within a few feet of the dark sea. Alex popped open the door and pushed out the raft pack. The yellow bundle hit the water, the cord jerked, and moments later a fully inflated yellow raft was bobbing on the surface of the Mediterranean Sea.

A loud warning siren wailed in the cockpit.

Alex glanced at the empty fuel gauge and red flashing light next to it. "Everybody out!" he yelled.

Sophie stepped out the door, followed by Dr. Farah. Alex handed Sophie the laser case. Before leaving, he grabbed a flashlight mounted by the door. He looked at Mike. "Dump this thing and get back here fast."

"That's the plan, boss."

Alex jumped into the raft and then used the raft knife to cut the lanyard to separate them from the aircraft. Mike banked the chopper away. Because of the darkness, Alex lost sight of the chopper, but he could still hear the sputtering engine.

Moments later, he heard a heavy splash, followed by the brief sound of rotors slicing the water. Then silence.

There was no time to worry about Mike's safety, as a bright spotlight lit up their raft from above. Alex squinted. He held a hand up to shield his eyes from the blinding beam. He narrowed his vision and caught sight of a man with a high-powered rifle leaning out the door of Sebastian's second helicopter.

Over a loudspeaker came, "Stay where you are. We will lower a ladder. Climb up and bring the laser with you. If you refuse, you will be killed."

This demand was followed by a loud 'crack' of gunfire. The bullet ripped into the water next to the raft. "You have thirty seconds to decide."

Dr. Farah yanked Alex's arm. "Alex, we can't give

up the laser."

"But if we don't," Sophie countered, "they'll kill us."

"Your thirty seconds are up," the voice on the loudspeaker said. "What's it going to be?"

"Hey, that wasn't thirty seconds!" Sophie yelled.

"I don't think that matters to them," Alex said.

"Then, what are we going to do?"

Alex looked at the chopper. He needed a plan and quick. As he twisted the wedding ring on his finger different scenarios flashed through this mind. None looked very promising. He calculated the odds of success of each and then came to a conclusion. He raised his hands in defeat.

"Alex, we can't!" Dr. Farah shouted.

"Listen to me. I want the two of you to climb the ladder and get into the chopper. When you're safely inside, I'll drop the case overboard and make a swim for it. Then I'll come and get you when I can."

"I can't go back there," Sophie said.

"We don't have a choice," Alex replied. "This is our only option to keep the two of you safe and to keep them from getting the laser."

Before anyone could move, the raft was hit by a series of giant, rolling waves. Alex held on and caught sight of what appeared to be a giant black sea monster rising up from the depths. The men in the chopper swung the spotlight off the raft and illuminated a rising submarine.

As the submarine leveled off, a hatch in front of the conning tower opened. A sailor popped up with a rocket launcher pressed to his shoulder. He took aim and pulled the trigger.

A red light streaked across the dark, nighttime sky and in mere seconds the missile slammed into the chopper and the aircraft exploded into a fiery ball.

As the falling debris dropped into the dark sea, Alex gestured to the submarine. "Ladies, I give you the Falcon."

"Not that I'm complaining," Sophie said, "but didn't they say they were over an hour away?"

"They did, but I don't know any Major in his right mind who would give his true location over open airwaves."

Sailors appeared on the deck of the submarine. A man stepped forward and tossed a rope to the raft. Alex caught it. Men aboard the Falcon pulled them in.

When the raft arrived alongside the hull of the submarine, the Captain of the vessel was there to greet them. He looked down. "Commander McCade?"

"Yes sir, Captain. I appreciate the help."

"Glad to be of service."

The Captain waved his men forward. His sailors lowered a net down the side of the hull. Dr. Farah climbed the netting, followed by Sophie. Once on deck, the two women had warm woolen blankets wrapped around their shoulders.

Alex stood in the raft and raised the laser case above his head. One of the sailors used a telescoping pole with hook slip under the handle. He lifted the pole and brought the case aboard.

"Captain, take good care of that," Alex said.

The Captain nodded. "Aren't you coming?"

"I can't. I've got a man down out here, and I can't leave without him."

"Understood. Let me get a team together and we'll

help."

"Thanks, I'd appreciate that."

The rear of the raft unexpectedly pulled downward, and Alex nearly lost his balance. He wheeled around and saw two hands grasping the back of the raft. A moment later, Mike's cheerful face emerged from the water.

Flinging back his wet blonde hair, he said, "You weren't thinking of leaving without me, were you?"

38

In the submarine's control room, Alex and the others stood by while all hatches closed.

The Captain gave the order to dive and the submarine's crew went into action. Less than thirty seconds later the long, black vessel slipped smoothly below the surface of the Mediterranean Sea.

At cruising depth, the Captain approached his guests. "As you can see it's quite cramped in here. We're not used to taking on guests, but we'll try to make you as comfortable as we can until we reach our destination."

"Captain, where are we going?" Sophie asked.

"We will drop you off the coast of Spain. A contact will pick you up and take you to a private airport where a jet is waiting to take you to Washington D.C.

"In the meantime, Petty Officer Berks here will take you, ladies, to get sandwiches and hot drinks. Lieutenant Garrison will be taken to get dry clothes, and Commander McCade will have his injuries looked at by our medic."

Alex peeked through his swollen eye. "Captain, I'm fine."

"Why don't we let our medic decide that?"

"Yes, sir."

The Captain continued. "After you've eaten, you

will be taken to my private quarters and stay there until we reach our destination." The Captain looked at his watch. "Our ETA is roughly six hours. Any questions?"

A sailor appeared behind the Captain. "Sir, Admiral Carr is on the line and wishes to speak with Commander McCade."

"Certainly. Commander, please accompany this man."

Alex followed the sailor to the radio room. He was given a headset by the radio operator; he put it on and adjusted the lip mic. "Hello Admiral, this is Alex McCade."

"Alex, my boy, glad to hear you survived another one."

"Thank you, sir. So am I."

"Oh, just a moment; Senator McDaniel is with me. I'm going to put you on speakerphone."

"Hello, Alex. Can you hear me?"

"Yes senator, I hear you fine."

"How did it go? Was the mission a success?"

"A complete success. I'm happy to report that Sophie and Dr. Farah are safe."

"And the laser?"

"That too. We also have the bio/chem. canisters and the computer flash drives."

"Bravo," he replied happily. "What about Sebastian and Veck?"

"Sebastian is dead, sir. Not sure about Veck."

"Alex, this is Admiral Carr, Congratulations. I tell you; this deserves a special celebration when you get back."

"By celebration Admiral, do you mean a poker

game?"

"I sure do. It'll give me a chance to win back some of that money I lost between you and that scoundrel friend of yours."

Alex laughed.

The admiral continued. "When you get some rest under your belt, call my secretary, and we'll set up a time to play before you leave Washington."

"Will do, Admiral."

Senator McDaniel's voice came over the line, "Alex, I'll be there to pick you up when your flight arrives at Andrews Air Force Base. Sorry, there'll be no ticker tape parade, though heaven knows you deserve it."

"Thank you, Senator."

"Well, take care and enjoy the trip back. See you when you land."

"Thank you, sir," Alex replied. "Before you go, any word on the president?"

The senator's voice turned solemn. "It's not good. He's on life support. I hate to say it, but it's only a matter of time now."

"Sorry to hear that."

"We all are," replied the admiral in the background.

The men said their goodbyes and Alex handed the headset back to the radio operator. From the radio room, he was taken to the medic.

Upon having his wounds cleaned and a few stitches put in above his eye, he was given a couple of ice packs and allowed to leave.

He was shown to the mess where Mike and the others were gathered around a stainless steel table bolted to the floor. They ate sandwiches, drank coffee, and chatted. When Alex stepped into the room, the talking abruptly stopped.

Sophie shot to her feet. "Alex, how are you feeling?"

"Fine and dandy," he replied and tossed the ice packs in the garbage.

Dr. Farah scolded him. "Alex, you need those. It'll keep the swelling down."

"I know, but it'll get in the way of my eating, and I'm starved." He yanked the ham and cheese sandwich out of Mike's hands and took a big bite out of it.

"Hey, get your own," Mike yelled and snatched the sandwich back.

With full cheeks, Alex grinned.

He went to the twenty-gallon stainless steel coffee urn and poured himself a steaming cup. He nudged Mike over with his hip and sat down at the table.

Mike reflexively moved his sandwich a safe distance away. Alex grabbed another sandwich off the central plate and took a bite.

"What did the admiral have to say?" Mike asked.

Alex held up a finger. He sipped his coffee to wash down the food, and said, "He and Senator McDaniel congratulated us on a job well done. Oh, and Admiral Carr mentioned he's looking for an opportunity to win his money back before we leave Washington."

"Win his money back? He's the worst card player I've ever seen," Mike said with a laugh, "but hey, I'll play anytime he wants to. I can always use the extra cash."

"Any word on the president?" Dr. Farah asked.

"It's not good. He's on life support, and they don't expect him to live much longer."

Dr. Farah slouched. "I feel so bad, but I created the laser system for humanitarian purposes. The laser was meant to only incapacitate the enemy; not to kill them." She shook her head. "It was President Grant's idea to experiment with those horrible chemical and biological agents."

Sophie had been quiet during this exchange. She took a sip of coffee with both hands wrapped around the mug. She set the cup down and said, "There may be a way to save the president."

Dr. Farah shook her head. "Dear, as much as we would all like to help him, I'm afraid there is no cure for Ricin poisoning."

"But I may know a way. I deciphered the Mayan codex at Alex's house, and I learned something quite extraordinary. The codex focuses entirely on the life of the greatest, richest, most powerful Mayan king ever known, Kan Ajaw K'uhul, a.k.a.--the Divine Serpent King."

"Okay, but what does this have to do with saving the president?" Dr. Farah asked.

"The codex also tells of the king's hoard of treasure he'd hidden in the city. And most importantly, the one item the king valued far above all others. A medicine that can cure all illness and disease."

Mike rolled his eyes and groaned. "You can't be serious."

She quickly scolded him. "I am—so hush. It's been documented that ancient Mayan healers made hundreds of medicines from rainforest plants in order to treat headaches, toothaches, earaches, stomach ailments, fever, diarrhea, burn ointments, and more.

"Even today, modern pharmaceutical companies are looking to rainforest plants to help them develop new medicines to treat AIDS, diabetes, and cancer, to name a few.

"So, I believe that it's not beyond the realm of possibility that the king, or one of his healers hit upon the right plant, or combination of plants to create some type of 'super-medicine'. And the more I think about it, the more I believe it could be true."

Dr. Farah nodded thoughtfully. "If this medicine does exist, what an incredible benefit it would be for all mankind."

Alex's mouth dropped open. "Doctor, you of all people must think this is a bit farfetched."

"Not really. As a woman of science, I believe that all things are possible until proven otherwise."

Alex paused. "Okay, for argument's sake, let's say this medicine does exist, and it's hidden with the king's treasure--how are we supposed to find it? The Spaniards couldn't find it. Sebastian couldn't find it. What makes you think we can find it?"

"Because we have something they didn't—two clues," Sophie answered. The first clue states that 'the pathway to the treasure starts where the king is born.'"

"Do you know where the king was born?" Mike asked.

Alex turned to his friend. "She didn't say *was* born, she said *is* born."

"What's the difference?"

"The difference between finding the treasure and not finding the treasure."

Sophie nodded. "Alex is right. And yes, I do know where the king is born."

Alex snapped his fingers. "The inner chamber of the pyramid."

"That's right," she replied. "Inside the pyramid is a painting representing the birth of the king."

"Do you think the treasure is hidden behind that painting?" Dr. Farah asked.

"I do."

"It can't be that simple. What's the second clue?" Mike asked.

"The second clue states, 'the key to finding the treasure lies with the golden scepter.'"

"What's the golden scepter?"

"A staff that once belonged to the king. It symbolized his divine right as ruler."

Alex asked, "How is this scepter supposed to help us find the treasure and lead us to the medicine?"

"I don't know," Sophie admitted, "but, if want to find the medicine we have to bring the scepter with us to the jungle city."

"Do you know where this scepter is?"

"I do. It's in a museum in Mexico City."

Mike interjected. "I see a pretty big problem. How on earth are you going to get a priceless artifact like that out of the museum?"

"I have a way."

"Mind telling us what that is?"

She grinned. "I'm just going ask for it."

Mike coughed. "You're just going to ask for it?"

Alex shook his head. "Sophie, even with your credentials, I sincerely doubt that you can simply walk into the museum, ask for the scepter, and expect to get it."

"I think I can. You see, the director of the museum happens to be my dear, old college professor, Dr. Rafael Montoya."

"Not enough."

"Maybe not, but I know what will be."

"That he's a sucker for a beautiful woman?"

"No, that he has spent his entire life searching for the lost Mayan city of Kan Ajaw K'uhul and I can show him right where it is."

Alex raised an eyebrow. "Maybe there's a chance after all."

"I think it's worth a shot," Mike said. "I'm always up for a good treasure hunt."

Alex agreed. He took one last sip of coffee and rose from the table.

Sophie looked at him strangely. "Where are you going?"

"Back to the radio room. If we're doing this, we're going to need some help."

39

The submarine surfaced off the coast of Spain just before sunrise and Alex and the others transferred to a waiting speedboat. The boat shuttled them ashore and left them standing at the edge of a forest.

When the speedboat motored away, a man stepped from the trees. "I am Sergio Lamas," he said with a Spanish accent. "Come with me."

The Spaniard led them through the woods, to a van parked a half-mile away. The four got into the back of the van. The man drove to a small local airport and dropped them off beside a waiting jet.

One minute, thirty seconds later, they were airborne and, on their way, back to the United States.

Nine hours later, the aircraft landed at Andrews Air Force Base, an airfield located just outside Washington D.C. The pilot taxied the aircraft to a remote location and stopped next to a black sedan with tinted windows.

Alex stepped from the plane with the laser case in hand, and Senator McDaniel got out of his car to greet him.

"Welcome home," the senator said and then he got a look at Alex's battered face. "My god, are you alright? You didn't tell me you were injured."

Alex brushed it off. "I'm fine. Veck and I got into a

little scrape, that's all."

"I hope he got the worse of it."

Alex smiled with swollen lips. "He sure did."

Mike stepped from the plane, followed by Dr. Farah and Sophie. The senator scanned them from head to toe. "I'm glad to see the rest of you made it in good shape."

Dr. Farah approached the senator. "I want to thank you. Alex tells me you were responsible for our rescue."

"I did what I could," he replied modestly. "I'm just happy you made it home safe and sound."

Alex motioned at the senator's sedan. "Do you want the case in the trunk?"

"No, no," he answered quickly, "the backseat will be fine."

Alex shrugged and walked to the side door. He opened it, set the case inside, and closed the door. Alex eyed the senator. "Were you able to do what I asked?"

The senator removed an envelope from his pocket. "The travel documents you requested."

"And the plane?"

"You'll be taking this same one you flew in on. A new flight crew is in route. After they arrive and the plane's been refueled, you'll be on your way to Mexico City."

"And our return trip?"

"The plane will be waiting for you at La Aurora International Airport in Guatemala City."

"Excellent."

The senator shook Alex's hand. "Good luck. I hope you find what you're looking for."

"So do I."

Senator McDaniel gestured toward the car. "Dr.

Farah, shall we?"

"Just a moment," she replied. She gave Alex a sweet kiss on the cheek as she hugged him. She did the same to Mike and then said, "I'll never forget what you've done. Thank you."

"You're welcome," they replied.

Then, the two women embraced. "I'm going to miss you, dear," said Dr. Farah.

"I'll miss you too," replied Sophie. "Take care of yourself."

"I hope you're right about the medicine."

"Me, too."

Dr. Farah got into the passenger seat, and Senator McDaniel got behind the wheel. Alex expected the senator to have a driver, but he supposed after years of having one, it was probably nice to get behind the wheel and drive himself for a change.

As the senator started the engine, Alex rapped his knuckles on the passenger window. It lowered. "Senator, I almost forgot. Will you pass on some information to the FBI for me?"

"Certainly, what is it?"

"Tell them Sebastian has another partner besides Dr. Valerius."

"Another partner? Did he say who?"

"Only that it was a prominent member of our own government."

"Well, that is interesting," the senator said. "I'll pass it on first chance I get."

"Thank you."

The senator tossed a wave. Alex backed away from the vehicle, and the senator drove away.

40

Four hours later, the jet carrying Alex, Mike and Sophie landed safely at the Mexico City International Airport.

After deplaning and passing through Mexican Customs and Immigration, the three exited the terminal and jumped into a taxi.

Sophie leaned forward and said to the driver, *"Nos lleva a 'Museo Nacional De Antropologia' por favor. Tengo mucha prisa."*

"Si," the driver replied. He set the meter and pulled away from the curb.

"How far to the museum?" Alex asked.

"Depending on the traffic; about thirty minutes."

"And you're sure the scepter is still at the museum?"

"Positive."

"What's this scepter look like, anyway?" Mike asked.

Her eyes lit up. "The scepter was made in the image of a feathered serpent. It's about three feet long and unbelievably beautiful. The head is made of solid gold, and the shaft is hardwood covered in thick gold leaf.

"The serpent's mouth is open and has protruding golden fangs. Its eyes are inset with fiery red gems that glow blood red when the light hits them just right. Some say, that when the eyes glow, it's the spirit of the serpent coming alive from within."

"Sound's incredible."

"It is."

"How did it end up in a museum?"

"It was stolen by a Spanish Captain named Alejandro de Aguilar. It's a heck of a story if you want to hear it."

Both men nodded.

Her voice took on a soft, almost magical tone. "It was the year 1502, and Spain's treasury had been nearly depleted by war. The king badly needed to replenish it, so he chose a cunning and ruthless man, Captain Alejandro de Aguilar, to take men and search foreign lands for treasure on behalf of the Spanish crown.

"The Captain was given one ship and fifty conquistadors. He chose his route and then set sail for the coast of Central America.

"When the ship arrived, they set anchor and used rowboats to go ashore. Immediately they came upon a group of poor Mayans. The Captain asked where riches could be found. The leader of the Maya told them of a very beautiful, very rich city located deep in the jungle, but--he added a stern warning, he said the king was very powerful, and he had thousands of fierce, unbeatable warriors who protected the city.

"The Captain's lust for treasure was so great that he ignored the leader's warning. The next morning, he hired a couple of locals to guide them to the city of Kan Ajaw K'uhul.

"After a long, treacherous trip through the jungle, they stopped in front of a river, separating themselves from the city. Mayan priests came to meet them. Captain Aguilar, as a ruse, asked to set up a meeting with their king to talk trade.

"The priests relayed the message and returned. Kan Ajaw K'uhul agreed to meet with the Captain.

"However, only the Captain and one aide would be allowed to cross the river and enter the city. The Captain agreed. He chose one trusted man to accompany him, and the Mayan priests led them across the river, into the city, and into the palace.

"According to the Captain's journal, they stepped inside the throne room and were astonished to see their magnificent king sitting upon a mighty throne cushioned by jaguar skins.

"The king was an impressive figure. He wore a colored feathered headdress, and a necklace of a two-headed flat snake, the Mayan symbol of royalty. In his hand, he gripped the magnificent golden scepter. The Captain said it was the most beautiful object he had ever seen.

"On a pretext to start negotiations, Captain Aguilar approached the king with a gift--a basket of colorful beads. The king's bodyguards stopped him, inspected the basket and then let him pass.

"When the Captain drew close to the king, he plunged his hand to the bottom of the basket and pulled out a sharp dagger. He lunged and pressed the blade to the king's throat.

"The Captain ordered everyone back and threatened to kill the king if his wishes were not obeyed. Captain Aguilar then ripped the golden scepter out of the king's hand and proclaimed himself ruler of the city."

Mike laughed. "That guy had some balls."

"He sure did," Alex agreed. "So what happened next?"

"The Captain brought the rest of his men into the city. Then they went about ransacking it and searching for the king's massive treasure vault. But there was a problem...they couldn't find it. So they began torturing the king's staff and other officials in order to learn of the treasures' whereabouts. However, this method didn't work either.

"The Captain was enraged. He threatened to kill the king's family if he wasn't told where the treasure was. Possibly thinking it was an idle threat, the king refused once again.

"Unfortunately, the frustrated Spanish Captain kept his word and murdered the king's two young sons and his pregnant wife in the center of the main plaza.

"When Kan Ajaw K'uhul learned of this horrible deed, he screamed an order for all to hear--all the Spaniards were to die even if it meant his own death.

"The Maya warriors responded and quickly overran the Spaniards. With so few in number, the Spaniards retreated from the city. The conquistadors made it as far as the river before the warriors overtook them. A violent clash ensued.

"Minutes later, thirty conquistadors lay dead, and twenty were taken prisoner and marked for sacrifice. Only one man escaped the onslaught--Captain Aguilar. And with him...the king's golden scepter.

"The warriors relentlessly pursued the Captain through the jungle, but he somehow managed to stay ahead of them.

"Eight days later, exhausted, hungry, and nearly dead, the Captain arrived at the coast. He planned to use one of the rowboats he and his men used to come ashore, but he discovered they had been destroyed. Then, he did the only thing he could do. He tucked the scepter into his belt and swam for his ship.

"Arrows rained down on him from shore, but none

hit him, and he made it safely to his ship."

"Incredible," Mike said.

Alex nodded in agreement.

"A month and a half later, the ship arrived in Spain. Upon hearing the news of the Captain's return, the king of Spain immediately summoned him to the castle. Captain Aguilar told the king of the amazing jungle city and of the incredible wealth just waiting to be taken.

"As proof of the city's riches, he presented the king with the golden scepter. The king was said to be overwhelmed by the gift, and he immediately offered the Captain a greater share if he would go back and get the treasure. The Captain agreed, but he said he would need many, more men to do it.

"The request was granted.

"As a gesture of his appreciation, the king presented the Captain with a silver medallion. On the front of the medallion was the image of the Virgin Mary, a religious icon meant to keep him safe on his journey. On the back was his engraved initials: '*A.d.A.*'

"A month later, the Captain, six ships, and a large army of men sailed from the harbor and…"

Mike was on the edge of his seat. "Then what?"

Sophie smiled. "…and they were never heard from again."

"You've got to be kidding!"

Sophie laughed. "Really. There was speculation, of course. Some thought the Captain's ships went down in a violent storm at sea. Others thought the Captain and his men got the treasure, but then kept it for themselves and never returned to Spain."

"What do you think happened?" Alex asked.

"I honestly don't know, but that same scepter that

Captain Aguilar stole and presented to the king of Spain is waiting for us at the museum."

41

The taxi driver turned off the busy street and continued into a hilly wooded area of Chapultepec Park.

The driver followed the winding road and a short while later pulled up to a large, white, two-story building with a sign out front that read, *'Museo Nacional De Antropologia.'*

It was getting close to closing time, so they had to hurry. Sophie paid the driver. She told him, in Spanish, to wait and they got out of the car.

The three went up to the museum and looked up at a large banner hanging over the main entrance. *'Must See! Today in the main exhibit hall! The Royal Spanish collection of Mesoamerican artifacts. Featuring—the priceless Golden Scepter of the Serpent King!'*

They entered the museum and stepped into a large central patio serving as the lobby. Sophie approached the ticket window and spoke to the lady behind the counter. "*Hola, Dr. Montoya esta aqui?*"

"*Su nombre, por favor?*"

"*Me llamo*, Dr. Sophie Marcus."

The young woman nodded and picked up the telephone.

Alex nudged Sophie. "Are you sure he's here?"

"He's always here. The man is extremely dedicated."

The woman spoke on the phone for a moment and then hung up. "*Ahora enseguida viene, Dr. Montoya.*"

"*Muchas Gracias,*" Sophie replied.

"What did she say?"

"He'll be with us shortly."

Sophie picked up a museum brochure from the stack on the counter and began paging through it while Alex and Mike strolled around the lobby. The two men stopped in front of an umbrella-shaped fountain, consisting of a single pillar with cascading water.

Alex noticed an elderly man coming down the stairs. He appeared to be well into his seventies. He had hunched shoulders and wore round spectacles. He was dressed in brown corduroy slacks and a wrinkled short-sleeve shirt that looked like he had slept in it the night before.

Alex called out, "Sophie, is that the professor?"

Sophie lowered the brochure, "That's him."

She and the others went to the bottom of the staircase and waited.

When the elderly man hit the bottom step, there were tears in his eyes. The man immediately embraced Sophie. "My dear, I can't believe you're here. When I heard your expedition went missing, I naturally assumed the worst."

"I'm alright professor, but my team wasn't so lucky."

"What happened?"

"I'll tell you another time, if that's okay?"

"Certainly," he replied and embraced her again. "It's so good to see you."

She gestured. "These are my friends, Alex McCade and Mike Garrison."

"Nice to meet you, gentlemen," he said and lingered on Alex's battered face. "What happened to you, young man?"

Alex smiled. "Fell down some stairs."

"You ought to be more careful," he replied simply.

The professor turned to Sophie. "Dear, I watched your National Geographic TV special over and over again just to see your face. I must say you looked wonderful."

"I doubt that. My hair was a mess, and I was caked in seven layers of mud."

"To me, that's when you look your best," he said chuckling.

"Professor, I'd like to talk to you about something. Can we talk in your office?"

"By all means, come this way. We'll take the elevator." He hiked a thumb at Alex. "I don't think your friend needs to be going near stairs anytime soon."

They rode the elevator to the second floor. They stepped out, and the professor led them down the hall.

Reaching his office, he escorted them inside. It was just the kind of office Alex expected out of an old college professor. The room smelled of pipe tobacco, and his desk was cluttered with papers, and stacks of open books. Dusty artifacts lined the shelves, and old photos of the professor on past digs hung in tilted frames on the wall.

The professor closed the door and gestured to a chair in front of his desk. "Please have a seat."

Sophie sat in the chair. Alex and Mike stood behind her.

Professor Montoya went behind his desk and sat down. He clasped his hands together on top of his desk and leaned forward. "Now my dear, what can I do for you?"

"I need to ask a favor."

"Certainly; what is it?"

"I want to borrow Kan Ajaw K'uhul's golden scepter."

"What?" he gulped. All the color seemed to drain from his face at once. "You mean...take it out of the museum?"

Sophie nodded. "Just for a few days."

He laughed weakly and then realized she wasn't kidding. "I'm afraid that's out of the question. Do you know what would happen to me if anyone found out?"

"No one will."

"But..." The professor took a deep breath. "Okay, let's just say I remove our priceless, star attraction from the exhibit. Don't you think people will notice?"

"You could say it is being cleaned, or something."

He appeared flustered. "Sophie, if you wish to examine the scepter, I will gladly arrange for that, but to take it out of the museum well...it's simply not possible."

"Not even if I told you that I found the City of the Kan Ajaw K'uhul?"

He waved her off. "Sophie, it's not kind to tease an old man like that."

"No kidding professor; I really found it."

His eyes burst open. "You found it?"

"I did."

"Oh my god," he said jumping up from his chair. "Where is it? Mexico...El Salvador? I always thought it was in Belize."

"Guatemala."

"Guatemala--I knew it!" Unable to contain his excitement, he came around the desk. "What's it like?"

Sophie stood and matched his level of excitement. "It's incredible! You should see..."

Alex tapped Sophie's shoulder. "We don't have much time."

She bit her lip and got herself back on track. "Professor, I'm sorry but we're in a big hurry, and I need to bring the king's scepter with us to the city."

"But why?"

"Because I have good reason to believe the scepter will lead us to Kan Ajaw K'uhul's treasure."

Alex was glad she didn't mention the medicine. No sense clouding the issue. He still had trouble believing it, and he didn't know what the professor would make of it.

"The treasure? You know where the treasure is, too?"

"I have a good idea, but I need the scepter to find it. Professor, will you let me take it?"

The professor slipped a wrinkled handkerchief from his pocket and mopped his brow. He muttered to himself and then looked at Sophie. "Wait here." He opened the door, paused, and then walked out and closed the door behind him.

Sophie beamed, "He's going to do it."

"Either that, or he's getting security to come and throw us out of here," Mike replied.

Ten minutes later the office door opened, and Dr. Montoya strode in with the king's golden scepter in his hands. Alex stared at the scepter. It was even more beautiful than Sophie described.

"Incredible isn't it?" She whispered.

The professor closed the door. "You have to

promise me that you'll have it back in three days."

"I promise."

"Also, I am attaching two conditions. Number one, when you find the treasure, I want my museum to be the first in line to show it."

"That goes without saying," she replied.

"Number two, the first chance you get--I want you to take me to the city."

"I'd love to."

The professor removed an old violin case from the closet. He swept aside some papers from his desk and set the case down. He fit the case with a strap, removed a violin from the case, and then carefully wrapped the golden scepter in black velvet used for displays.

With the scepter safely swaddled, he gently placed it inside the case and closed the lid. He flipped the latches and then handed the case to Sophie. "Don't let anything happen to this."

"I won't."

The professor pushed aside a large potted tree in the rear of his office. The space revealed a door. He opened the door and turned on the light to a descending stairwell.

"Press 7-9-3-1 into the security pad at the bottom of the stairs. That door will lead out the side of the building."

Sophie kissed him on the cheek. "Thank you, professor."

"You're welcome. Good luck and be careful."

The three hurried down the stairs. Alex punched in the code, and they exited the side door of the museum.

They followed the sidewalk to the front of the building and then hopped inside the waiting taxi. Sophie gave the driver the directions to their next destination.

With the taxi underway, she leaned back in her seat and let out a big sigh of relief.

Alex chuckled. "When you asked to borrow the king's scepter, the professor's face turned so pale I thought he was going to pass out."

She laughed. "Poor professor, I don't think he's going to get much sleep over the next few days."

"Then again, neither are we."

42

The taxi stopped on a dirt road on the edge of a farmer's field. Sophie paid the driver. They got out and watched the taxi drive away.

In the dark, amid the sound of chirping crickets, Sophie turned to Alex and asked, "Who are we meeting?"

"His name is Hernando Lopez; an old friend of my father's. The man runs a helicopter charter service in Belize. He was the one flying Mike and I to the jungle resort when Dr. Farah's plane went down."

"What's he like?"

"He's a good man, but most importantly he can get us what we need and take us to the city-- no questions asked."

A flashlight beam flickered from across the field "There he is," Alex said, "let's go."

The three made their way across the field to the tree line where they were met by a man in his 60's with brown, weathered skin.

He was dressed in worn leather cowboy boots, faded blue jeans, and a big shiny belt buckle. With a slight tip of his cowboy hat, he said, "*Hola amigos*, it is good to see you again."

"*Hola Hernando,*" the men replied.

The man raised his flashlight beam on Alex's face. "What happened to you?"

"I wish people would stop asking me that. I'm fine."

"I bet the other guy wasn't."

"You got that right."

Hernando turned and raised his eyebrows dramatically. "My, who is this beautiful *senorita?*"

Alex gestured. "Hernando Lopez, meet Sophie Marcus." Hernando grinned and shook her hand.

"*Con mucho gusto,*" he said.

"*El gusto es mio,*" she replied.

"You are a woman of many talents. You speak Spanish and, you are a musician as well."

"Musician? What?"

He nodded at the violin case she had strapped on her back.

"Oh, um...yes."

"Maybe you could play for me sometime?"

"Maybe I will."

Alex addressed Hernando. "Did you get everything I requested?"

"*Si,* come with me; I'll show you."

By flashlight, Hernando led them through the trees and into the next field where his helicopter sat.

Reaching the chopper, Hernando opened the rear door and pulled out two large green duffle bags. Alex and Mike each took a bag and inspected the contents.

"Looks good," Alex said.

"Here too," Mike replied.

Hernando eyed the men. "With this kind of

hardware, you must be expecting trouble."

"I hope not," Alex replied, although he knew that running into the natives was a real and frightening possibility.

Alex and Mike put the bags in the chopper. Alex handed Hernando a piece of paper. "Here are the GPS coordinates that I got from the DELTA chopper pilot."

"Very good."

"Another thing Hernando," Alex said. "Fly low, we don't want to attract attention."

Hernando grinned. "*Senor*...that is what I do best."

When everyone boarded, Hernando started the engine and then guided the chopper into the air.

Once the helicopter reached cruising altitude, Alex unfastened his seatbelt and met the others in the rear cargo section. He opened the first green duffle bag and dug in. He handed out camouflage fatigues, tactical vests, socks, and boots.

After getting dressed, Alex reached into the same bag again. This time he removed lighters, flashlights, emergency locator beacons, and water-filled canteens. The last items: radio earpieces and throat mics.

He made sure everyone had a set, including Hernando, and then he made a quick test to ensure they worked properly.

From the second duffle bag, Alex removed two AK-47's, along with two .45 caliber pistols with holsters, two boot-knifes, and extra ammunition.

After he and Mike inspected the weapons, the three stretched out on the floor, closed their eyes, and tried to get a little shut-eye before they arrived.

Shortly after midnight, they arrived at their destination. Hernando lowered the aircraft and hovered above the treetops. "*Amigos*, we are here."

Alex got up. He immediately strapped into the harness. He slung the strap of the AK-47 over his shoulder and turned on his headlamp. He exited the aircraft and a few moments later, pressed his throat mic. "I'm ready."

"Good luck," Hernando replied. He started the winch, and the cable lowered.

Alex slipped through the artificial vegetation mounted on top of the retractable roof. After descending twelve feet through the foliage, his boots met a solid structural beam.

He pushed off the roof framing and continued downward until he landed on the grassy surface of the Mayan ball court.

He swung his headlamp, aimed at the base of the stone wall and then raised it to the top. He turned in a complete circle and scanned the surrounding jungle. Seeing nothing, he slipped the AK-47 off his shoulder and got out of the harness.

He spoke into the microphone. "Bring it up." The cable retracted.

Sophie was next. She landed on the ball court with the violin case strapped to her back. Mike followed. When all three stood side by side on the ball court, Alex radioed Hernando and the cable retracted for the final time.

An eerie silence fell over the jungle as the chopper flew away. Alex felt uneasy. It was probably his imagination, but he suddenly felt a thousand eyes staring at him from the darkness. "I'll take point," he said. "Mike, you in the rear, Sophie in the middle. Sophie, if we run into trouble, get down and let Mike and I handle it."

The two nodded.

Alex led the way off the ball court with the others following. He paid close attention to his surroundings and swung his headlamp to both sides of the trail as he walked. He listened carefully and smelled the air. He needed all his senses working at their best to avoid an ambush. In the dark is where they were most vulnerable to attack. He would have preferred a daytime mission, but they did not have the luxury of waiting. The president was dying.

They continued down the trail. Ahead, Alex held up a fist. The group stopped. After ten seconds of silence, he waved them forward.

When they arrived at the wall of skulls, Alex eased through the doorway with his AK-47 pushed out front. He scanned the area and then waved his friends through. As they neared the palace, Sophie screamed.

Alex wheeled around and what he saw scared him more than native warriors charging. There was an empty spot behind Sophie. Mike was nowhere to be seen.

"Where did he go?" Alex asked.

"I don't know. I just looked back and he was gone."

Alex dashed back down the trail. His head was on a swivel. His eyes darted to the ground, through vegetation, and up in the trees. There was no sign of him. How the hell could someone disappear like that? Those damn natives were deadly as snakes and moved as quietly as ghosts.

He ran through the doorway of the wall of skulls and charged into the vegetation. The shaft of light from his headlamp snapped back and forth. He beat back palms and searched around trees. Still no sign of him.

He didn't care how much noise he made now; the natives already knew they were there. He cupped his hands around his mouth and yelled, "Mike? Mike?"

Sophie caught up to him. "Alex, we'll find him."

He whirled around. "Before or after they kill him?"

She laid a calming hand on his shoulder. "We still have time. The Maya don't kill their captives right away."

Alex swore under his breath. What chance did they really have? He knew he could never find the natives if they didn't want to be found. There are millions of places in the jungle to hide. He paced back and forth, twisting the wedding ring on his finger as he walked. He had to calm himself down and think clearly.

He paced for a few more moments and then it occurred to him. He spun on his heels and began hiking back toward the city center.

"Alex, where are you going?"

He stopped and turned. "We don't have to look for the natives. We do what we came here to do. We find the king's treasure--and they'll come to us."

"And then?"

"We'll figure that out when the time comes."

As they arrived at the pyramid, the two immediately hiked up the steep staircase.

Once on top, Sophie led the way inside the temple, stepped into the hole and descended the ancient inner staircase. Alex followed.

When she reached the bottom of the stairs, she walked directly to the back of the chamber. She aimed her headlamp at the Mayan painting of the nude figure rising above a crack in the earth which represented the king's birth. "This is it," she said.

Alex stepped up to the painting. "How do we open this thing?"

Sophie carefully examined the outside edges of the

painting and then backed away in disappointment. "I was hoping to find some cracks or something around the painting indicating a passage, but there's nothing."

"What do we do now?" Alex asked.

"Look around the chamber for some type of lever; something that might cause it to open."

Minutes passed as they searched.

"I didn't find anything," Alex said.

"Neither did I," Sophie replied.

She went back to the painting of the rising king. "I hate to do this, but it's the only way."

"What is?"

"I want you to place your hands on the middle of the painting and push. But please be careful, this is a very rare and valuable painting."

Alex leaned his AK-47 against the side wall. Then, standing in front of the painting of the rising king, he placed his hands in the middle.

"Alright," Sophie said. "Push."

Alex put his back into it and pushed, but the wall didn't budge.

"Push harder," she urged.

He reset his feet and pushed harder.

"More," she yelled. Then she joined him and pushed. They gave it all they had. Soon the plaster around the painting began to crack and chip.

"Keep going--it's moving!" she shouted with excitement.

Alex and Sophie kept pushing and the painted stone block began sliding inward. A one-inch gap soon appeared.

"Keep pushing," she shouted. She peered into the

widening space with her light. "There's a room back there."

Alex kept pushing by himself. It was difficult, not only because the stone was heavy but also because it moved on an incline. He gave it all he had, and soon the gap grew into a two feet wide space.

"Hold it, right there," she said. She squeezed her shoulders through, then pulled the rest of her slender frame into the opening and disappeared behind the wall.

"What do you see?" Alex asked.

"A room."

"Treasure?"

"No," she replied sadly, "it's empty."

"Maybe that Spanish Captain and his men found the treasure after all," he said.

"Wait, I see a flight of stairs in the back of the room."

Alex grunted. "Sophie, hurry up. This stone keeps trying to slide back into place. I don't know how much longer I can hold it open."

"There's a latch back here. If you push the stone in another foot, it should catch."

Alex strained his muscles and managed to push the slab inward another ten inches. Then he heard a soft 'click.'

"That's it," she said.

He removed his hands and the block of stone stayed in place. He snatched his rifle. As he stepped through the opening, his boots crunched on something hard lying on the floor.

He shone his light down and found it littered with small bones. He picked one up. "Stingray spines? What are these doing here?"

"They were used in Mayan blood rituals," Sophie replied. "Men of royalty used the spines to poke holes in their penises and draw blood."

Alex's face contorted. "You've got to be kidding."

"No, I'm not," she said with a twinkle.

Alex and Sophie crept forward and gazed down the back staircase; even with the bright beams of their headlamps, they couldn't see the bottom.

From behind came a loud '*Crack*!' Then the grating sound of stone-on-stone.

The latch holding the doorway had broken loose and the stone block was sliding back into place. Alex dashed to the wall.

He wrapped his fingers around the edge and pulled, but the large stone was too heavy. It slammed shut. His eyes darted around the area looking for another way to open the doorway.

"Damn, we're sealed in," he said.

Sophie turned toward the rear staircase. "Looks like we have no choice but to see where this staircase leads."

43

Alex was content to let Sophie lead the way. This was her world, and she knew it better than anyone.

He watched as she brushed aside thick layers of cobwebs and descend the staircase. When they reached the bottom, Sophie shone her light down an eerie passage. It was lined with smooth stone blocks coated in centuries of accumulated dust.

She eased forward scrutinizing her surroundings as she went. There was no telling what kind of booby traps the Maya engineers had laid.

Ahead, in the middle of the pathway, the beam of her headlamp landed on a skeleton strapped to a wooden frame.

A sharp, obsidian-tipped spear was strapped into one hand and a shield made of tortoiseshell was strapped into the other. Wisps of black hair still clung to the yellowing skull. Its jaw hung open as if stopped in the middle of a terrifying scream.

This was a guardian of the tunnel; a sentinel meant to scare away intruders. Sophie stopped for a moment to inspect the skeleton and then moved past it, unfazed.

Twenty steps ahead, she stopped in the passage and held out her hand. "Let me have your backpack."

Alex took off his backpack and handed it to her.

Like a bowler, Sophie brought her arm back, slid her foot forward and let the bag go. It slid down the tunnel, skipping over barely visible stone nubs in the floor.

Poisonous darts shot out from holes and then ricocheted off the opposite wall and dropped to the floor.

Alex took in a deep breath. Sophie on the other hand, acted like she had seen something like this a thousand times before. Without speaking, they continued down the passage.

They came to a short flight of steps, walked down and entered an octagonal-shaped room with extraordinary and vibrantly painted stone walls. But the centerpiece of the whole display was an exquisite statue of a coiled serpent.

The serpent's body was curled into four tightly wrapped coils, with a short tail. The statue measured four-feet high by eight-feet in length and was placed directly in the center of the room.

Sophie strolled around the statue, and her headlamp reflected off the beautifully painted surface of reds, blacks, greens, and gold colors.

She stopped and examined holes bored into the stone coils. The holes went in a circular pattern around each coil with each hole about an inch and a half in diameter and approximately six inches deep.

"What are those holes for?" Alex asked.

"I'm not sure," she replied. She blew dust away from some holes and as the dust cleared tiny etched carvings appeared. "Hieroglyphics," she muttered.

"What do they mean?" Alex asked.

"This one means bird. The one below it means star." She stood back and cast her eyes on the statue. "Images were an important part of the Mayan culture.

Their images had specific meanings, so there must be a reason for this serpent statue to be here."

"What does the serpent represent?"

"There are a couple of meanings. The Mayan's believed that the serpent represented renewed life. For instance, when a serpent or snake loses its skin, life begins anew. The serpent also represents the link between the living world and the underground world; a place where their gods live."

Her face lit up. "This could be the transition point; the point we leave the living world and enter the underground world of the gods."

"But it's a dead end."

"I don't think so. I think there must be a doorway somewhere."

Alex moved around the room pushing on the wall. It worked once, maybe the same method could work again. After one unsuccessful turn around the room, he leaned his back on the wall, frustrated.

He had absolutely no idea how to open the passage. And what did he really know about the Maya? Not much. If they were going to solve this mystery it was up to Sophie.

He watched her studying the statue and thought about Mike. Was he dead? Was he hanging from a tree? Maybe it was a mistake to come here after all. Finding this 'cure-all' drug was a long shot from the beginning. And what did they have to base it all on? A 500-year- old book? What the ancient Maya considered a 'cure-all' drug might be today's equivalent of an aspirin.

"Did the codex mention anything about a statue?" Alex asked.

"No," she replied. "The codex provided us with two clues: The first being, 'the pathway to the treasure starts where the king is born'. That got us this far. The second clue: 'the key to finding the treasure lies with the golden scepter'."

Sophie knelt beside the statue and stared at it for nearly two minutes. Alex was about to speak when her eyes widened, and her body jolted upright. "Oh, my God!

"What?"

"I get it."

"Get what?"

"I can't believe I didn't think of this sooner."

"What?"

"The statue must have a locking mechanism to open a hidden doorway." She turned and smiled. "And how do you open a locked door?"

"With a key. The scepter is the key!"

Sophie carefully removed the golden scepter from the violin case.

Kneeling beside the statue, she raised the scepter above a hole in the first hump. Cautiously, she lowered it into the hole and twisted the serpent headpiece. The bottom of the shaft locked perfectly into place.

Grabbing the shaft with both hands, she pulled downward--and the stone hump began to rotate.

Alex cheered. "You're a genius! The snake's humps are like tumblers of a lock. All we have to do is line up the right symbols on top of each hump, and the door should open, right?"

"Right," she replied, "but we still have a problem. We don't know the combination. One wrong symbol might trigger a cave-in."

Sophie stood back from the statue and began pacing back and forth. "The statue is a serpent," she muttered.

"The serpent image was also used to represent the Mayan god Kukulkan."

"Who?" Alex asked.

She lifted her eyes. "Kukulkan is the all-powerful god of the four basic elements--earth, air, fire, and water."

Alex pointed at the statue. "Four elements--four humps."

Sophie closely examined the hieroglyphics on the serpent's coils. "They're all here."

"Then let's do it."

"But what if we're wrong?"

"We'll never know until we try," he said.

Sophie nodded. She grabbed the shaft of the scepter and pulled down until MAIZE, the symbol for earth, appeared on top. She removed the scepter, placed it into the second coil, and rotated it until VULTURE, the symbol for air was on top.

Next, she located the hieroglyphic symbol for fire, LIZARD, and rotated the third coil. On the fourth and final coil, she pulled down and watched as FISH, the symbol for water, rotated to the top.

The moment all four symbols aligned--there was a deafening--'CRACK!'

They cringed and waited for either the doorway to open or the ceiling to come crashing down, but nothing happened.

"Maybe the doorway is stuck," Alex said. "It's probably been centuries since it was last opened." He noted the direction the eyes of the serpent statue and followed its gaze to the wall. He began pushing.

While he struggled with the wall, Sophie considered the situation from another angle. She scanned the statue and stopped at the tail.

Without thinking, she grabbed the tail with both hands and pulled. There was an explosive crash, and she fell back under a thick cloud of dust.

As the dust settled, she sat up looking bewildered. Then she saw the open doorway and yelled, "We did it!"

Alex brushed the dust from his hair. "Good job, but next time… how about a little warning?"

She coughed. "I swear, I didn't think it would actually work."

Alex helped her to her feet. They moved to the open doorway together, and Sophie stopped to inspect it. She shone her light downward and shadows played off the recess in the floor where the heavy stone door had dropped.

She ran her hand along the inside edge of the doorway and felt small droplets of water seeping under the side slabs.

She turned to Alex. "This is ingenious. When I pulled on the serpent's tail, it released a pin, causing the stone door to drop into the floor. The weight of the dropping door caused these thinner stone plates to slide upward. These plates sealed off water stored in the walls, probably diverting water from an underground river."

"So if we tried to blast through, or put in the wrong combination, the tunnel would have flooded, and we would have drowned."

"Exactly."

Sophie retrieved the scepter and repacked it in the violin case. She slipped the straps over her shoulders and joined Alex.

Together, they stepped through the doorway and entered the mysterious underworld of the Maya.

44

Leaving behind the smooth walls of the pyramid, Sophie led him through a tunnel lined with jagged rock walls and uneven flooring.

She pointed out that the Mayan's often built their temples atop natural tunnels, as they believed it provided direct access to their gods.

As they ventured deeper into the tunnel, the walls narrowed and the ceiling began to slope downward, forcing them to bend at the waist.

Soon they had to drop to their hands and knees to keep moving forward. The ceiling continued to slope downward until all that remained was a single tunnel to crawl through.

Sophie shone her light into the hole. It was filled with a thick veil of stringy webs and crawling spiders.

"This has to be the way," she said. Without hesitation, she crawled into the narrow tunnel.

Alex took a deep breath, squeezed his shoulders together and entered the tunnel behind her. As he inched forward on his hands and knees, he felt spiders being squished under his palms. Spiders crawled inside his shirt, and he could feel their tiny legs skittering on his bare skin.

Twenty feet ahead, he burst out of the hole. He

jumped to his feet, raked his fingers through his hair and shook the spiders out of his shirt. As he did, something glittered under the beam of his headlamp.

He looked up and stared at enormous piles of treasure. Beautiful ceremonial masks lay with discs of pure gold and silver, intermixed with ornate obsidian knives, mirrors, bundles of green feathers, and exceptional beautiful terra cotta pots. There were shields made from tortoise shells, gold rings, gold necklaces, jade bracelets and much, much more.

"Sophie, you did it!" he exclaimed.

Sophie appeared to be in a trance; mesmerized by the dazzling display. She finally mumbled, "We found it."

Alex's light beam wasn't strong enough to see to the other end of the cave. There was no telling how large the cave was or how much treasure there actually was here.

He spotted unlit torches fixed upright on the walls. Taking out his lighter, he walked around the cave and lit each one until the entire cave was ablaze in the flickering torch light.

Sophie swiveled her head. "This place is enormous," she said and then began to inspect the piles of treasure.

"Sophie, we need to look for the medicine."

"That's right," she said after being temporally sidetracked.

"So how do we find it?"

"Look for a clay pot or urn with dried plants or powder inside." She pointed. "Let's start on the far end of the cave and work our way back."

The two hiked to the far end of the cave, passing huge mounds of treasure.

When they reached the end of the cave, Sophie spotted a figure in the shadows. At first glance, it appeared to be a skeleton tied to a wooden frame, like the one they passed earlier in the passage. But this one was different somehow.

She moved in for a closer look and examined it. "Alex, look at this. There is still skin on the bones. This one looks to be mummified."

Alex shone his light upon it. She was right. The skin looked like dried, crinkled parchment.

She pointed to strands of blondish-brown hair attached to the skull and then to the remains of a beard and mustache. "This is odd. This man isn't Maya. He's European."

She lifted tattered cloth covering the throat region. Underneath she found a medallion hanging by a chain. She slipped the medallion over the skull and examined it.

She rubbed tarnish off on the medallion. "It's made of silver," she said. She rubbed more and the image of the Virgin Mary appeared. She flipped it over, rubbed tarnish off, and read the initials engraved in the back. '*A.d.A.*'

Suddenly the man's eyes snapped open.

Sophie jumped back and screamed, "He's alive!"

Alex jumped back, too.

He raised his weapon, but the man didn't move. Alex leaned in for a closer look. The eyelids had opened, but the eye sockets were empty. He had definitely been dead a long time.

"Maybe it was a muscle reflex or a trick of the light," Alex said. Either way, it gave him the creeps.

She composed herself. "Do you know who this is?"

"Should I?"

"This is Alejandro de Aguilar, the Spanish Captain. The man who stole the king's scepter."

"From the story you told us about."

"Yes, and this proves beyond a shadow of doubt that the Captain and his men made it back here. Their ships didn't sink or sail off somewhere after stealing the treasure.

The Maya warriors must have captured him. And knowing the Mayans like I do, he was probably kept alive down here for years, made to stare at the treasure he so desperately wanted but could never obtain."

A fitting end, thought Alex. He stared at the remains of the Captain. This was the bastard who killed the king's pregnant wife and sons, and who knows what other atrocities he committed. It was a harsh end, but in Alex's opinion, the man got what he deserved.

Sophie pocketed the medallion and pointed to a tunnel opening behind the Captain's remains. "Let's see where this leads."

45

Alex and Sophie slipped by the remains of the Captain and hiked into the dark passage. The tunnel went for fifty feet and then opened into a large cathedral-like cavern. The space was filled with hundreds of stalactites and stalagmites.

In the darkness, they could hear the sound of rushing water from a subterranean river. They followed the sound of the river, passing shards of broken pottery, stingray spines, and clay dishes once used to burn incense.

They weaved between rocks and arrived on the edge of a cold, black river. Water rushed by and disappeared through the base of a rock wall some forty yards to their left.

Sophie looked right and her headlamp lit up a small structure on the riverbank. "It's an altar," she said. The altar was simple in design with one long flat stone slab atop two smaller ones.

She hurried to it. Alex followed.

When she arrived, she found a stone urn at the base of the altar. She lifted the heavy urn and shone her light upon it.

She read the hieroglyphics. "*Ah Uincir Dz'acab.*"

"Who?"

"The Mayan god of healing," she replied. She rotated the urn. On the back of the urn she read, "*Cit-Bolon-Tum*. The god of medicine. This has to be it. This has to be where they kept the medicine."

She set the urn on the stone altar and with great excitement she pulled on the lid, but it didn't budge. She tried again with the same result.

"Let me try," Alex said.

He leaned the rifle against the altar. He pulled on the lid, but it failed to move. Taking his knife, he slipped the tip of the blade under and pried upward. The lid lifted, slightly.

With a grunt of effort, he used his fingers, pulled, and the lid came off. He thrust his head over the opening, shone his light in…and his stomach dropped. The urn was empty. It had all been for nothing.

Sophie pulled the urn toward her and looked inside the urn. She bit her lip and stoically turned away. Alex felt as bad as she did. He didn't know what to say.

Noise on the far side of the cave drew their attention. They wheeled around just as torch-carrying native warriors stormed into the cavern. They were the same type he and Sophie had run into at the waterfall. They had the same severely wrinkled brown skin, deeply sloped heads, and black shoulder-length hair.

Approximately thirty warriors fanned out in a semicircle around the altar. They raised their weapons and stared at them with bulging yellow eyes.

Sophie pointed. "Alex, there's Mike."

Alex's eyes shifted to the back of the group and he saw a native holding a sharp, obsidian knife to his friend's throat. His calculation had been right. There was no need to look for the natives after they captured Mike. He knew that once they found the kings treasure, they'd come to them. But now that they arrived, he wasn't sure what he could do.

The warriors split their group in half, and a regal-looking man appeared wearing a stunning feathered headdress and a long cape made of snakeskin. In his ears hung large jade earrings and wore thick gold bands on his ankles and wrists. Around his neck hung the necklace of a flat, two-headed snake--the sign of Maya royalty.

The king walked through the middle of his warriors and stopped within twenty feet of the altar. The king eyed Alex and spoke in a language he had never heard before.

When he finished, Alex glanced at Sophie and whispered, "Did you catch any of that?"

"Some, but it's a very old dialect. From what I could tell, he said he wants the scepter that was stolen from them long ago, or we will be sacrificed to their gods."

Alex knew what he had to do. "Sophie, give me the scepter."

"Alex, we can't give it to him. I promised the professor I'd bring it back."

"We don't have a choice," Alex gestured, "as you can see our circumstances have changed."

Sophie reluctantly slipped the violin case off her shoulders. She laid it on the stone altar and opened it. She removed the wrapped relic.

As she pulled away the black velvet, the scepter's golden surface glistened in the torchlight. The natives gasped, and the leader's eyes widened in delight.

Sophie gave Alex the scepter.

As if in a trance, the king stepped forward and extended his hands to receive it.

Alex lifted the scepter to eye level. Without

warning, he turned, dashed to the edge of the subterranean river and thrust the golden scepter over the dark rushing water.

The horrified leader shrieked. He stumbled forward, clutching his heart.

Alex held the scepter firmly over the river and pointed to Mike. The Mayan leader understood immediately. He snapped an order and Mike was set free.

Mike hurried to Alex's side, rubbing his throat where the blade nicked him. "Thanks, buddy," Mike said. "Now, what?"

The angry leader moved in closer and thrust out his palm for the scepter.

Alex maintained his grip on the scepter over the water and said, "Sophie, tell him I'll give him the scepter if he lets us go."

Sophie nodded and apprehensively approached the king. She spoke.

The man in the headdress appeared surprised she could speak his language. "*Maktxel mi a k'ul?*" he asked.

She responded, and a dialogue ensued. Minutes later, she returned to the men with a big grin, which seemed completely out of place considering their dire circumstances.

Alex was perplexed. "What are you grinning about? Did you tell him our terms?"

"I did." She replied and then turned to look at the Mayan leader. "Do you know who that man is?"

"I assume he's their king."

"Yes, but not only that. He claims to be the Kan Ajaw K'uhul--the Serpent King."

"It can't be," Alex said. "I mean, he's extremely wrinkled and old looking, but that would make him over

500 years old."

"Yes, but if it's true, it means the medicine works; not only to cure disease, but also to prolong life. Think about it. Their awful appearance may just be the result of long-term use of the medicine."

Mike was impatient. "Fine. But what did he say? Can we go?"

"Yes, but I altered our demands, slightly. I told him we will give him the scepter if he gives us the medicine and allows us to go free."

"The medicine, too?" Alex said. "Good thinking. But can he be trusted?"

"Knowing how much he wants the scepter, I think he can."

Alex had his doubts. He didn't know if the man could be trusted, but he didn't have another way out of their situation.

They could jump into the subterranean river; after all, that's how he and Sophie escaped the natives at the falls. However, at the falls he saw an exit strategy. But here, there was no telling where this river let out. It may just run deeper into the earth, and they'd all drown. With no other option, he pulled the scepter from over the water and handed it to Sophie.

Sophie held the beautiful glimmering Mayan object in her hands. She approached the ruler. And with the dignity and honor befitting a king, she presented it to him.

A wide smile broke across the king's wrinkled face. For the first time in over 500 years, the golden scepter of Kan Ajaw K'uhul was back in the hands of their own people.

The king turned and lifted it high above his head.

Instead of shouts of joy that Alex expected, the

warriors dropped to a knee and bowed their heads in reverence. Silence followed, and the three waited tensely. It was unclear whether or not the king was going to keep his word.

The king lowered the scepter and turned to face the three. He pulled a small snakeskin pouch from his belt and handed it to Sophie. The warriors lowered their weapons. The two spoke briefly, and she backed away.

"What did he say?" Alex asked.

"He told me that he and his people have lived in this city for hundreds of years, but now, too many outsiders know of its existence. It's time for them to move on. He told us to take the medicine and go, and to never come looking for them."

"That's easy," Mike said, "I never want to see them again anyway."

Holding the medicine bag in one hand, Sophie pointed to the side of the cavern with the other. "He wants us to leave that way. It's another way out."

The three walked cautiously to the side of the cavern. The large, yellow eyes of the warriors followed their every step. Only when they neared the wall, did the passage become visible in the rocks.

Without looking back, they entered the tunnel. They hiked single file through the man-made tunnel. As they hiked, Sophie raked her hand along the rough wall. She could feel the chisel marks left behind by Maya diggers.

She said, "Kan Ajaw K'uhul must have ordered this tunnel dug right after the scepter was stolen. Because without the scepter, even he couldn't enter the original way without the tunnel being flooded."

The three continued hiking. As they walked, Alex turned to Mike. "So, how they did they do it? How did they capture you without making a sound?"

"It happened fast," Mike replied. "I was just walking. Then I felt a rope around my neck; so tight I couldn't breathe or yell for help. At the exact same time, two men grabbed my arms, two men grabbed my legs, and they dragged me off the trail. I must have passed out from lack of oxygen because when I woke up, my arms and legs were tied, and I was sitting on the ground with a hood over my head. I couldn't see a thing. The only time they took the hood off was when I was in the cavern."

"Did you hear them say anything?" Sophie asked.

"I heard them talking, but I couldn't understand a word. At one point their voices raised. Something caused quite a commotion."

"That's probably when they realized we had the scepter," Alex replied.

The three came to the foot of a rising staircase. Alex climbed first. At the top, he reached up and pushed aside a heavy stone slab. He pulled himself up and then reached down and helped Sophie through the hole. Mike followed.

"Sophie, any idea where we are?" Alex asked.

She glanced around and said, "I recognize this room. We're on the first level of the palace."

"The palace. That makes sense," Alex replied. "That way the king's diggers could work in secrecy."

Mike put his hands on his hips and stared down at the hole in the floor. "So that's how they did it."

"Did what?" Sophie asked.

"How the natives got by Sebastian's sentries and the motion sensors without being detected. They simply came up through the floor and captured Sebastian's men, all without a shot being fired. Those bastards never had a chance."

They left the palace through a rear door and hiked

to the ball court. Once there, Alex pulled the tab on the emergency locator, sending a beaconing signal for the helicopter's return.

With time to kill, they sat on a low stone block wall to wait. It was an uneasy wait. Alex was sure they were being watched. He scanned the area. He didn't see any natives, but that wasn't surprising; the natives were practically invisible in this environment. His only hope was that the king and his men would honor their agreement.

Sophie suddenly groaned.

"What's wrong?" Alex asked. "We got what we came for, right?"

She looked up. "I know, but there I was face-to-face with a real Maya king, possibly even the great Kan Ajaw K'uhul himself, and I didn't ask him a single question. Think of what I could have learned. I have hundreds of questions I could have asked." She huffed. "I had an opportunity of a lifetime, and I blew it."

"I wouldn't say that. We'll never know if it that was the real Kan Ajaw K'uhul or not, but it doesn't matter. How many archeologists that you know, have ever met a real live Maya king?"

She smiled a little. "You know...that was something, wasn't it?"

"You bet it was."

Mike interrupted, "I hate to mention this, but what are you going to tell the professor about losing the scepter?"

She plopped her face in her hands and huffed. "I haven't the faintest idea."

46

At the White House, Vice President Calvin Jeffords sat on the couch inside his cushy office. He was with his new public relations director, Christy Nishimoto, a stunning Asian American woman that Calvin had more than a passing interest in. Yes, he was married, but that never stopped him before.

He inched closer.

"As I was saying," the vice president said, "when I am officially declared president, I want to personally address the children all across America in their classrooms via TV. I will give messages of hope, etc."

She jotted down notes.

"I need you to encourage the children to write songs about me. I also want the nation's best poets to write poems about my presidency…how blessed the country is to have me, etc."

He inched closer.

The door to his office burst open, and the Vice President's wife Heather strode in. A statuesque, raven-haired beauty, Heather wore a tight-fitting dress and high heels. She carried fabric swatches in one arm and her little dog in the other. "Oh, darling, I didn't know you were in a meeting."

Calvin gritted his teeth and slid away from his PR

director. "Yes, you did. Anytime my door is closed you know I am in a meeting. That means I am not to be disturbed."

She shrugged. "I brought some fabric samples for you to look at. I'll be doing a lot of redecorating when the old man dies."

Calvin furrowed his brows. They only called the president the "old man" in private, not in the presence of others. God, she was irritating.

Heather set the dog on the floor. "Muffin, go give daddy a kiss."

The white Maltese dog ran to the vice president and jumped on his lap.

"Get him away from me!" Calvin said, struggling to keep the dog from licking his face.

"Don't be like that, you'll hurt his feelings."

The public relations director rose from her chair. She tucked papers under her arm and headed for the door and said, "I'll be leaving now."

Calvin pushed the dog off his lap. "Wait, I have one final item," he said.

She turned around.

"Before the president dies, I want a photo taken where I'll be holding his hand while he's on his deathbed. It'll make me look sympathetic. Then I want it distributed to all the major papers worldwide."

Miss Nishimoto nodded and left the room.

Heather turned. "Who is she?"

"She's our new public relations expert. She's helping me transition into the presidency." That part was true, but he was interested in her for other reasons as well. Even though Miss Nishimoto was thoroughly professional and showed no interest in him as a man--he was working on changing that. Very few could resist his charms.

Heather set the fabric samples on his desk. "Darling, take a look at these and let me know what you think. I have to get going. I have a hair appointment."

She bent at the knees and held out her arms. "Muffin, come to mama."

The dog ran and jumped into her arms.

Calvin sneered. How he hated that dog.

Heather turned, gave a backwards wave over her right shoulder, and left the room.

Calvin loosened his tie. He took a seat behind his desk and poured himself a drink from a new bottle of scotch. He held the glass for a moment and then downed the liquor in one gulp. He felt the liquid searing his throat and then set down the glass.

He removed a notepad from his desk drawer. It had the list of everything he wanted to accomplish during his presidency. He'd had this list for years and added to it every so often. He had put a lot of thought into it.

Deep down he hated the way this country was run. Calvin came from the ruling class and carried a pedigree, for god's sake. After all, his father was the great Holton Jeffords and, his father before him was the great Malcolm Jeffords. Calvin was determined to never bow down to lesser mortals again.

He looked at the list. By following it, he'd change America for the better--in his image. He wasn't a communist per se, but he did admire some of the finer qualities of communism.

He would be a top-down ruler and planned to dictate his will through presidential executive orders, bypassing Congress, in order to do what he wanted to be done. At first, people might not agree with his decisions, but once they saw his plans in action, more would agree than disagree. This is how a real leader acted, not like that imbecile Thomas Grant. Calvin was confident, that in the future, people will build monuments dedicated to his greatness.

He pushed the button on the intercom. "Diane, get Dr. Von Ruden on the line for me, immediately."

"Yes, sir," came the response.

Dr. Vincent Von Ruden was the president's personal physician. A few moments later, Calvin's secretary's voice came over the intercom, "Dr. Von Ruden is waiting for you on line one."

Calvin picked up the phone. "Hello, doctor."

"Yes, Mr. vice president, what can I do for you?"

"I want an update on the president's condition?"

"As I told you a few hours ago, he's dying, and there is nothing I can do except to manage the pain."

"How long would you say he has to live?"

"He could go at any time."

"Thank you, doctor. Let me know immediately when his condition changes." And by that Calvin meant--death. The vice president hung up, smiling.

He swiveled his chair to face the window. He gazed outside and began thinking of the perks of the presidency: riding in Air Force One, golfing at exclusive clubs, vacationing on Martha's Vineyard, summit meetings at Camp David, appearing on late night talk shows, hanging out with celebrities, and so much more.

He shivered with excitement. Everything he planned was finally coming true.

301

47

The helicopter returned to the Maya ball court. Hernando picked up Alex, Mike, and Sophie and then he flew it at top speed to their destination. They had the medicine; they only hoped the president was still alive when they got there.

The sun had been up about a half hour when he set the helicopter down at Guatemala City's La Aurora International Airport. Alex and the others said their thanks and goodbyes to Hernando.

They left the helicopter and hurried to the waiting jet plane. Less than ten minutes later the jet was in the air, and they were on their way back to Washington D.C.

After a seemingly never-ending flight, the pilot brought the jet in for a smooth landing at Andrews Air Base. He slowed the aircraft and then turned off the active runway.

He taxied the aircraft to the same remote location they had met the senator the day before. The plane stopped. The door opened and air stairs lowered.

Alex rushed out expecting to see the senator, but neither the man, nor his vehicle could be seen. Where is he? He wondered. The man was never late.

Mike stepped from the plane and immediately sensed what his friend was thinking. "Maybe he got caught in traffic?"

Alex sneered. Every second counted. They had to get to the White House immediately. He borrowed the pilot's cell phone and dialed the senator's private number. Strangely, there was no answer.

The senator always answered his phone. With no one else to turn to, he dialed the chief of staff's phone number from memory. It rang twice.

"Hello?"

"Mr. Lawson, this is Alex McCade. Is the president still alive?"

"He is, but just barely."

"I don't know if Senator McDaniel told you, but we have a medicine in our possession that can possibly save the president."

"You have a medicine? But the doctors say..."

"I know what the doctors say, but you have to trust me."

"Alright, what can I do?"

"We need a ride to the White House right away."

"Where are you?"

"Andrews Air Base. Once we get to the White House, we'll need immediate access to the president."

"Stay put; I'll arrange it," replied the chief of staff, and he hung up.

Alex returned the cell phone to the pilot.

"What did the senator say?" Mike asked.

"He didn't answer, but I spoke to the president's chief of staff. He's arranging a ride for us."

"Is the president still alive?" Sophie asked.

"He is, but according to the chief of staff, he's barely hanging on."

Minutes later, a police car, with its lights flashing,

burst onto the airfield. It skidded to a stop, and the police officer waved for them to get in. The three piled in the back seat, and the officer looked back. "I hear you need to get to the White House ASAP."

"Faster, the better," Alex replied.

The police car raced off the airfield with the siren blasting. It got onto Pennsylvania Avenue and headed toward the White House.

They crossed the bridge over the Potomac River, and a short while later the police car came to an abrupt stop two blocks from the White House. Traffic was at a standstill. Horns honked, and people began getting out of their vehicles to see what was holding things up.

Alex leaned forward. "Officer, what's happening?"

"Accident," he replied, "just came in over the radio."

"Can you get around it?"

"I could go back and take another route, but that will take some time."

"We're only two blocks away," Alex said. "We'll take it from here. Thanks for the ride."

"You bet."

The officer got out of the car. He opened the back door. Alex, Mike, and Sophie got out and ran in the direction of the White House.

Less than five minutes later, Alex, Mike, and Sophie arrived outside the White House gates. Alex approached a guard at the gate. "Sir, my name is Alex McCade. We have an emergency meeting with the president's chief of staff, David Lawson."

The guard eyed them warily.

They still had on their sweaty jungle fatigues and muddy boots. They had been so focused on getting the medicine to the president that it never occurred to them to change back into their regular clothes. "I know how this must look, but please contact the chief of staff. He will explain."

"Move along, you're not getting inside."

"No, please call him," Sophie said. "It's an emergency."

The guard decided to humor them. "So you know the chief of staff personally?"

"We do, and he's expecting us."

"And I suppose you know the president, too."

"No, not him," replied Alex. "We're not crazy, and the chief of staff is waiting for us."

The guard snickered. He sauntered to the guard house and came back with a clipboard. "What's your name?"

"Alex McCade."

He scanned the list. "Well, Mr. McCade...I don't see your name anywhere on the list."

Alex noticed a pedestrian walking by using his cell phone. Alex yanked the phone out of his hands. "Sorry, I need this."

He began to dial the chief of staff's cell number when Mike tugged his arm. "Here he comes."

Alex saw a security cart driving to the gate with the chief of staff behind the wheel. Alex tossed the cell phone back to the bewildered man.

The cart stopped, and the chief of staff shouted at the guard. "Let them in."

The guard hesitated.

"I said let them in now!"

The guard stumbled over himself. After a brief pat-down, he let them in the gate.

"Is he still alive?" Alex asked as he hopped on board the cart.

"Not for long."

The chief of staff raced the cart up to the East Wing entrance. When it came to a stop, they bailed out and ran inside the building. The elevator was waiting.

When the elevator doors closed, David said, "Alright, now fill me in on this medicine."

Alex said, "Sophie learned of an old Mayan medicine that supposedly cures all illness and disease."

Sophie held up the old snakeskin pouch.

If David had doubts, he didn't show it. He was at the point of trying anything to save the president.

The elevator doors opened.

David Lawson led them across the hall. As he reached for the doorknob, the secret service agent stopped him. "I'm sorry Mr. Lawson; no one is allowed inside to see the President."

"But we have to see him."

"I'm sorry sir, no one is allowed in."

"Is the first lady in there?"

"Yes, she and a priest. The priest is administering the last rites."

Sophie put her mouth close to the door. "Mrs. Grant! Mrs. Grant!"

The agent pulled her back. "Be quiet, or I'll have you removed."

"Mrs. Grant!" she yelled again.

The man waved another agent over. "Escort Mr. Lawson and the others out." The agent nodded and gestured firmly toward the elevator.

Sophie screamed in defiance, "But we have to see the President! We can save him!"

The door to the President's room flung open. Mrs. Grant stood there with her hands on her hips, her eyes puffy and red. She had been crying. "What on earth is going on out here? My husband is dying—don't you people understand that!"

"Mrs. Grant, I have to talk to you; it's urgent," said the chief of staff.

"David, can't it wait?"

"No, it can't. These people say they have a medicine that can save your husband's life."

"And you believe them?"

"I trust them, and if they believe it's possible, then I say we have to let them try."

She turned to them. "Is this true?"

"It's true," Sophie replied.

"Don't tell me the medicine is in that filthy bag you're holding?" asked the first lady.

Sophie nodded.

Millicent Grant began to close the door.

"Wait!" Sophie shouted. "Your husband is dying, right? If we're wrong, then there's no harm done, but if we're right--we can save him."

The President's wife looked at David who nodded his approval. She took a deep breath and then turned to the agent. "Alright, let them in."

The first lady showed them into the room. The president's personal physician and a nurse stood solemnly at the president's bed as a priest was saying prayers.

Alex had seen the president on TV countless times,

and it was hard to believe that the person lying in bed with all the hoses, tubes, and wires attached was really him.

The president's personal physician, Dr. Von Ruden, turned tartly. "Mrs. Grant, what are these people doing here?"

"They say they have a medicine that will save my husband's life."

"That's preposterous!"

"But..."

The doctor looked into her eyes. "Millicent, you must accept the fact that your husband is dying, and there is nothing that can be done about it. They must leave at once."

"It will work," Alex assured her.

The doctor saw the old snakeskin pouch Sophie was holding. He furrowed his brows, and said, "Let me see that."

Alex stepped in his way. "No."

Dr. Von Ruden wheeled to the first lady and huffed. "Millicent I'm sorry. If you go through with this, I will have no choice but to report this."

The first lady looked at Sophie. "Please, do what you have to do."

The doctor slammed his stethoscope on the table and stormed from the room.

Sophie placed the pouch on the table beside the bed and loosened the drawstring.

Alex looked inside. The bag was less than a quarter full of a grayish powder. It suddenly occurred to him that they had no idea how much to give him, or even how to administer it.

"His vital signs are dropping," said the nurse.

"C'mon, Sophie, we have to hurry," Mike said.

Sophie accessed the situation. The president's throat was full of tubes, and she couldn't risk pulling them out, it might make things worse. She saw the saline bag hanging beside the bed, and she had an idea. She pulled the saline bag off the hook and cut the top off with a pair of scissors.

She took the king's pouch, poured all the powder inside the saline bag and mixed it well with a thermometer. "Nurse, I need something to fasten the end," she said.

The nurse removed a bed linen clip from a cabinet and handed it to Sophie. She clipped the end of the saline bag and hung it back on the hook beside the bed. All eyes watched the grayish liquid drip into the plastic tubing and slowly flow toward the president's arm.

The door to the room suddenly slammed open. Dr. Von Ruden and Calvin Jeffords charged in. "Millicent, what the hell is going on?" yelled the vice president. "Get these people out of here—now!"

"No, they're staying."

The vice president puffed his chest. "Dr. Von Ruden told me they came in here with some crazy notion of giving your husband some sort of 'miracle' drug."

"You're too late Calvin; they've already given it to him."

The hard tactic didn't work, so the vice president softened his voice, "Millicent, listen to reason. Dr. Von Ruden has been caring for your husband since the first day he took office. You can't really believe these strangers over him, now can you?"

"Calvin, I will do whatever I feel is necessary to save my husband's life."

The vice president gave up trying to appeal to her

good senses and turned to the nurse. "What did they do?"

The nurse pointed to the snakeskin pouch lying on the table and then to the saline bag hanging above the bed.

The vice president strode to the table and picked up the open pouch. His face twisted, "This thing stinks to high hell. What was in here?"

"Leave that alone!" Sophie yelled.

She made a grab for the pouch, but the vice president pulled it behind his back. "No, you don't, missy. I am confiscating this bag. It will be used as evidence at your trial."

"Trial? On what charge?" David spouted.

"Attempted murder--all of you!" He turned to the medical staff. "And you are my witnesses."

"You've got to be kidding," David said. "We were trying to save his life, you fool."

"Fool? You're the fool, and you are going to pay dearly for what you have done." He turned to the Secret Service agent. "I am the acting president, and I want these four removed—immediately!"

"Yes sir," the agent replied. "Let's go," he said motioning toward the door.

As Sophie passed the first lady, she said, "Don't worry Mrs. Grant, he'll get better soon; I'm sure of it."

After being escorted from the room, the four reconvened in the hallway. Alex bit back his fury and said, "That vice president. What a bastard."

"You'll get no argument from me," David replied.

They paced in the hall, expecting at any time to hear that the president had recovered. Time crawled by.

A half hour later, the door of the president's room

opened. The vice president smiled. "I thought you'd like to be the first to know--the president is dead."

48

The news of the president's death hit them hard. They had risked their lives to acquire and bring back the medicine for the president. For all their effort, he died anyway, and they felt miserable.

Sophie sniffed. "Maybe if we got to him sooner."

"Don't blame yourselves," David replied sadly. "You did all you could."

Alex, Mike, and Sophie stared at the floor, not knowing what else to say.

David put his hands in his pockets. "Well, there's nothing left to do here. Looks like you three need to get cleaned up. Do you have a place to stay?"

"Not yet."

"If you don't mind, I'll have my secretary make hotel arrangements. And my driver can take you."

"Thank you, Mr. Lawson, we'd sure appreciate it," Sophie said.

"Call me David."

On the way to the hotel, Mike took a whiff of his jungle fatigues and cringed. He lowered the limousine window and said, "Man, we stink. This car's going to have to be fumigated after we leave."

"I beg your pardon," Sophie replied.

Mike backtracked. "Of course, I was only speaking of Alex and myself. You, on the other hand, smell of only the finest roses."

"I rather doubt that," she said with a laugh. "I can't wait to get to the hotel and take a nice long bubble bath."

The limousine stopped in front of the Four Seasons Hotel. The three tired souls exited the vehicle and pushed through the revolving front door of the luxury hotel. Customers and staff stiffened at the sight of them.

By their reaction, it was obvious that people dressed in dirty jungle fatigues, wearing muddy boots, and reeking of jungle sweat was not the kind of clientele the hotel catered to.

The three ignored the horrified looks and proceeded to the front desk where a well-coiffed woman stared into a computer screen.

"Excuse me," Alex said.

The woman's eyes lifted at the same time her mouth dropped open. "I'm sorry sir; you must have a reservation to stay in this hotel."

"We do; the name is Alex McCade."

She cast a doubtful look and then glanced at her snickering co-workers. She turned back. "Mr. McCade, was it?"

"Yes."

She reluctantly typed his name into the computer. She waited a moment and then her eyebrows rose. "My, I do have a reservation in your name. It also says your reservation was made by the secretary of the president's chief of staff."

"That's right. Is there a problem?"

She perked up. "No sir, no problem at all. I have

you down for three rooms, king size beds, non-smoking. Is this correct?"

Alex nodded.

"And how long will you be staying?"

"One night."

"Very good." She tapped the keyboard and then handed over electronic keycards to their rooms. Without a word, the three got in the elevator.

When they arrived on the top floor, they got out. With keycards in hand, they went to their separate rooms. Alex trudged into his room and locked the door behind him. All he wanted was to take a long, hot shower and then crawl into bed.

He jumped into the shower and let the jets of hot water pulsate on his neck. In time he felt the knots begin to loosen. After cleaning himself up, he stepped out of the shower and toweled off.

He brushed his teeth and then slipped into bed. With a moan, he reached over and turned off the lamp. He lay back and pulled the covers up to his chin. The moment he closed his eyes--the phone rang.

Unbelievable, he thought.

The phone kept ringing, so he curled up and used the pillow to muffle the sound. Fifteen rings later, it stopped. He removed the pillow from his head and settled onto his back. He had just started to relax when the phone rang again.

He cursed under his breath and snapped up the phone. "What?"

"He's alive!"

"Who's alive? Who is this?"

"Alex, its David. The president is alive."

Alex sprang upright in bed. "What do you mean?

How?"

"The medicine worked. The president is alive. I'm sending a car to the hotel. I want you three back at the White House immediately."

Alex hung up the phone. A surge of energy shot through his veins. He suddenly had more energy than he could remember. He threw back the covers and jumped out of bed. He dressed into his dirty clothes and headed out the door.

He banged loudly on Sophie's and Mike's door, and they opened it with a kill-or-be-killed look on their faces.

"What the hell is going on?" Mike asked. "I just got to sleep."

Across the hall, Sophie opened her room door with a towel wrapped around her. "What's going on? I was in the bath."

"The president is alive!" Alex said. "The medicine worked. Get dressed. David is sending a car to pick us up. He wants us back at the White House right away."

Mike and Sophie slammed their doors. A few minutes later they came out fully dressed. The three rode the elevator down and ran out the door of the hotel where the chief of staff's limousine was waiting.

They arrived at the White House in record time. They cleared security at the front gate and drove up to the doorway of the East Wing. David Lawson met them inside. "Welcome back," he said.

"It's true?" Alex asked.

"It sure is. The doctors are at a loss to explain it. You should have seen him, it was the damnedest thing," he said with a laugh. "Ten minutes after he was pronounced dead, he sat up and scared the hell out of everyone in the room."

David ushered them into the secret bunker and right into the president's room. Alex took one look at the president and couldn't believe it was the same man he'd seen earlier. He was sitting up in bed, strong, alert, and the color in his face had returned. He looked great. All tubes, wires, and machinery he'd been hooked up to was now gone.

Millicent Grant was standing beside her husband and heard them enter. "You made it," she said happily. She went over and gave each one a heartfelt hug. Wiping away fresh tears she turned to her husband. "Tom, these are the people who saved your life." She glanced back. "I'm sorry, but in all the excitement I've forgotten your names."

Alex stepped forward. "Mr. President, my name is Alex McCade, and these are my friends Mike Garrison and Sophie Marcus."

"Please come closer," the president said. He warmly shook their hands. "I can't thank you three enough. David told me everything you did and all I can say is--it's a miracle."

The president took in a deep, clear breath and let it out. "I can't believe how good I feel." He suddenly tossed aside the sheets.

"Tom, you mustn't exert yourself," cautioned the first lady.

The president waved her off and slid out of bed. "I've never felt better in my life."

He energetically pranced around the room. He stopped and did a few deep knee bends and said, "Look--my arthritis is completely gone!"

He snatched a hand mirror and stared at his reflection. "I look pretty darn good too, except maybe for a few new wrinkles."

Alex and the others exchanged knowing looks.

The president set the mirror down and turned. "I have to know. What was in that medicine of yours?"

"To be honest sir, we don't know," Sophie said.

Alex nudged Sophie closer. "Mr. President, Sophie is the reason you're alive. She deciphered an old Mayan codex that spoke of an ancient medicine. Mike and I were skeptics, but she convinced us it was possible to save you."

The president took Sophie's hand and looked sincerely into her eyes. "Thank you." Then he glanced at the others, "Is there any of the medicine left?"

"No sir, we didn't know how much to give you, so we used it all," Alex replied.

"How about the container the medicine came in? There's bound to be some residue left behind. I'll get our nation's top scientists on it and have them determine what it's made of. Can you imagine what a medicine like this could do for all the sick and suffering in the world?"

"I'm sorry, sir. The vice president took it from us."

"He what? Why?"

"He said that..."

The room door suddenly swung open and in walked the vice president.

"Speak of the devil," David muttered.

Calvin Jeffords strode into the room with a strained smile. "Mr. President, I-I can scarcely believe the good news," he gushed. "Sir, you look remarkable."

"Calvin, I want that medicine container you took from them."

The Vice President looked stunned. "Well, that's impossible."

317

"And why is that?"

"I-I had it incinerated."

"You what?"

"Well..." he stammered, "when I heard you were alive, I realized I wouldn't need it for evidence at their trial, so I threw it in the incinerator."

"Trial?"

"The murder trial," he replied sheepishly.

"You've got to be kidding me."

"Mr. President, what was I to think? These obscenely dressed people come in here with some smelly old bag and saying there's some sort of miracle medicine in it."

The president huffed. "That old smelly bag you're referring to, contained an extraordinary medicine with the potential to cure all the world diseases—and guess what? You destroyed it."

The Vice President began to sweat heavily. "But Dr. Von Ruden will back me up; he thought these people were nuts too. I-I... was only trying to protect you."

"Protect me? I was dying, you idiot! What harm would it have done?"

"But..."

"Shut up Calvin!" The president turned to his secret service agent. "Get him out of here." The agent gladly escorted the mumbling vice president from the room. "I can't stand that man," the president said.

When Calvin Jeffords left the room, President Grant faced his wife. "Millie, where are my clothes?"

"Oh no, you're not leaving," she protested.

"Yes, I am. I've got a lot of things to do. No telling what Calvin screwed up while I've been out of action."

The first lady, knowing it was no use to argue, walked into the next room and returned with a fresh suit and a tie and laid them on the bed.

The president lifted the pants off the bed but stopped short of putting them on. He looked at Alex and the others. "In a little over a month, I am hosting a state dinner in honor of the Queen of England and the Duke of Edinburgh. It'll be white tie and tails, and I'd like you three to join me."

"Thank you, sir," replied Alex, "but...".

"Good, I'll have my secretary make the arrangements."

The first lady smiled and put her hand tenderly on Alex's arm. "It won't do any good to argue. He's as stubborn as they come, and he won't change his mind."

"In that case sir, we'd be honored."

"Good, good. Now if you'll excuse me, I'd like to get out of this hospital gown and into some real clothes."

The first lady walked Alex, Mike, Sophie, and David out of the room. She thanked them again for all they had done and then went back into the room to be with her husband.

"Time to celebrate?" Sophie asked.

"I'm all for that," Alex replied. "David, you have to join us."

David smiled. "I know just the place."

49

The limousine driver dropped them off in front of a seedy bar in a rough part of town. As they walked inside the smell of stale beer overtook their senses.

The interior had a sticky, linoleum tile floor and faded wood paneling from the 1970s. Some might call it a hole-in-the-wall, but Alex called it perfect. He could see why the bar appealed to the chief of staff. Here, no one would bother you. No cameras, no media, no one asking questions. It was also a place where three people wearing jungle fatigues could fit in.

Mike and Sophie went to the restroom while Alex took a seat at a back table. David went to the bar and placed an order with the burly bartender.

The bartender was big, overweight, and heavily tattooed. He wore a red bandana on his head and a stained t-shirt so tight it rode up and exposed his hairy gut.

Alex used his forearm to clear peanut shells from the table and sat alone with his thoughts. In recent memory, he couldn't remember being happier. They had made it out of the jungle alive, they saved the president's life and most of all he had Sophie in his life. She was obviously beautiful, but a far greater beauty resided within.

He glanced down at his wedding ring. He loved his

wife beyond anything he could ever imagine, but it was time to admit to himself that she was gone, and it was time to move on. No one could replace his wife, but as simple as it sounds, he finally realized it wasn't about finding a replacement; it was about finding someone new to share his life with. Sophie was a unique and very special person in her own right, and he was lucky to have her.

He grasped the ring, and with effort, managed to work it from his finger. He held the platinum ring in his forefingers and stared at it one last time. Then he stuffed it into the front pocket of his pants.

David returned to the table with a pitcher of beer and four mugs. As he filled the mugs to their foamy tops, Mike returned. Sophie followed a few minutes later.

She glanced at his ring-less left hand on the table and then she met his eyes. As she sat, she reached over and gave his other hand a loving squeeze, acknowledging what he had done. He appreciated her silent gesture and the fact that nothing needed to be said.

Alex raised his mug. "I want to make a toast. To Sophie, we couldn't have saved the president without her."

The four cheered, clinked mugs and drank.

David held up his mug for the next toast. "To the president…"

His phone rang.

"I'm always on the clock," he said and answered it.

He didn't speak. He listened and hung up. "That was a report from a crew of specialists who went to Sebastian's island after you left and removed any trace that could prove you were there."

"Did they find Sebastian's body?" Alex asked.

"They did. They found him lying in a pool of his own body fluids. Not a very dignified way to go."

"But one he richly deserved. And Veck?"

David smiled. "This is interesting. They found his body impaled on an iron weather vane atop the aircraft hangar. The black spear-like vane went right through his stomach. I'm told he looked like a bloated frog splayed on a skewer.

"Apparently, he hung alive for hours before finally dying. It must have been a long, painful death. When you've got time, I'd like to hear how you accomplished that."

Alex smiled. "Be glad to." He took a sip of his beer and said, "But you know it's still not over. We still don't know who Sebastian's unknown partner is."

"Any ideas?" David asked.

"Sebastian said it was someone high up in our own government. So, who had the most to gain from teaming up with him?

"With the kind of money we are talking about, that could be anybody."

"True, but who stood the most to gain from the president's death."

"That's easy, Calvin Jeffords, the vice president."

David shook his head. "It couldn't be him; the man is a complete moron."

"But it wouldn't take a Rhodes Scholar to team up with Sebastian. All he had to do was strike the right deal. And what did the vice president want more than anything in the world?"

"That's easy, to be president."

"And in a general election would he stand a chance of winning the presidency?"

"Absolutely not."

"Which means the only guaranteed way to become president is for President Grant to die in office. Then, according to the 25th amendment, the vice president would become president after a vote by Congress. My question is...would he get those votes?"

David thought a moment. "They don't know him like I do. I hate to say it, but I think he would."

"That's why I believe the vice president struck a deal with Sebastian. If Sebastian shot the president with the laser, then Calvin Jeffords becomes president.

"The vice president in return would order no strike against Sebastian which leaves him free to sell the weapon without any interference or threat of retaliation. It's a win-win scenario for both of them."

"Not a bad theory," David replied. He picked up his cell phone. "I'll call a friend of mine in the FBI and see where this leads."

50

After a few pitchers of beer and a lot of laughs, the small group left the bar. Alex, Mike, and Sophie were dropped off at their luxury hotel. Once inside, they headed directly to the elevator. There was no need to stop at the front desk as they still had their keycards.

People stared as they strolled across the lobby in their dirty, smelly jungle fatigues. Alex noticed a gray-haired woman and her husband whispering to each other, obviously not approving. He didn't care.

They took the elevator up to their floor, and each went to their own room and went straight to bed.

Alex woke the next morning at 11:05 a.m. He couldn't remember the last time he slept-in. He hadn't even bothered to take off his clothes.

He walked into the bathroom and brushed his teeth. After rinsing, he wiped his mouth on the towel.

He left his room and knocked on Sophie's door. She answered. She had already showered and was ready to go. They got Mike and headed down to the lobby. They talked about catching a flight back to Seattle after they bought new clothes. The ones they were wearing were filthy. No airline would let them fly looking like they did.

They returned their keycards at the front desk and checked out. As they turned to leave, they saw David

Lawson enter the hotel looking quite disheveled.

"David, what's wrong?" Alex asked.

David ushered them into a corner where they could talk in private. "That friend in the FBI I told you about called me back this morning. A maintenance worker at a small airstrip in Virginia reported seeing a woman matching Dr. Farah's description being forced into a private jet at gunpoint.

"The FBI reviewed the surveillance video and positively identified the gunman."

"It was the vice president, wasn't it? Alex asked.

"No...but it is someone you know."

"Who?"

"Senator Charles McDaniel."

"Senator McDaniel?" Alex blurted out. "It can't be. There must be another explanation."

"I wish there was," David replied, "but it's beginning to make sense. My friend at the FBI told me that two agents are missing, and they were last seen with the senator on his way to pick Dr. Farah up at the airport."

Alex was confused. "But there were no FBI agents with him. He showed up alone." Then it occurred to him. "You know...he did act strange when I asked if I should put the laser in the trunk of his car."

"Which may be right where those FBI agents are now," Mike added.

Alex slammed his fist against the wall. "That bastard! And we just handed Dr. Farah and the laser right over to him."

"Did the FBI say where the plane was heading?" Sophie asked.

"No idea," David replied. "The plane left from a

private airport with no tower. Also, no flight plan was listed and the tail numbers on the plane were false. He could be anywhere by now."

Alex thought a moment and said, "I may know where he's going. It was something his daughter said to me long ago."

"Where?" Mike asked.

Alex headed for the hotel exit. "Come on, I'll tell you on the way."

51

On a bright sunny morning, on the lush tropical island of St. Martin, Senator Charles McDaniel turned the corner in his black Mercedes convertible and took the drive leading into the hills. Cresting the hill, he took a winding tree-lined road and then turned into the driveway of his secluded villa.

The villa, his private getaway, had a white stucco exterior, red tile roof and large plantation windows with shutters. The elegant home boasted six bedrooms, four bathrooms, and an infinity pool that claimed breathtaking views of the bright blue Caribbean water below.

The senator parked the car and stepped out wearing khaki shorts, a colorful tropical shirt, and sandals with black socks. With a cheery disposition, he pulled a bag of groceries from the trunk and strode up the stone walk. He stopped at the front door, unlocked it with his key, and stepped inside.

He reached to enter the security code to the alarm, but the alarm was turned off. Puzzled, surely, he engaged it before he left. No matter, he closed the door and continued across the living room.

He entered the kitchen--and froze. There was a silhouette of a man sitting at his kitchen table. The figure was leaning back in the chair, with feet on the table and hands behind the head. With trembling fingers, the senator snapped on the light.

"Morning Senator," the figure said.

"Alex? My god, you startled me. What are you doing here?"

"I see you shaved your beard."

The senator paused for a moment to regain his composure. "Um, yes. The climate here really isn't suitable for one. So, enough about my beard, why are you here? And how did you find me? No one knows about this place."

"Your daughter does."

"Kimberly?"

"The night my SEAL team rescued her. She was quite shaken as you can imagine. While I was trying to calm her, I asked her to think of a happy place; a place where she always felt safe and would like to return someday. She mentioned your villa in St. Martin."

He set the bag of groceries on the counter. "You've got a good memory."

"By the way, President Grant is alive and well?"

He looked genuinely happy. "The medicine worked?"

Alex nodded. "It did. But imagine my surprise when we got back to Washington and no one could find you. Then I heard that Dr. Farah and the laser were missing as well as those two FBI agents that accompanied you to the airport."

"I don't know what you're talking about."

"I think you do. You were Sebastian's other partner."

"That's preposterous!" he said sliding to his left. "Why in the world would I associate with a mad-man like him?"

"For the money, of course. I did some checking and, apparently, you aren't doing as well financially as you let on. You've accumulated a lot of debt, and a share of five billion dollars would certainly cure your financial ills, wouldn't it?"

Alex swung his legs off the table and sat upright in the chair.

"Now, tell me if I got this right. Sebastian planned the entire operation and then he brought you and Dr. Valerius in as his partners. The plan was to steal the laser after the final tests had been performed at the White Sands Missile Range. But instead of waiting, Sebastian and Dr. Valerius double-crossed you and intercepted Dr. Farah's plane and crashed it in the jungle.

"When you heard the news of the plane crash, you were livid. You knew what he'd done. You wanted the laser back for yourself. But how? Being on the outside was no good; you needed to get on the inside of the investigation to learn what was going on. So you decided to contact your friend the president and offer your services. Being that he trusted you, and that you were well acquainted with the laser system, he agreed.

"Now, once inside of the investigation you learned Sebastian was selling the laser to the Chinese. You knew you had to move quickly or lose it forever. That's where Mike and I came in. You used us to get the laser and Dr. Farah back. And like fools, we handed them right over to you."

The senator nonchalantly slid further to his left. "You've got it all worked out, haven't you?"

"Yep."

"Well, don't feel bad Alex, I've been fooling people all my life. In fact, you could say that it's one of my greatest strengths. By the way, you're right about everything except that Sebastian wasn't the mastermind—I was."

The senator yanked open a drawer. He pulled out a black revolver and thrust it at Alex. The ex-Navy SEAL never flinched.

"I had been in the Senate only a few months when I was struck by how much of taxpayers' money is wasted every year, and I figured...why not some for me? So, over the years I carefully helped myself to every opportunity that came my way, which, by the way, is not uncommon in Washington.

"Many years later, the opportunity of a lifetime came. I became Chairman of the Finance Committee; a very powerful position. One day the military came asking for additional funding for the development of a revolutionary new weapons system.

"I was given first look at the details of the proposal and quickly realized the enormous profit to be made if it was successful. So, I made sure they got their funding; all with an eye toward getting my hands on it in the future."

"Now that you have the laser what are you going to do with it? Will you do like your buddy Sebastian and sell it to the highest bidder?"

"Heaven's no, son. You've got it all wrong. I am, first and foremost, a patriot of the United States. My plan has always been to steal the weapon and then sell it right back to our own government."

"Some patriot," Alex spat. "And you think they'll pay?"

"Of course they'll pay."

Alex looked around. "Is Dr. Farah alive?"

"Yes, she's alive, and the laser is in a safe place. They're far too valuable to let anything happen to them."

The senator smiled. "I take it by coming here you intend to stop me?"

"Of course."

"You're a brave man Alex, and I like you. I'm just sorry it has to end this way."

The senator tightened his grip on the pistol. "Goodbye Alex." He pulled the trigger, but it clicked on an empty chamber. Shocked, the senator squeezed two, three, four more times, but heard clicking each time.

With a wide grin, Alex raised his clenched fist over the kitchen table and slowly opened his fingers. The shells from the senator's pistol hit the table with a sharp, *tick, tick, tick*...

Horrified, the senator dropped the pistol and frantically raced into the living room. He threw his hand inside a cigar box on the mantel and removed another revolver. He wheeled around expecting Alex to be on top of him, but he was still sitting calmly at the table. A relieved breath escaped the senator's lips.

He strode into the kitchen with a renewed sense of confidence and aimed the pistol at the fearless man sitting at his table. Alex opened his other hand, and more shells dropped onto the table with *a tick, tick, tick*... "You really should find better places to hide your weapons."

Frightened, the senator dropped the pistol and stumbled backwards. "Even if you bring me back; no one will believe you. I-I have powerful friends in Washington. My case will never go to trial."

Alex slid the chair back and rose from the table. "Senator, no one likes a traitor, and once those friends of yours learn the truth, they won't clear away fast enough."

"But they'll never learn the truth. I'll deny everything."

"That won't work, because our whole conversation

has been recorded."

"You're bluffing."

Alex glanced to the side. "Gentlemen…"

Two men exited a side room and entered the kitchen. Senator McDaniel saw them, and his face went pale.

"I'm sure you remember the FBI director Meyers and the president's Chief of Staff, David Lawson," Alex said.

"Jim, David, what are you doing here?"

"Mr. McCade told us his suspicions, and we had to come and see for ourselves."

The senator gulped hard. He turned and dashed for the front door. He flung open the door and was stopped by the sight of two large FBI agents. The senator backpedaled. "You can't arrest me! This is a French territory."

The FBI director held up a sheet of paper. "This says I can."

"If you take me in, I swear I will never tell you where to find the laser or Dr. Farah."

"We already have. We found her tied up in the guest house out back, and the laser hidden under your bed." The FBI director shook his head. "I bet you weren't very good at hide-and-seek as a child, were you Charles?"

Alex opened the back door of the kitchen. In walked Sophie and Dr. Farah followed by Mike with the laser case in his hand.

"Hi senator," chirped Mike, "something wrong? You're not looking so good."

The FBI director handcuffed the pale looking senator. With a hand on his shoulder, he walked him outside. He handed the senator off to the two agents, and they escorted him to the backseat of a waiting car.

Alex and the others stepped outside. Before leaving, the FBI director came up to Alex and Mike and shook their hands. "Thanks, guys. I owe you one."

"Our pleasure."

Dr. Farah gave Alex and Mike each a hug, and then a kiss on the cheek. "What can I say, you're angels. Thank you."

"Have a safe trip back," Alex replied.

Dr. Farah took Sophie's hands in hers. "Sophie dear, take care of yourself."

"You too," replied Sophie. The women embraced.

David Lawson escorted Dr. Farah to the car. The two got in and the car drove away.

Alex walked off to the side and pulled out a cheap prepaid cell phone he bought at a local store. He dialed.

The call was answered. "Is it over?"

"It's over," Alex replied. "The FBI just hauled him away."

"I still can't believe he did it."

"I'm sorry; I know he was a good friend of yours."

The president sighed heavily. "Like a brother to me. Alex, I can't thank you and your friends enough."

"Glad to help Mr. President."

"Should you need anything in the future, don't hesitate to ask."

52

Two days later, Sophie stood trembling outside the front entrance of the *Museo Nacional De Antropologia.*

She looked Alex in the eyes and said, "I don't know if I can do this."

"Just go in there and tell him the truth. That's what we came for."

The two walked inside the museum and went straight to the professor's office. Outside his door, Sophie took a deep breath and knocked.

Dr. Montoya opened the door with a combination of surprise and concern. "Sophie, I was so worried. Are you okay? Come in."

Sophie walked in. "I'm okay."

Alex followed.

As the professor closed the door, he said, "I expected you days ago. What happened?"

"I found the treasure."

"You did? That's wonderful! But wait, why don't you look happy about it."

"I am, but…"

He noticed her empty hands. "Oh my, god. Sophie, where's the scepter?!"

Sophie spent the next fifteen minutes explaining

everything that happened. By the time she was done, the professor was pale, shaking, and slumped heavily in his chair.

It wasn't until the professor got a call from the president of the United States, confirming what Sophie had told him was the truth, that he was able to calm down a bit.

As the professor repeatedly mopped his brow with his old, wrinkled handkerchief, he said, "Sophie, I appreciate the president's willingness to help, but this is Mexico. Even if he puts in a good word for us, we can still go to jail for losing a priceless piece of history."

Sophie laid a gentle hand on his. "Not you, professor. I took complete blame. I made some calls and said I took the scepter without your permission. So, if anyone's going to jail, it's me. But if I'm lucky, and my proposal works out, all charges may be dropped against me."

"And if it doesn't work out?"

"Then I'll be expecting you both to come visit me in the big house."

Sophie reached into her pocket. "In the meantime, I want to show you something." She placed the tarnished silver medallion in the professor's hand. The elderly man adjusted his spectacles.

He looked closely at the medallion and saw the image of the Virgin Mary on the front. He excitedly turned it over and read the initials, 'A.d.A.' His eyes snapped up. "Where did you find this?"

"With the king's treasure. It was hanging around the neck of Captain Aguilar's remains."

"His remains? He made it back to the city?"

"He did. We found him tied to a pole in the king's treasure chamber where he was made to stare at the king's treasure until the day he died." Sophie wrapped his fingers around the medallion. "You keep it," she said. "Let this be the first item displayed in your museum."

The professor was at a loss for words.

Sophie's cell phone rang. She looked at the caller ID and went pale. "This is it. Wish me luck."

She answered the phone and walked to the other side of the room.

Alex heard the voice on the other end but couldn't make out what was being said, and Sophie's expression provided no clue how it was going, one way or the other.

His eyes shifted to the professor who looked as nervous as he was. After what felt like an eternity, she hung up. Then a slow smile appeared on Sophie's face.

"I'm in the clear."

Alex hugged her.

"No prison?" the professor asked.

"Nope. The Spanish government, owners of the scepter, and the board of directors here at the Museo Nacional de Antropologia agreed to drop all the charges against me for losing the scepter."

"That's fantastic! But how did you do it?"

"Because I guaranteed them each twenty percent of all artifacts found in the jungle city."

"That's 40 percent. The Guatemalan government would certainly never agree to that."

"You're right, they refused at first, but then I reminded them that unless they agreed to my terms, they could wait another 500 years to find the city themselves."

Alex smiled. "Very cunning of you, Dr. Marcus."

"Why, thank you, Mr. McCade."

"What about the missing scepter? Will the loss be

made public?"

"No, it was agreed that it would only encourage treasure hunters to search the jungle for it and we don't want anyone running into those natives again.

"Instead, the Spanish government agreed to secretly create a replica of the scepter and use that in the traveling exhibition. Hopefully, the world will never learn the truth."

She stepped close to the professor. "I have more news. I was named director of the site."

"That's wonderful," the professor replied, "congratulations."

"...and my first decision as acting director is to name you my co-director."

He paused and then his expression saddened. "I'm sorry dear, but I can't accept."

"Why not?"

"I'm afraid jungle conditions aren't suited for a man my age."

"Not so fast professor. Believe it or not, there is a room in the palace that has all the creature comforts of home; expensive furnishings, French paintings, Persian rugs, and a large comfortable bed for you to sleep in. The room has a refrigerator. And we can set you up with air conditioning."

"Air conditioning? How in the world?"

"I'd rather show you. How would you like to go to the jungle city of Kan Ajaw K'uhul?"

His chin dropped open. "You mean...?"

"Like I promised. We've got a helicopter waiting."

"Oh my goodness, t-this is so sudden," he replied nervously.

"How fast can you get ready?" she asked.

The seventy-nine-year-old ripped open his desk drawer. He pulled out a clear plastic bag crammed with prescription pills and then slapped a floppy hat on his head.

"Ready when you are."

Special Note

Three weeks later, at the request of the President of the United States, Alex McCade, Mike Garrison, and Dr. Sophie Marcus attended a state dinner at the White House. After dinner, President Grant invited the three to stand, and he proudly presented them with the Presidential Medal of Freedom. The medal, the nation's highest civilian award, is given to those who have made outstanding contributions to the security or national interests of the United States. Details of their heroic feats were not provided and remain classified to this day.

About the Author

I was born in St. Paul, Minnesota and currently live near Dallas, Texas with my wife, two sons, a dog and a turtle. If you would like to contact me, please email: stevekroska@gmail.com.

If you enjoyed this book, please post a review on Amazon. Thank you for your support.

Made in the USA
San Bernardino, CA
08 February 2020